# ROA

# MAVIS

# GRIND

SIMON
MARLOWE

CRANTHORPE
MILLNER
PUBLISHERS

This book is a work of fiction. Names, characters, places and incidents are either products of the author's imagination or are used fictitiously. Any resemblance to actual events or locales or persons, living or dead, is entirely coincidental.

First published by Cranthorpe Millner Publishers (2026)

ISBN 978-1-80378-377-2 (Paperback)

www.cranthorpemillner.com

Cranthorpe Millner Publishers

Printed and bound by CPI Group (UK) Ltd
Croydon, CR0 4YY

FSC www.fsc.org MIX Paper | Supporting responsible forestry FSC® C013604

*For Christine, James and Jessica.*

"*Crosby's gonna sing, folks. Now's the time to go out and get the popcorn.*"

– Bob Hope, from the *Road to*… movie series.

# IF ONLY I KNEW WHAT WAS COMING

# CHAPTER ONE

## THE DISCREPANCY

When you hear there has been a discrepancy, there are three options open to you. The first is to fess up and comply with Compliance. But beware, you're going to lose your job, your self-respect, your wife, your partner, and your cat, dog, goldfish, and sadomasochist gerbil kept in a garden shed. Also, your friends, who were never really your friends, will stop talking to you, plus your aunts who never remembered you, your uncles who might just remember you, your cousins who you've never met, your nephews and nieces, who you never knew all lived next door, and your half-brother, the one you never knew existed until your mum told you after a sniff of Dubonnet.

You will also need to add impoverishment to the list after maxing out your credit cards, dealing with long-term unemployment, criminal prosecution, incompetent legal defence, public humiliation, and extortionate fines that force you to file for bankruptcy, complicated by 10 years in purgatory – also known as the one-star accommodation in His Majesty's prisons. (Just so you don't have too many surprises, I do have a bit of previous history with HMPs, which I will explain later.)

However, for now, rushing to fix your moral compass is not rewarded by society nor the company you've just defrauded.

Instead, you will be punished, and your little "discrepancy", if followed by contrition and honesty, will be rewarded with misery and servitude. Choose option one, and you may think you have become a better person, forever the reformed sinner, but others will consistently refer to you as "the idiot" behind your back.

Option two is denial. It was not you who was responsible for this minor discrepancy, this opportunistic white-collar crime that happened to present itself on your dual-screen desktop. Deny all knowledge when confronted with the definition of a discrepancy: *(Noun) An illogical or surprising lack of compatibility or similarity between two or more facts.* Also known as evidence. Your hope is that incredulity will be sustained for the next 40 years of your stunted career without invoking any form of sanction.

This may seem as idiotic as option one, but it is possible that some greater power or mysterious deity may be working on your behalf. This option has a wheel of fortune that may be spun in your favour: companies hate looking stupid, especially when an accounting discrepancy exposes their own lack of risk-management controls.

However, if you were to take option two as a solution to your problem, you would need to keep in mind that there is a high probability that denial is a bit like the bereavement curve: you could easily slip into acceptance, lowering your guard and feel comfortable with the company's cost-benefit analysis of not punishing you. This is the path of delusion. You are a cog in the wheel, a socket in the machine, and time – the company's time – will play the long game in order to penalise you. As you become wracked with guilt, a diminished person, witless and vacuous, addicted to alcohol, drugs, and prescriptions for athletes' foot, you will be made to walk the plank. The company was just biding its time, looking for the right moment, and wham! Redundancy arrives. Off into obscurity, poverty, a nobody's nothingness of irrelevance.

In other words, don't bother existing, because no one wants to know you exist.

And so remains the third and final option: attack! Turn the discrepancy into an opportunity. Express surprise that such a despicable betrayal of the company has been brought to your attention, besmirching the reputation of the department. In fact, you will work tirelessly with the investigators, the auditors, the stock-takers, the police, the fraud officers, the lawyers, the Vatican, and the church, to get to the bottom of this appalling betrayal of trust. Whoever this person or persons are, they will be rooted out, exposed, and hung, drawn, and quartered.

Then, when Compliance has left your office, breathe a sigh of relief and phone your co-conspirator. Head straight to the bar, which is packed with city workers in a post-Christmas, post-New Year first-month-of-the-year blues way, to plot a way out of the mess you are in.

Because this is how it all started for me.

'You're an idiot!'

'What?'

'I said' – my anger surrounded by a public cacophony of excited alcoholics – 'you're an idiot!'

At this point, we need to pause, because before I go any further, you need to know who the guy in the bar is. Trust me, he is an effing idiot, and his name is Matt Chubb.

He's the type of guy who goes bald just before he leaves school, so he shaves his head to avoid mockery and laughter at the evidence of alopecia. His face looks very much like a monkey's prolapsed anus, although that is a disservice to the chimpanzees that hang their arses out over the edge of artificial timber enclosures.

As you can tell, I am not happy with him, and you probably still have no idea what he looks like. Well, let's just say Matt Chubb has the look of a trader, a city boy, built like the Terminator, linear in thought and incapable of understanding guilt, shame, embarrassment, or nuances of social interaction.

'First off,' he replied, 'don't call me an idiot. And second, don't start acting like a baby just because Compliance knocked on your door.'

'They didn't just knock on my door,' I said, leaning forward as I gripped the rim of my lager, 'they sat in my office and asked me questions.'

'That's their job, that's what they're supposed to do.'

'About the fund.'

'Don't be so dramatic, Jamie. It's not the Spanish Inquisition.'

'Wrong,' I replied, easing back on my chair. 'They are worse than the Inquisition, and it's all because you're an idiot.'

'There you go again!' he howled, raising his arms up indignantly. 'Calling me names for no good reason.'

'I have every reason, Matt! Do you know what they said to me?'

'No, I wasn't there.'

'Exactly! So I'm going to tell you what they said to me.'

Then, as tends to happen in these kinds of situations, I

didn't say anything. I just stared.

'Do you want another drink, then?' Matt asked, getting up from the table and waving his empty glass.

'A pint,' I said reluctantly, as I realised there was nothing I could do. I was powerless to change the facts. I just had to accept the consequences, the consequences of our little "discrepancy".

I drank like a fish for the rest of the night, avoiding Matt Chubb and circulating like a puppy worrying if I ever would be fed again. Out of fear and loathing, I offered people bets on the moon being made of Edam and Mars harbouring life.

On the second bet, I had a few takers.

I then headed outside to nick a cigarette, only to find Matt Chubb, the idiot, puffing on his vape.

'You do know,' I began, swanning up to him with my cigarette poised like a weapon, 'they have discovered a black hole not just in the centre of the Milky Way, but also in the reconciliation ledger.'

'Yeah,' he said, puffing some foul-smelling vanilla smoke in my face.

'The deal,' I said, to remind him of our viable and low-risk strategy, 'was to siphon off at a barely imperceptible amount, charging discretionary fees that would be under the radar for even the most assiduous auditor whose nightly pleasure was fondling coloured felt tip pens. But you have taken an industrial hoover and sucked up every shekel like it's money to burn to keep your monkey's arse face warm on a cold winter's night.'

'You should get yourself a girlfriend,' Matt replied, blowing out a cloud which floated down ye olde lane of financial pubs and coffee shops. 'Get yourself back in the sack. It's not good for you. It makes you anxious and tense… Paranoid.'

'For Christ's sake, Matt, you need to get a grip!' I hissed, annoyed about the girlfriend dig. 'I would get a girlfriend, but I think my prospects have gone downhill rapidly. I mean, I'd need to find someone who's willing to wait 10 years while I get sodomised on alternate nights by my cellmates Jack and Bill.'

'I have a plan,' he said, like he'd had it all worked out from the beginning.

'You mean a plan for you,' I replied, already imagining that somehow Matt was going to get away with it and I'd be the one who'd get postcards from the Bahamas telling me to hang in there because it would all be worth it in the end.

'I'm not a total psychopath, Jamie.'

'Liar. You've shopped me, haven't you? My life is ruined because you've told them it was me who's been jerking them off and taking the money.'

'Jamie,' Matt said, pretending he was offended, 'this is a plan for both of us.'

'I don't want your plan, Matt. I don't need a plan from you to get me out of this mess. I just need you to go and see Bridges and tell him it was a terrible mistake. He can have the money back, and if we all keep quiet, everybody's reputation, including his and the company's, will be protected. This kind of thing is bad for business. It can't get out.'

'He's already seen me.'

'Who, Bridges?'

'Yeah.'

'Christ!'

I then did a full body turn, repeating Jesus and Christ in an alternate pattern, until I was feeling dizzy and exhausted.

'Christ!' I said one last time, just to make sure I had the word well and truly out there. 'Why didn't you tell me in the bar?'

'Because you were angry and you weren't in the mood to listen.'

'I still am angry,' I argued, wondering why Matt didn't think that was evident.

'You know,' said Matt, remaining cool, calm, and collected, 'I think that's what Bridges was trying to say to me – how angry he was. All he did was stare.'

'What do you mean?'

'That's all he did. I got called up to the boardroom, got told to stand there at the other end of the table, and he just looked at me, minute after minute.'

'You're kidding!'

'Nope.'

'And he said nothing?' I asked.

'Nothing, he just stared, because he couldn't say anything.'

'Why couldn't he say anything?'

'Because he knew if he said anything, he would start something that he didn't want to start. He'd be telling Compliance that he knows who did it, who took the money, and then the house of cards would all come tumbling down over his head. Better to take the hit, that's what he was saying.'

'You mean option two?'

'What's option two?'

'Nothing,' I replied, not wanting to reveal my tense, anxious, and paranoid thinking. 'So, that's it? We just go back to work like none of this ever happened?'

'No, I didn't say that. I can't go back to work because they sacked me.'

'They've sacked you?'

'That's what I said.'

'Blimey,' I mumbled, almost feeling sorry for him until he gave me the other part of the breaking news.

'And they've sacked you.'

'What are you talking about? They haven't sacked me.'

'Are you sure? When did you last check your messages?'

I pulled out my phone. There it was. The message, the employee notice. Your time is up, we know what you've been up to; you are a very naughty boy, so piss off back to your scummy little housing estate, move back with your mummy and your useless dumb arse sister, and don't ever, *ever* come anywhere near the citadel of money again.

'Told you,' said Matt, reading upside down as I scrolled.

'That's your fault,' I replied, feeling despair and terror rip through my alcohol-drenched brain.

'No, it isn't. It's both our faults.'

'Wrong. It's your fault, because yet again you went totally off-piste.'

'Listen, Jamie, are you going to be a loser all your life or are you for once going to get some balls and take on a bit of risk?'

'I did!' I screamed. 'And look what's happened.'

'OK, Jamie, you tell me what you think has happened.'

I was about to explain that I had carefully constructed a very minor scam that took advantage of a software glitch when calculating the commission between buyers and traders.

At every transaction, the numbers were rounded off, and the 0.001% reconciliation was dumped into a suspense account. I had steadily accumulated a significant but unaccountable amount of money, and this error was never corrected following the release of the accounting software – Version 2.0.2 – because the programmers had forgotten to remove it. However, it was at this exact moment, I realised I had made the biggest mistake of all: I had told Matt about it.

'I think,' I said instead, 'I have ruined my career and my life, and I will be condemned to working night shifts in a haunted mortuary that lets vampires suck blood from the dead and hospital porters sit in nappies playing poker with human toenails.'

'That sounds interesting, but my plan is better.'

'You mean, the one that has got us sacked, and now looking over our shoulders, wondering if a knock on the door means the fraud office or contract killers hired by Bridges?'

'Bridges wouldn't do that, he's a pussy.'

'The guy is a psychopath… And you're a sociopath,' I retorted.

'Yeah, you know, I always thought we had something in common.'

'You do know both are serious personality disorders, right?'

And then, whether I liked it or not, the same thing happened to me as it does every time I am mad at Matt: a strange calmness overwhelms me, brought on by stress fatigue and emotional exhaustion.

I grabbed half a pint abandoned on the table next to us and drank it down in one, then readied myself for Matt's revelations. If my jaw touched the ground, it would be par for the course, but in this instance I was preparing to tunnel all the way to Australia.

'When did you last check the suspense account?' asked Matt.

'Last week.'

'So you haven't looked at it for over a week?'

'No.'

'OK. So you won't know that all the money in the account has gone?'

'No. Has it? Where has it gone?'

'I've moved it.'

'Please don't tell me you transferred it to your personal bank account,' I groaned.

'No, Jamie, I am not an idiot.'

'I think the jury's out on that one.'

'Yeah, anyway, all is not lost, Jamie boy,' he said, looking cheerful as he sidled past me heading back towards the bar. 'And a sensible head like yours will be pleased to know I have invested our illegally acquired funds in order to realise its full financial potential.'

'What do you mean?' I shouted.

'I'll tell you later. First, we need to see Samira.'

'Samira?'

'Yeah. Don't you want to see her?'

'No, why would I want to?'

Then Matt paused, like he was about to say something, but instead changed his mind and disappeared back into the bar.

# CHAPTER TWO

## THE ROAD TO ILFRACOMBE

Against my better judgement... No, let me rephrase that. With no hope, no future, no avenues, no pathways, no options, no nothing, I agreed to Matt's useless plan to see Samira. I also agreed to let him drive us down to Ilfracombe to see her, even though he was severely intoxicated, because there was a good chance we would veer off into a crash barrier, bringing my sense of hopelessness to a fatal and inappropriate conclusion.

However, Matt's intoxication was super infused with a gram of coke. This, so he told me, gave him hyper-sensitive and acute directional driving skills, also known as heightened night vision. I didn't need to worry, he told me, because there was no way we were going to crash.

'But why Ilfracombe?' I asked, sank down in the passenger seat, already thinking about the need to relieve myself after consuming copious amounts of alcohol. 'She lives in London.'

'Yeah, I know. She has a flat in London, and yeah, I go around to it two nights a week, and we are at it like rabbits, but right now she is staying down in Ilfracombe.'

'There's no need to brag,' I grumbled, watching the orange lights of the M25 northbound flick by.

'That's your fault, Jamie. You gave up on her.'

Now, no doubt you will have all heard that there are two sides to every story, and in the case of Samira and me, there are three sides. There's the way Matt sees it, the way I see it, and there's the way Samira sees it. I know what Matt thinks, I know what I think, but I still have no idea what Samira thinks. From my perspective, if I could turn back time and do it all over again, I wouldn't make the same mistakes, which is something along the lines of not reading the messages.

For instance, had I known that when Samira talked to me about marriage and how it reinforced patriarchal power over women, and when she had stressed the need to ensure that possessive concepts did not infiltrate our conscious and subconscious interactions, what I was supposed to say in reply was: Will you marry me? At least, that's what I think from a patriarchal point of view. But I also thought that there might be specialised codes, and the opposite meaning could be concluded from when your girlfriend demonstrates a firm grasp of post-feminist irony. Then, I might have taken a different approach.

However, I can never be sure.

And it was too late once I had called time on the relationship with Samira.

It didn't prevent Matt from making a beeline for her, as he left me sobbing into my 12th pint of lager because I thought I'd made a terrible mistake in dumping her.

Post relationship, post-reactive depression, Matt was soon telling me how he had proposed, and how Samira was euphoric, but it was an engagement that had a caveat, what he called a 50% proposal, as opposed to a full monty.

'Do you mean you only said, 'Will you,' and left out the 'marry me,' bit?' I had asked when I found out.

'Yeah, we got engaged in Rome.'

'But there's no wedding?'

'No, there's no wedding, just the engagement.'

'I thought the point of getting engaged was to get married?'

'Well, I'm not ruling it out, but I'm certainly not ruling it in.'

'Does Samira know this, that she's engaged to you but you're probably never going to get married?'

'Yeah,' Matt had insisted, and that had been the end of it.

Of course, as I hadn't spoken to Samira since we'd split up, I had no way of knowing that Matt's proposal to get engaged to Samira meant exactly as he described it.

I didn't attend the engagement party, and I didn't give them an engagement present, but as things stand, Matt and Samira were spending a life of engagement together.

Anyway, I just thought you'd like to know that before I get back to Matt's useless plan.

'All right, so what's this plan of yours? Are we going to become lobster fishermen?'

'It's genius!' said Matt, overtaking another very fast car and ignoring me as I sank deeper into the passenger seat.

'Oh, hang on,' I said, pulling out my phone and looking at the message, which read: Termination of contract of employment with immediate effect. 'Let me open this Einstein app. It will listen to people's ideas and give a verdict. It can tell you if your idea is genius, bullshit, or if you're just an effing idiot!'

'You know, Jamie, your problem is you don't inflate.'

'What does that mean?'

'Inflation theory. Did you know the universe came into being at an unimaginable rate, a rate of inflation that, even before a second had passed, was burning hot and breathing fire? The big brain that pressed the button to get things going didn't ponder the what-ifs and maybes – they inflated. And they ran with it.'

'Are you sure that astrophysicists think the Big Bang was caused by someone pressing a button?'

'I'm not being literal. I'm giving you the motivational analogy. You have good ideas, Jamie boy, but you never press the button… Let the seedling grow and inflate.'

'It was me who told you about the glitch.'

'Yeah, but then it was me who did all the inflating. Your problem, Jamie, is if you had to be carbon neutral, you'd start with a bonsai tree, when what you need is a forest.'

'Yeah, well, you do know that even if you plant an acorn, it takes 200 years to mature into an oak.'

'Listen,' said Matt, continuing to make illegal driving manoeuvres, 'horticulture is not the issue.'

'It's *your* analogy,' I said meaningfully.

'The point is,' he continued, because he was the only one who knew what the point was, 'we need to get there on time.'

'Is that the space-time continuum, or just bog-standard Greenwich Mean Time?'

'Time,' said Matt, struggling with the concept, 'is what matters.'

'Well, they do say don't do the crime if you can't do the time.'

'And I've got news for you, we both did the crime, and now we need to make up time. So shut up.'

And so I did, because I didn't want to know. I didn't want to know what mattered, what time it was, what time we needed to be there, why we needed to be there on time, and why on earth we needed to be on time just to meet Samira. And I also didn't want to know what Matt had planned, what Matt did with Samira two nights a week, or what Matt did five nights of the week alone in his bedroom.

I just didn't want to know.

I stared out of the passenger window, watching the lights of the motorway go by, up and down, up and down, watching the cars and lorries fall behind us, watching my life pass away into an alcoholic stupor, fragmented with fear, anxiety, and more fear, condemned by the consequences of our actions.

Sleep, at least for a bit of time, was full of disturbed imagery.

What happened next happened without me knowing anything about it, apart from the sound of screeching, followed by a thump, a thud, a bump, a thud, another bump, and a crash.

That's my memory of Matt flying out of control using his hyper-sensitive, acute directional driving skills. And I do mean fly, because as the ear-splitting brakes screamed like a constipated banshee, I opened my eyes to see a foggy mist of horizontal fields and disinterested cow faces munching away and waiting to have their udders soothed by warm hands.

That's what I always thought about dairy farming, and that's exactly the strange kind of thing that can pop into your head when faced with an existential crisis. A moment of pure unadulterated powerlessness, strangled by your seat belt, your arms and legs waving in pseudo gravity, waiting patiently to die.

It is often said that in such life-threatening moments, time slows down. It did for me, as I had time to review my life choices, with my mum, my dad, and my sister – all of whom told me I would end up being killed by Matt Chubb in a car crash.

But for now, at least, I was wondering why the world was upside down, why everything was so eerily quiet, why there was a large white balloon in my face, and why the cow fields smelt of petrol. They don't normally, I decided, still unsure why the cows should remain so passive after watching a wingless BMW fly and miss their cow cousins, aunties, and uncles by a couple of feet.

For once, Matt was unable to speak, offer a plan, or destroy my life any further (other than pending criminal fraud charges and life-threatening, drug-addled daytrips to North Devon). We were like two dazed monkeys hanging awkwardly by our seatbelt straps, contemplating the absurdity of life in the jungle of cow dung and dew drops.

However, I did take the initiative, because I suspected we could have just as easily stayed like that whilst challenging a cow about the meaning of life. With no bones broken, I took my weight off the seatbelt, unbuckled, and then banged my head on the upturned car roof. I think Matt must have taken a blow to the head because he carried on being silent as I pulled him out of his predicament and then dragged him away as far as I could from the wasted, smouldering German flagship.

I looked into his eyes and asked if he was concussed, and Matt just slowly shook his head as if he was oblivious and living with the fairies. But he looked sadder, defeated, something I had rarely, if ever, seen in Matt. I thought about saying something consoling and soothing… Such as the word "insurance".

Then he appeared to emerge from his temporary coma, and we both said something together that summed up our collective experience: 'Blimey.'

At last, we agreed on something, as the smoking car fully realised its combustible potential and caught fire. Initially, the heat was warming, as the flames spread rapidly through the vehicle, gutting the interiors, and boiling the bodywork. The cows took a bit more interest, then scuttled off to another patch of grass.

'Well,' I said to Matt, watching the flames roar and listening to things go pop and bang, 'at least we're alive.'

Matt shook his head slowly again, and I was wondering if he was going to tell me we were dead, and our bodies were floating off to Heaven. Or slipping down to Hell.

'We're stuffed,' he said instead.

'Again?'

'No,' Matt replied, demonstrating increasing levels of consciousness. 'I mean, we're really in the manure.'

I was confused. 'Eh, so what's the difference between just being close to a urinal or sitting in a field of cow dung?'

'You don't want to know.'

'Yes, Matt,' I said anxiously, 'I really do want to know what "really stuffed" looks like.'

'Really stuffed,' he said, with a distorted grimace, 'is being skinned alive, your toenails pulled out by rusty pliers, your balls cooked in olive oil, and your eyes sucked out by a Dyson V12.'

'That sounds like torture.'

Unfortunately, for both of us, Matt nodded.

What I am now about to tell you is a short précis of a very long conversation that took place in a field of cows and burning rubber.

Matt had seen the writing on the wall. He knew Bridges had smelt a rat and would have Compliance performing forensic audits on what we were up to, so he had decided to siphon off as much as he could and get the money out. In total, he had scammed about £250k, which was way above the few thousand I had in mind to pay for the annual skiing trip.

Between us, so Matt rationalised, that was close to two or three years' salary, and by Matt's risk-ratio calculation and opportunity cost, we were well short of an adequate return. Therefore, he had arranged, at short notice, a deal to significantly multiply our acquired sterling, split two ways, which was enough to disappear, invest, and sustain a quiet life off the grid, such as a log cabin in British Columbia.

At that point, I was thinking Matt would tell me about his investment in high-risk cryptocurrencies, junk bonds, or currency exchanges in Argentine pesos. Then that naïve hope met the reality of Matt's colossal idiocy. You see, Matt knew someone who also knew someone who also happened to know someone else, who was a big-time coke dealer. Now, in the world of city finance, coke is not a novelty, but what Matt had managed to secure was a significant investment in the commodity. He had also arranged, via someone who knew somebody else, to supply the commodity to an interested party. Therefore, we had been on our way to meet our trading partners who had travelled from Dublin to the North Devon coast (it needed to be vague, so Matt assured me) but we were to meet in Ilfracombe to finalise the exchange.

I was stoical, probably because I was still recovering from our near-death experience, but Matt had not finished, because he still had to explain why we were shafted.

To secure the deal with our Irish friends, he had borrowed an additional £250k from them. Half a million had been invested. And that's when the cog wheels in my brain began to whirr and clank, a gear shifted, and everything began to spin out of control.

'So we are stuffed,' I agreed, closing my eyes to absorb the fatalism overwhelming me. 'Because the coke was in the boot of the car that's now incinerated. That now means we owe £250k to a bunch of Irish drug dealers, and a loan of dubious provenance. That effectively pays for our torture, our eyes being pecked out by seagulls, before we are cut up into fish bait. On top of being unemployed and unemployable, and facing potential prosecution for financial fraud. In other words, in less than 24 hours, we have graduated from white-collar crime to organised crime.'

'Well, as long as I get a 2:1, I'm not that bothered.'

'I wonder if my mum will keep my bedroom as a shrine, or just erase all evidence of my existence?'

'Don't worry, your mum loves you, even if you do piss your pants. Still, there is one good thing.'

'Yeah, what's that?'

'This is the road to Ilfracombe.'

# CHAPTER THREE
## THE PINK HOUSE

Samira was staying in the Pink House overlooking the harbour. However, before we knocked on the door, there were two things Matt wanted to show me, just in case we didn't make it out alive.

One was a shop that sold hoovers, and the other was a Damien Hirst sculpture at the end of the harbour. He said he had to show me, because whilst he knew the pregnant woman with a sword pointing upwards was probably art, he thought the display of hoovers in the shop might also be a Damien Hirst, or an artwork by another artist. He needed my opinion before he could decide for himself, before he made peace with the world and faced his full appraisal with our maker.

'Do you know that Damien used to come here on holiday to Ilfracombe? That's why he did the statue, because of his memories of coming here as a child.'

'When did you last speak to Damien?'

'What do you mean? I've never spoken to Damien Hirst.'

'Well, you sound like you met him in the pub last night and you told him we were going to Ilfracombe, so he told you how much he loved the place as a kid.'

'No, I read about it. Anyway, what do you think?'

'Of the hoovers?'

'Yeah. Is that just a really strange shop, or is it art?'

At first, I didn't want to know, because I didn't know why we were casually wandering around a picturesque North Devon seaside town on our way to be beaten and murdered by a very angry drug gang from Dublin. Why were we not running as fast as we could in the other direction?

But I suppose I knew why: because we would be abandoning Samira to a fate worse than death (or lots of horrible things that eventually ended in her dying).

I looked at all the hoovers spread out across the floor, row upon row, all the way to the back of the shop, and I had to agree, it was strange, but I couldn't work out what was strange about it.

'The display,' I realised, observing them like a hard-headed art critic. 'There are no display stands. That's what's odd.'

'Heh, you're right. So it's not art, it's just a shop that puts no effort into displaying their goods in an appealing manner.'

'Well, we don't know for sure that it's not art. Have you ever tried to go in and buy a hoover?' I asked.

'No, the place is never open when I come here.'

'Suspicious,' I said, stroking my chin.

'Yeah, you're right, Jamie, very suspicious.'

'Which means it's inconclusive. But then, everything about this place feels… Inconclusive.'

'Now you're freaking me out,' said Matt, still staring into the shop full of hoovers with no display stands.

'Come on,' I said. 'I'm cold, and I don't think we can put off being murdered any longer.'

We left the pseudo-artwork hoover shop and carried on down Ilfracombe High Street, wondering if Damien Hirst had fossilised the whole place, because it was quiet, so quiet, that everything looked like it belonged in another age. *Perhaps Damien loved it here so much he'd had it pickled*, I thought. It was our last hope, because it felt like we were trudging through formaldehyde before reality struck inside the Pink House.

'You're late,' said Samira, who opened the door as we stood waiting under a wooden porch.

'We know,' Matt replied, who, like me, was reluctant to go in.

Samira was younger than us, in her late 20s, and she had the self-confidence of a woman who knew she was attractive enough not to put up with men if they didn't come up to scratch. I'd missed her since I'd dumped her, and I couldn't help gawping at how beautiful she looked. Her face and her hair were all perfectly proportioned, as if she had been sculptured out of marble. Her skin was as translucent as ever, tinged with healthy cheeks, crisp, darting eyes, and lips that I always thought should be kissed automatically. It was just odd that she had spent time with me, and now with Matt, because we were the same in one sense: the man-boys who didn't know how to grow up.

Then she turned to me. 'Did he show you the hoovers?'

'How did you know?'

'He shows everybody the hoovers,' she said, as she looked at me with her characteristic disdain. Matt just kept quiet.

'They're here, by the way. Waiting,' she added after a moment, widening her eyes to indicate we had our mission to fulfil.

And this was when things got a bit awkward.

Waiting for us in the large open-plan kitchen – very

nice interiors in the Pink House – were the members of the Dublin gang, also known as the Boss Man, the Henchman, and Danny Boy. We looked like two naughty schoolboys who had played truant all day and knew we were going to get into serious trouble.

We kept quiet as the Boss Man sarcastically welcomed us like we were his distant cousins back from America.

'Well, well, well, if it isn't the bad boys of London, here to fulfil their side of the bargain and deliver on their contractual commitments,' said the Boss Man, who looked as if he had been standing there stewing ever since he stepped into the house.

He was short and stubby, with a big, fat protruding stomach that I stereotyped as an outcome of copious amounts of Guinness. It might also be worth mentioning that he reminded me of one of my uncles who had been claiming disability benefits for the last 40 years, bet on the horses every Thursday, and hated cricket. I was fearful but also felt some kind of familiarity with the man, even if he was more than likely going to bring the curtain down on my pitifully unhappy life.

However, I didn't think it was my place to say anything, because it was Matt who should die first.

'Sorry we're late,' he said, trying his best to sound genuinely sorry. 'We had an accident on the way down here.'

'Did you now?' asked the Boss Man, who nodded thoughtfully at the Henchman to his right, and the guy to his left, who we got to know as Danny, (although for the purposes of this chapter I will continue to refer to him as Danny Boy). 'And what kind of accident did you have on your way down to this lovely Pink House by the sea?'

'A car accident,' said Matt, which of course was true.

'A car accident,' the Boss Man repeated as he addressed our informal circle in the large open-plan kitchen with its nice interiors. 'Well, I hope you boys are all right. You do look a bit beat up, but still in one piece, I see. Which is good, because we wouldn't want anything to get in the way of you two eejits delivering on what we are expecting from you.'

That's when things started to go downhill. Because there's no way you can bring bad news, especially to gangsters, that can be sugar-coated, massaged, or filtered, without it sounding like bad news for them, but mainly for you, in terms of consequences.

'We've lost the coke.'

What happened next is a little bit of a blur, so I will just focus on the ending. I ended up with a very long blade across my throat courtesy of Danny Boy, and Matt's hand was rammed into a toaster by the very, very big Henchman. He then began trying to toast Matt's fingers, but the toaster wouldn't stay down.

'You need to turn it on,' said Samira, who helpfully flicked the plug switch.

*Interesting*, I thought. Samira was either trying to demonstrate some kind of loyalty to the Dublin gang, or she was so angry with Matt that she was more than willing to facilitate any kind of punishment.

For a second, I felt sorry for him, but then remembered I hated the bulbous pus-ball for ruining my less-than-ambitious life. I think it took approximately five seconds before Matt started screaming like a baby. I could tell that Samira was quietly raging inside, because she pushed a tub of butter towards the heated toaster, checked the timer, and turned it all the way up to human finger Welsh rarebit.

Ouch!

Which is not the sound of Matt complaining about how the flesh on his fingers was melting, but the sound inside my head as I realised Samira was not just angry, but disappointed. Now this may not sound like a significant deviation, but I have learned in the subsequent years of my life that a partner's disappointment has far greater meaning than pure rage or anger. And for now, at least, Matt was still Samira's partner – engaged, but not to be married – and evidently a disappointment.

As Matt's fingers burned, and Matt's face turned red and oozed pain, suffering, and an acute sense of anguish, the Boss Man got up close and personal.

'Now,' he said, in full threatening mode, drool dripping down the side of his mouth, 'where is my money!'

For some insane reason, I decided to seek further clarification. 'Don't you mean the coke?'

Fortunately, the Boss Man stayed focused on Matt's desperate and agonised face whilst providing the clarification I was seeking.

'No!' he said, all mean, nasty, and full of vengeance. 'The coke is gone, so you tell me. So now I want me money back. The question is, how are you going to pay me?'

I randomly calculated in my head that I was just below the credit limit on all my cards and had spent the bulk of this month's salary on a new squash racket – trust me, they're seriously expensive. All Matt could offer in remuneration was a heartfelt scream of pain, which must have meant his fingers were beginning to brown quite nicely. He then looked at me with his eyes bulging and a desperate plea for me to come to his aid. All I could do was indicate with a sideways glance at Danny Boy that my throat was about to be cut, which was a far greater worry to me than his toasted fingers.

It was at that moment that my life flashed before my eyes, as the hideous, eternal truth that all life eventually comes to an end, nailed itself to an image of a crucifixion. This would have happened were it not for St. Samira's intervention.

Having believed, probably quite fairly, that both Matt and I should suffer for being two wholly inadequate man-boys, who had failed emotionally and materially, she turned off the toaster and announced the following.

'I have the money.'

Sweet Jesus, Holy, and Mary! Hallelujah! Praise the Lord, his disciples, his uncles, aunts, cousins, nephews, and nieces!

Samira has the money!

But how? It is at this point that you should know that Samira is a personal trainer. Her annual income is typical of a personal trainer – about enough to keep a rabbit in lettuce for a week with very little declared to His Majesty's Revenue and Customs. She worked part-time in the gym around the corner from our offices, whilst also maintaining a running machine in her living room that constantly annoyed her fellow flatmates with the pounding feet of an insomniac. So, that said, unless her numbers had come up on her lottery ticket or a long-lost uncle had bequeathed his entire fortune, I could not see how she had suddenly acquired £250k.

The Boss Man was also sceptical. 'And where, pretty lady,

have you suddenly acquired 250,000?'

Before Samira could answer, Matt began pleading for his hand to be released from the toaster by the Henchman.

'Shut up!'

Which meant no.

'Take his hand out,' said Samira assertively. 'And then I'll tell you how to get your money back.'

I don't think it was what the Boss Man wanted, or the Henchman, who must have felt he had barely gotten started, but Matt's hand was removed.

He held it out in front of him. We all stared at it, curious to know what a toaster could do to human fingers. They were red, slightly browned, and could have done with at least another minute.

'I suggest you run it under the tap,' said the Boss Man, who was surprisingly sympathetic.

Matt was in shock, shivering like a petrified prolapsed anus.

Samira, out of the generosity of her disappointed heart, ran the cold-water tap. She even helped Matt hold his hand as he let out a deep-felt sigh of relief. It was a touching moment. Love restored; engagement rehabilitated; first aid performed.

Although I did wonder if cold water was still the correct treatment for skin burns. I did vaguely recall a first aid course I attended while I was a respected employee, and the urban myth-busting advice that you should wrap clingfilm around such a wound before heading off to A&E. But I could be wrong. Plus, I wasn't sure why Matt should be given special treatment when I still had a knife to my throat.

However, I was going to keep quiet as I hoped Samira was

not seeking to delay the inevitable and was ready to write a cheque.

She left Matt to keep his hand in the cold water and looked at each of us, one by one, before she then explained where and how she had obtained the money we all needed.

'Truth is,' she began, with a faint flutter of her eyelids, 'I bought the coke for 50% less.'

'But it was Matt who bought the coke!' I blurted out, feeling the pressure of the knife Danny Boy still had pressed against my skin.

'Is that what he told you?'

I nodded. Matt kept his back to everyone and made strange soothing noises as the cold water poured over his hand.

'What do you think makes you city boys run like demented lemons on those treadmills all day? I have the best contacts in the gym and plenty of willing suppliers.'

'So,' intervened the Boss Man, 'you cut the coke you were going to give us?'

'No, I just got a better price than Matt thought he had negotiated. That's why I have £250k tucked away.'

I had to ask, 'What's the conversion rate, sterling to euros?'

'Heh, shut up!' said the disciplinarian Boss Man. 'Listen to the lady who has more balls than you two useless urchins.'

He had a point, I suppose.

'We'll take sterling,' he said. 'Now, how do we get our money off you, then?'

'I don't have it on me, so I'll need to go and get it.'

'You haven't been as stupid as these two eejits and put the money in one of them banks?'

Samira shook her head, like an all-knowing, all-seeing

goddess of salvation for severely challenged and thoroughly contrite man-boys.

'My gran's got it,' she said, with assurance.

'OK, and where's this gran of yours at? Has she stuffed it under her pillow?'

'No. She doesn't know, of course, but the money is secured and in her possession.'

'You mean, you've hidden it in her house?'

Samira moved her head sideways, indicating she was revealing something, but not everything.

'Now, don't you mess with me. Where does she live?' he asked.

'The Shetlands.'

'Scotland?'

Samira nodded.

The Boss Man paused, weighing up the evidence and contemplating a judgment. 'OK,' he said, as if he had come to a decision. 'And what's your gran's name?'

'Mavis,' said Samira, without hesitating. 'Mavis Grind.'

'Mavis Grind, you say,' replied the Boss Man, in a tone that suggested he didn't believe everything he was being told, but there was some tangible authenticity to it.

There was another pause as the Boss Man calculated, as Matt turned around and looked at Samira with a large question mark hovering above his head.

I hoped he would keep quiet and think about the toaster rather than opening up a panoply of uncertainty.

'OK, so this is what I have decided,' the Boss Man said, with a degree of finality. 'Today is Monday, which means you can be there by Friday.'

'I can fly there today and get it sorted,' Samira countered.

'No, you can't. Seeing as none of you can be trusted, Danny Boy here will be coming with you to see your gran, but you'll be driving up there because he has a bit of a fear of flying, don't you, Danny Boy?'

I assumed Danny Boy was agreeing as the Boss Man continued with his offer.

'When you get there, you give the money to Danny Boy, and then that's it, you don't ever have anything to do with me or any others like me… And you don't ever come to Dublin.'

I nodded enthusiastically, Matt remained perplexed, and Samira maintained a steely self-confidence.

'Right, and there are rules. No social media. No Tik-Tok-X-Flock-Facebook-social-bollocks crap. You're off the radar, got it?'

Relief! There is a god.

I always believed in you, dearly beloved god of all things magnificent, and beautiful, and if there is a history of atheism in my personal belief system up to this moment in time, I can only offer my most profound apologies and will happily spend the rest of my life in a monastery, in silence, contemplating the great benevolence that shines from out of your wonderous heart and sacred eyes.

I know, up against it and in a crisis, you always turn to "you know who".

At this point, the knife was sheathed, and Danny Boy stepped forward.

Dressed in black army fatigues, black army boots, and a skull cap, he cut a figure of purpose, single-mindedness, and what I suspected was a ruthless determination to see things through. Even though he'd had a knife poised to carve across my throat, I didn't detect in his face a man who was as hardened as I supposed him to be. I don't know what it was, instinct perhaps, but there was a glint in his eyes, a casual mischievousness that probably endeared him to others – perhaps as they were about to meet their maker. But it seemed a pleasant way to go.

'Right, I'll be getting the wheels then,' he said, and walked out without saying goodbye.

Fair enough, it seemed as good a time as any to settle down and have a nice cup of tea.

Phew.

# ON THE ROAD

# CHAPTER ONE

## ON THE COASTAL ROAD

Whilst Danny Boy went to get some wheels, I have time to tell you everything you need to know about him. The first thing you will need to know is that his real name is not Danny Boy, but Michael O'Brien. However, in order for you not to become unnecessarily confused with the gradual accumulation of characters and nicknames who join us on our little road trip to Mavis Grind, Danny Boy will now be referred to as Danny. This is mainly because he said it was not for the English to call him Danny Boy and would constitute a derogatory and stereotypical naming of Irish men.

Now, much of what I am about to tell you was acquired during our long and arduous trip up the spine of our crumbling state of nations. It is information I gathered in conversations I had with Danny, either sat behind him as he kept his eyes on the road, during and after we had eaten, at the urinal, or in moments when there was a pause in general levels of absurdity – trust me, this will become apparent sooner rather than later. In fact, there is a fair degree of absurdity that characterises Danny, as he revealed various truths about himself, which, over time, I realised I should have viewed with a thick sceptical lens, but at the time seemed perfectly plausible.

He told me he was born in Belfast and was a Protestant,

so he grew up knowing how to hate Catholics, but his parents moved down to Dublin before his prejudices could become deeply embedded in an intractable sectarian psyche. Removed from the boiling pot of divided neighbours, Danny experienced an epiphany, a conversion that led to him adopting the Catholic faith. Whether this was an instinctive response to rebelling against his parents or a genuine moment of self-revelation, Danny was reticent in discussing the specifics, but it all meant a 180-degree turn and a hatred of discrimination and oppression.

And such was Danny's enthusiasm for taking the fight to the oppressor, he decided to dedicate himself to the cause of a united Ireland – Erie, Gaelic – and political and military activism. It is at this point that Danny acquired his nickname, because his codename within the IRA, and post IRA, the Real IRA, was Danny Boy. It was through his freedom-fighting days that Danny moved between the legitimate and illegitimate worlds of freedom fighting, and how he slowly but surely got dragged more and more into gangsterism and less and less into uniting Ireland. In fact, disillusioned with "the struggle" and increasingly attracted by the money, it seemed the only profitable and viable future for him was to go all in with the gangs who helped fund the cause.

Towards the end of our journey, the views Danny expressed to me on the road were rather jaded and distorted, and akin to my own encrusted cynicism, so much so that I thought we were like kindred souls or distant cousins. Surprisingly, he said, he hated the Irish as much as he hated the English. He said what he hated about Ireland were the priests, the nuns, Guinness, Ryanair, Gaelic games, folk music, the Giant's

Causeway, and garden gnomes. That, I said, seemed to be a hatred for all things Irish, or some of the things that culturally define Ireland, at least.

And he agreed.

The last thing you might find interesting about Danny was he had just completed an Open University degree in English Literature. He was well-read, having finished his dissertation on the Joycean synapse in a Beckettian stream of consciousness.

'No way,' I had said.

'Yes way,' he'd replied.

Back in the kitchen of the Pink House and having made a cup of tea for the Boss Man, the Henchman, a whimpering Matt, and a disappointed Samira, casual conversation had been exhausted after we had worked out who wanted milk and who wanted sugar.

Relief came when Danny pulled up outside the Pink House in a 12-seater mini vehicle with the North Devon NHS Community Trust Transport logo embossed along the sides.

As we all stood outside the Pink House, feeling the January cold cool our house-warm flesh, we were further stunned into more temporary silence as we all considered the viability of such a vehicle.

'It's the best I could do,' said Danny, leaning his arm out of the driver's seat. 'With the time and all and the need to get going.'

Matt had no doubts, desperate to escape the Boss Man and the Henchman. Samira seemed to agree, because she said it meant she wouldn't have to sit next to either of us. My own assessment consisted of options again.

Option one: we seek a more appropriate, less conspicuous mode of transport. Whilst desirable, it would mean spending more time with people who clearly had nothing to say to each other. And even if we did stay in the Pink House until a BMW or Mercedes had been acquired, we would all be dead, lying in pools of blood, inflicted by others, and self-inflicted as the easiest way out.

The second option was to do as we were told.

'Right,' said the Boss Man. 'You three get in there and do everything that Danny Boy tells you to do. Any shenanigans, and I'll have your eyes pecked out by seagulls before we cut you up into fish bait.'

Ah ha! Just as I had predicted.

'What are you smiling about?' Matt asked, with his toasted hand wrapped in clingfilm.

I kept my insight to myself, as one by one, looking like something along the lines of Noah's Community Ark, we took our seats as far away from each other as possible.

Danny took one look at all of us, grinned, as he no doubt considered me and Matt as low-hanging fruit, and pulled off into the fading light. In other words, as the Boss Man and the Henchman stared grievously at our departing vehicle, the day of "our greatest trauma" was coming to an end.

At least, that's what I thought.

Sat in silence, winding through the narrow roads on our way out of Ilfracombe, I did manage to glimpse the pregnant sword of the Damien Hirst. As we drove down the High Street, I was able to look down into the obscure shop window with artistically arranged hoovers. And so I wondered: was there some symbolic meaning in the pregnant sword and random artwork that was probably not artwork?

No, I decided.

Instead, I began hastily processing a few things.

First off, I was nervous about Samira. She had demonstrated a determined resilience, a malice aforethought, that I had never equated with her character because I had rather derogatorily assumed she had no greater concerns beyond running, weightlifting, and squatting. But the toaster incident, a discreet background in city drug deals, and the sleight of hand in acquiring a significant amount of money, suggested I had missed something – if not a lot – when I was going out with Samira. Within a few hours, she had demonstrated there was an individualism, a self-reliance that meant men, such as Matt and me, were instantly disposable if we failed to come up to scratch. She was no longer demure but positively proactive. It was not a bad thing in itself; I was just surprised that I had missed it and felt guilty for failing to look beyond the surface of her attractiveness.

I was genuinely surprised that she could place herself at the heart of mildly substantial drug deals, navigate her way out of death by seagulls and fish knives, and put us on the Yellow Brick Road to salvation. But it was probably not the first time I had underestimated Samira. She was a bit of an enigma, even after explaining how a young Indian woman had to jump through hoops, crawl under fences, and climb over brick walls just to get noticed, and also known as isolated incidents of a racist variety that accumulate from small acts of exclusion to fascist ideology.

However, when it came to her family, she dismissed them

as boring, conventional, and thoroughly uninteresting, and she had to put a lot of time into keeping them at arm's length because they always wanted her to do something far more predictable with her life, rather than watching men and women running up and down on a treadmill. I just wondered if it was possible that Samira had a Scottish granny.

Was she telling the truth?

And did Matt know more than he was letting on?

That was top of my list of priorities, but required a separate conversation with both of them, away from Danny's big ears. (By the way, Danny does not and never has had big ears. His ears are perfectly proportioned, aligned with his eyes and his nose.)

My next priority was far more practical. If we were to spend the next few days on this journey, I would need a toothbrush, toothpaste, clean pants, and socks. Minimum. Not that I'm obsessive about personal hygiene, but a line needs to be drawn regarding what is acceptable among travelling companions. Being smelly, rather than odourless, is going to grind on the road trip to see Mavis Grind.

Which reminds me – deodorant.

As we left Ilfracombe behind, I plucked up the courage to move from my one seat back and sit behind Danny, who I noticed had been using his mirror to keep an eye on Matt in the middle of the vehicle, and Samira sat at the back.

So I knew that he knew I was now right behind him.

'My name's Jamie,' I said.

'I know,' Danny replied, as he sped along the country lanes.

'I was just wondering...' I began with a degree of

trepidation. 'Two things, really. Like, we don't have any personal items – toothbrush, toothpaste, clean pants and socks, deodorant. You know, that kind of thing. I was also wondering if we have made ourselves a little bit conspicuous. I mean, won't the police find it easy to spot our stolen vehicle with that big logo embossed along the sides?'

Initially, I got the silent treatment, telling me that I was asking questions that were outside the scope of my responsibilities.

'Are you trying to say I smell?' asked Danny, who had clearly picked up on the former rather than the latter

'No, no,' I said hastily and awkwardly. 'It's me. I mean, you know, I can emit odours... Especially the feet... If that makes sense.'

That was bad. I should have kept my mouth shut. And just for the record, I don't spray deodorant on my feet unless they're really smelly.

'Forget it,' I muttered, wincing at my pathetic attempt to play a constructive part in our criminal escapade.

'Don't you worry,' Danny replied, arching his back. 'If you start to smell, I'll be sure to strap you to the roof so none of us have to suffer from your smelly feet.'

'Thanks,' I answered sheepishly.

'Oh, and just so you know, I don't think borrowing a vehicle like this is as conspicuous as crashing a car full of coke.'

'That was Matt,' I said, wanting to make sure that my own idiocy was passive rather than active.

Danny grinned and then offered some degree of reassurance. 'We'll be taking the coastal road and keeping off the motorway. We'll take the A39. That way we won't be so *conspicuous.*'

'OK,' I replied, wishing I had just kept my mouth shut. After all, I was only a white-collar fraudster. Danny was the professional.

I turned around to see that Matt had his head against the window and his eyes closed. *He must be in a lot of pain*, I thought to myself, and took great pleasure in thinking about that for a few seconds. Then I looked at Samira, and she stuck her tongue out at me.

I turned away, looked forlornly through the windscreen as Danny shifted gears, whilst coming to the obvious conclusion that Samira really didn't like me.

I used Google Maps to check how long it would take us to get from Ilfracombe to Lerwick on the Shetland Islands. 23 hours and 18 minutes via the quickest route, but we were already starting to take the long way round. That was generous of the Boss Man to give us time to get all the way up to see Samira's gran, sit down with her, and sip some broth, while Samira gave Danny a bag of sterling to the tune of £250k.

I didn't believe it.

Or, I should say, I couldn't imagine such a scene.

Life isn't that simple. The solution couldn't be that simple when it was already profoundly absurd, having gone to work yesterday, being freaked out by Compliance, meeting Matt in the pub and establishing yet again that the guy is a wide-ranging liability, getting sacked for a minor discrepancy with the suspense account, driving down to Ilfracombe to see my ex-girlfriend after crashing a car with a boot full of coke, then facing death by seagulls and a rusty fishhook by a Dublin gang boss toasting Matt's grubby hand.

I turned around again to check on my partners in crime, and Matt was firmly with the fairies, and Samira had also closed her eyes – although I suspect she was probably keeping one eye open. As much as I wanted to shut my eyes and wake up the next morning in my mum's house with breakfast waiting for me downstairs, the adrenaline was keeping me alert.

There was nobody I could trust, I realised. There was nothing predictable about what lay ahead. Also, the more I thought about it, there didn't seem to be any good reason for having Matt or me around, seeing as it was Samira who had the money. I was almost tempted to ask Danny if he could drop me off at the next bus stop, on the basis that, in reality, I was surplus to requirements.

Then the thought occurred to me that if there was no logical reason to retain myself or Matt, the only other reason for keeping us on board was to peck our eyes out and use us as fish bait once the money was retrieved. It made sense, in a classical crime thriller kind of way, that loose ends are tied up once the objective has been completed. There would be no risk of loose lips blabbering stuff to impressionable young ladies in sweaty nightclubs, perhaps in a slightly inebriated state, propping up a bar as you spent the last few pennies from your fortnightly benefits income. There would also be no risk if you had a visit from the local constabulary, who were looking into reported discrepancies at a highly respectable city firm. You can't save your neck and spill the beans if your arms, limbs, torso, and head are buried in remote parts of the Atlantic.

As these mildly paranoid thoughts preoccupied me, I unconsciously drifted off into a distorted REM sleep, chased by fat-headed seagulls swooping down to steal my ice cream and fish and chips.

The nightmare only stopped when I heard the following from Danny: 'Heh, wake up!'

And so I did, pronto and obediently.

Fortunately, he didn't have a knife to my throat, but neither was he offering me a nice cup of tea. 'I need you to go up front,' he said, his eyes looking slightly mean and aggressive.

'What?'

'We've messed up.'

'What?' And then, as my brain began to find its way out of the menacing flock of seagulls, I realised we had come to a stop.

Danny then nodded at the side of the window.

It was dark, very dark, so dark the darkness was pressed up against the window.

'That's the edge,' he said, offering a fatalistic shrug.

'The edge? The edge of what?'

'The world,' he said, less than impressed. 'No, the edge of the cliff, you eejit!'

'What cliff?'

Danny sighed. 'Just to remind you, you daft city boy, this is the coastal road we're on, and we are right close to the edge, and I can't see where that edge is, even with these headlights, so I need you to get in front of the vehicle and guide us along.'

'What?'

'Stop saying what. You'll wake the babies back there.'

'What babies?'

'What did I just say to you?'

'Don't wake the babies.' Then the penny dropped, as I turned around to see Matt and Samira fast asleep.

As you may have guessed by now, I have a fundamental aversion to risk, threat, and danger –apart from the odd white-collar crime that has been carefully calibrated – and I didn't see why it should be me walking off the edge of the cliff into a watery grave with my eyes pecked out by seagulls and my skin nibbled by disgruntled seabass.

But there was no debate, drawing straws, rock-paper-scissors, or strip poker to ensure some degree of democratic allocation of risk-taking.

Instead, I was handed a torch.

'Now,' Danny began, setting himself at the steering wheel again, 'you shine the torch along the edge and point me to the angle I should be taking. Walk to the limit of me headlights, and no freaking out just because we're next to them moors.'

'What's wrong with the moors? If I fall to the right, I won't fall off the cliff.'

'*The Hounds of the Baskervilles*... Mad dogs,' he said sombrely, like he had lived with this fear since the day he was born.

'That's fiction,' I said, convinced rationality was yet again on my side.

'That's what you think. Darkness plays tricks.'

This was not encouraging me, but then I suppose I was hardly in a position to argue.

I was the chosen one, whether I liked it or not.

So with a degree of trepidation, I stepped outside and shone the torch... And man, was it cold, dark, and eerie!

The edge of the world was approximately one or two yards away, as the headlights and my torch picked out the green crumbly precipice, which, having looked things up in Google Maps earlier, I knew to be hundreds of feet above sea level.

I cursed Matt because he was my default curse, and buried my head in my hood as the wind whipped around and the air bit into every exposed pore of my skin. I heard Danny start up the engine, and rather like guiding a plane into landing, I stuck out my hand. Hard right.

Of course, I'll admit, the thought kept popping into my head that it would only take extending my arm hard left, for all my troubles to suddenly be driven off the cliff edge. Admittedly, I would have to adopt an alias and live on the fringes of society with a bunch of Emperor Penguins, but it was tempting – even if incompatible with my slightly wonky moral compass. Plus, I suppose I would miss the idiocy of the prolapsed anus known as Matt, and I would never know if Samira still held a small candle for me, fluttering in the westerlies ripping through my crumpled heart.

Apologies for that vomit-inducing romanticising, but I have been struggling for months trying to get my head around Samira choosing Matt over me. All right, it's true, it was my mistake, and I let it happen because it was me who dumped her, but she didn't have to go galloping over to Matt, who, for all his faults, was the one person I could call a friend. You were lucky to find anyone close to being a genuine friend in the city.

There was hope, I thought. Fate may have played a hand, based on fragmented connections that only make sense in multiverse-type situations like these, because Samira was now closer to me, in terms of physical proximity, than she has ever been. There were things I had discovered about Samira today that I had never seen before. There was fortitude, resilience, planning, and cunning; something unexpected and as intriguing as the potential outcome of our journey to the farthest reaches of this green and pleasant land (I will also accept that the word "pleasant" can be replaced with other descriptors, and please feel free to say them aloud to yourself while chortling into a £1.50 two-litre bottle of cider).

Right, now, where was I?

Oh, yes, about to fall to my death.

However, before that could happen, the howling wind began getting seriously windy, and rain had now started battering my face, my body, my frozen hands, and my frozen feet. I could barely see any better than Danny, hunched over the steering wheel and beeping at me to get a move on.

He was welcome to fulfil a death wish, but I was diligently performing my task as assigned when I looked into the deep dark vista of the moors and was spooked by two green slanting eyes, peering inexplicably at me.

I immediately held up my hand, as if I were "on point" in an army recon patrol, hoping Danny would stop and not run into me as I stared back at the piercing green eyes that were unmistakably translucent.

Was it the mad dog of Baskerville, as Danny had ominously warned? Would it rip out my throat and toy with my intestines, before tossing me over the cliff edge for seagulls to peck out my eyes?

What the eff was it?

That's when I made another mistake.

I shone the torch on the green eyes and lit up the fangs and whiskers of an enormous cat.

'What the—' I managed to blurt out, before the beast of Exmoor leaped towards me.

I ran.

I ran along that tarmac road pooing my pants. I ran like the wind, like a demented wailing banshee. I didn't care about the cliff edge. I was wetting myself with fear because I'd just had fangs and claws fly at me out of the abyss.

In fact, I would have carried on running all the way to Minehead, but for the fortuitous sight of another car coming towards me. At least, I thought it was a good sign, until I realised that it had luminous markings, blue lights, and a policeman who looked as confused and bewildered as I probably did.

He stopped, and I stopped as I heard the North Devon NHS Community Trust Transport pull up behind me.

I was filled with a sense of relief and despair. Even though I had committed mildly heinous fraud, I broadly considered myself a law-abiding citizen, and so the sight of a policeman at a moment of distress was a welcome sight. On the other hand, it probably also meant I was going to have to reflect on how often I would be sodomised at His Majesty's pleasure.

There was only one option.

I had to lie and use the poker face I had used staring down the barrel of Compliance, and hope the police were not searching for a stolen North Devon NHS Community Trust Transport vehicle.

The policeman got out of the car and shone a torch directly into my face. As I put up my hands, he came closer and asked a highly appropriate and reasonable question.

'What are you doing out here?' he said, in a tone of disbelief.

'Sorry,' I said, trying to refocus after being effectively blinded. 'We took the wrong road.'

He looked over my shoulder and shone the torch into the windscreen behind me. I looked back to see Danny wave and shrug. It might reinforce the rubbish I was about to make up.

'Are you with this vehicle, sir?' the policeman asked, pulling a face that had admonishment written all over it.

'Yes, sorry,' I said, shaking my head so as to project my own sense of dismay. 'We are escorting two psychiatric patients back to Minehead. We took a wrong turning and ended up on the coastal road. We thought we could make it while it was still light, but got caught out. I'm just trying to help guide us back, you know, so we don't fall off the edge.'

He paused, as all good diligent policemen should, assimilating the stupidity of our situation.

'You do know that what you are doing is extremely dangerous?' he said, pointing out the obvious, again, as all good policemen tend to do.

'I know,' I admitted, hoping he wouldn't start asking for things such as ID cards.

I also momentarily named myself Dr Jekyll just in case he asked.

'Looks like you'll need some help,' he said, shaking his head.

'Yeah, thanks, that would be great,' I replied, relieved I was not going to be arrested just yet, and relieved we might safely avoid crashing to our deaths.

'I'll reverse,' he said. 'And you can follow.'

Now that was a very nice man.

Which I also communicated to Danny, Matt, and Samira, demanding they appreciate the sacrifice I had made to ensure we made it off the coastal road.

However, the rest of the journey into Minehead was taken up with Danny requesting I reiterate, a number of times, exactly what I had said to the copper, and Matt incredulously querying the detail of the big cat.

'Puma,' Matt said eventually. He then went on to tell all of us that it was a well-known fact that big cats had been abandoned on the moors by irresponsible pet owners, and that I was lucky not to have had my throat ripped open. However, Danny unhelpfully added he'd seen nothing, told Matt to shut up, and went back to asking me what exactly I had said to the copper. It was not until we arrived in Minehead that the exhausting cross-examination of my brief interaction with the law ceased.

Mistrust was the word that came to mind.

Danny had turned his attention to finding a place we could park for the night.

I didn't care.

I shut my eyes, because if anyone deserved a good night's sleep, it was me.

# CHAPTER TWO

## THE CHE GUEVARA SUGAR SACHETS

If I slept, I didn't know I had, because my dream world seemed like a reality. Mr Blobby was sitting on my face letting one rip and suffocating me whilst singing *Follow the Yellow Brick Road* from *The Wizard of Oz.* Then things heavily turned urinal, like public toilet urinal, permeating my nostrils and boring into my brain. As I struggled to wake from this nightmare – kicking out with both feet to stop Matt urinating on me any longer – a very old woman was staring at me, a bit like my mum would do when I had to ask if she had managed to wash my favourite *Snoopy* T-shirt.

That's when I knew I was still dreaming, because there were multiple faces of old women all staring at me in the same way. But on the other hand, I wasn't dreaming, because when I looked outside the window, there were cars and lorries, vans, trucks, and coaches running parallel or going past us. Which meant we were moving. Which meant we were on the motorway. Which meant I probably wasn't dreaming.

And this was real.

'Ahh… Ahh.'

'All right?' said Matt, who was sitting next to me.

'What the…'

'Yeah, I know,' he said, which was OK for him because I definitely didn't know.

So I had two questions. 'Have you been urinating on me? And why do we have loads of old women staring at us?'

'Listen, mate, you may think I urinate all over you, but that's not me that stinks.'

'Who smells of piss, then?'

'Who do you think?' he replied, inviting me to survey the old women.

'OK, so why are they—' I started to say, but struggled to finish my sentence as I looked around to see Samira sitting behind us listening to an old woman talking about her local butcher and the succulent beef cuts she gets from him.

The only sense of normality came from seeing the back of Danny, still diligently at the steering wheel, motoring along.

I looked at Matt with my eyes so wide open that he would understand I needed some kind of vaguely rational explanation.

'Right,' he began, sighing deeply. 'Where we parked last night was in the car park of some care home. We were all asleep when this woman, like a matron, started shuffling these ladies onto the vehicle.'

'You're kidding?'

'Nope'

'You mean…?'

'Yep. We had to pretend we were the transport they get every Tuesday and Thursday morning to the Minehead Day Centre.'

'OMG.'

'You know what,' said Matt. 'I never liked that abbreviation. I think we're getting too old for it.'

He was probably right.

'But,' I said, as I assimilated the intel from the prolapsed anus, 'are we actually going to the Day Centre?'

'No,' Matt explained, shaking his head, resigned to something that was beyond our control. 'Don't worry, they've all got dementia, so they haven't got a clue what's going on.'

'You mean, we're taking a dozen old ladies with dementia to see another old lady called Mavis Grind on the Shetland Islands?'

'Who knows. The way I see it, anything's possible.'

I felt a tap on my shoulder, and then my ear being flicked.

It was Samira.

'Just so you know,' she said, as I turned around again, 'I have already told Matt, and I am now telling you: I will not be talking to either of you for the remainder of this trip. The only exception will be life or death situations that require mutually beneficial cooperation.'

'Does that mean you're not going to talk about kidnapping old ladies from a care home?'

'We didn't kidnap them,' Samira replied, nodding at her friend sitting next to her, recalling the best choice cuts. 'Danny made the only decision we could. Anyway, it's a nice day out for them. Better than sitting there all day in front of a TV.'

'Trust me,' I said. 'With a bus load of dementia patients, we will not get further than the two centimetres up the M1, and just past the third centimetre we will be arrested, vilified, and locked up for a very long time for involving little old ladies in the crime of the century.'

'Jamie, you've always been a drama queen. We will' – Samira paused as she leaned forward – 'toilet them at the next service station, and there they can be left safely and collected.'

I also leaned forward and whispered like a drama queen, 'If you think I'm pulling down little old ladies' knickers and wiping their bums, you've got another thing coming. Also, don't you think driving off with little old ladies, even just for five minutes, is still along the lines of abduction? The police will not only be looking for a stolen North Devon NHS Community Trust Transport vehicle, but there will be international arrest warrants out for the Beasts of Bodmin, who kidnapped and then dumped these frail and vulnerable little old ladies in a car park next to a burger van.'

Samira rolled her eyes, which is something she used to do a lot when we were an item. 'Danny has a plan,' she said, and returned to maintaining purdah whilst in the presence of the man-boys.

I looked at Matt, hoping for some kind of support. He looked back as if to say, 'Don't look at me, I've got nothing to do with this.'

*Well,* I thought to myself, *if Danny has a plan, then we are under the direction of the master planner,* and to some extent, I had more confidence in a professional gangster than Matt trying to perform the role.

'How's your hand?' I asked him whilst wondering why we should be toileting old ladies and not just leaving them and doing a runner.

'It stings,' Matt replied, holding up the hand that had been wrapped in clingfilm and looked like a pulverised jellied eel.

'You should go to A&E,' I said, whilst wistfully thinking about coffee and toast.

Then, from behind us, the purdah was broken.

'He's not going to the hospital. It will attract attention.'

'And kidnapping a dozen little old ladies doesn't qualify as attention seeking?'

'Shut up, Jamie! Don't make me have to talk to you!'

Matt, despondently, lowered his hand.

Samira, whether she liked it or not, was going to have to talk to me before we got anywhere near the Scottish border.

I rubbed the sleep out of my eyes and then stared back at one of the old ladies who had been permanently gawking at us since my rude awakening. Her cracked and wrinkled face, her dry lips, and sullen eyes were mildly disturbing.

*It all comes to this*, I thought. *After all the trials and tribulations of failing at everything in life, old age creeps up on you and slaps a sell-by date on your forehead. You are then dumped in some remote seaside care home, kidnapped by a bunch of desperate, heartless city workers, taken for a ride to a remote service station, and then abandoned in your urine-soaked incontinence nappies.*

Unfortunately, the woman then spoke.

'I don't know you,' she said to me, in a mildly officious, querying type of way.

I ignored her and looked for a sign on the motorway that signposted the mileage to the nearest service station.

I then felt another prod in my back, and the whispering temporary purdah was broken yet again. 'You need to speak to her.'

'Matt, Samira wants you to talk to old ladies.'

'Jamie,' Samira hissed, squeezing out my name in barely disguised disappointment. 'She's talking to you. Matt can't talk. He's injured. Plus, he doesn't know how to.'

That was encouraging. Does that mean Samira thinks I have far more potential than Matt as something resembling a human being?

'Talk!' The prod came promptly.

'My name's Jamie,' I offered, rubbing the wound just above my gluteus maximus.

The old woman replied by continuing to give me a fixed stare. 'But I still don't know you.'

'No, well, we're replacements. Volunteers for the day.'

'Oh, that's nice. Thank you so much,' she said. 'Do you have a proper job as well?'

I puffed out my cheeks.

'We did,' I said, glancing at Matt. 'I mean, my friend here and I, we used to work in the city.'

Another prod. 'You gave up your jobs?'

'No,' I said, out of the side of my mouth. 'We were sacked.'

'You didn't tell me,' the nun of purdah, incapable of keeping her vows, butted in.

I ignored Samira because the old lady seemed to be a lot nicer.

'In banking?' she asked pleasantly.

'Yeah, well, it involved lots of money. A bit like banking.'

'But that's not a proper job,' she said astutely. 'You need a trade. My husband was a shoemaker. He made lovely shoes. He could also repair shoes.'

I nodded thoughtfully, wondering why we didn't have shoemaker shops anymore, and if this was a niche market that might provide for me, having done the requisite prison time as a guest of His Majesty's and having been released from the bondage imposed by Jack and Bill.

'You know,' the old woman began, 'I don't think this is the way we normally go to the Day Centre.'

'Isn't it?' I asked innocently, wondering why her dementia wasn't as advanced as it seemed to be in all the others.

'No,' she replied, shaking her head, demonstrating a level of lucidity that was not in anybody's interests.

'I tell you what,' I said, standing up and slipping past Matt's legs. 'Let me speak to the driver and find out why we've gone a different way.'

I used both hands to steady myself along the aisle as Danny seemed to be hitting 80 in the fast lane. As I wobbled between speeding, braking, and overtaking, I made my way to our driver. 'Please don't take this as a criticism, but we do appear to be conspicuously driving on the motorway… I suppose there is a good reason for that, and Samira says you have a plan.'

'Does she?' he replied, as if he didn't have a plan.

'Does that mean you don't?'

'Aye, I have a plan,' he said, suddenly veering across three lanes of the motorway.

I was thrown back into the lap of two old ladies, who were understandably shocked and woken from their stupor.

I apologised and pulled myself up to see us driving around a tight bend and then into a large car park and service station.

Relief.

Which was temporary.

As Danny pulled up, he turned to me. 'Right, get them off the bus and just leave them over there.' He pointed to the service station entrance, with a long list of well-known franchises offering refreshment.

'So we're not going to toilet them?' I asked, with a heavy intake of urine still in my nostrils from lying my head in the laps of the two old ladies.

'No, you're not going to toilet them,' Danny hissed, looking confused and frustrated. 'Who said you had to toilet them? You're not bloody nurses; you're daft city boys who've probably never done a proper day's work in your lives. Now, you take that other eejit with you, walk them ladies over to one of them cafes, sit them down, and then get back here.'

'What about Samira? She's a woman. It would look odd just us two being with them.'

'No, she stays here with me. Now, get moving.'

I cursed Samira for making me sound more stupid than I actually was, and pointed at Matt.

He didn't seem to understand what pointing at him meant, so I announced it to everybody on the transport.

'OK, ladies, we're just going to stop here for a little break. That means everyone off the bus and follow me and my friend Matt.'

Unfortunately, the only movement from the somnambulant ladies was a very, very small woman, possibly even shorter than a very short person, who stood next to me and asked, 'Can I have a cup of tea, please?'

'Yes, we're all going to have a cup of tea,' I announced to the non-compliant.

Fortunately, this was the trigger for sound and movement as, like a separate but connected organism, they rose and shuffled towards the door I had yanked open.

As I corralled and organised like a schoolteacher on a daytrip, Matt appeared looking mildly distraught, something

I hadn't seen since I once came close to beating him at squash.

'Cameras,' he said, moving his head like a cartoon conspiracist. 'There's CCTV in these places. We'll be seen.'

He was right.

'Pull your hood up,' I said, pulling mine up.

'I don't have a hood,' he replied.

'OK, it's cold, so pull your jumper over your face.'

Not that I cared, as Matt assumed the look of a headless chicken.

'OK, ladies,' I said, moving in front of the gaggle. 'Follow me, please.'

It was at this point that I wanted a flag or an umbrella, like those annoying tourist guides penetrating the throngs like an ice-breaker, as I took a direct line of approximately 50 metres from transport to service station entrance. I was focused, avoiding the looks of amusement and puzzlement our little gathering had created among fellow travellers, and laser-like in finding three tables in a corner where we could deposit the little ducklings.

They seemed happy enough, yet confused, of course, as I encouraged and supported each one of them to sit down on the plastic chairs. I then wondered where Matt was, because I was the only one taking my voluntary duties seriously.

I found him sitting down near the burger bar, fiddling with the sugar sachets.

'Thanks for your help,' I said sarcastically, as I did the nervous conspiracy head movement. 'If I go first, then you follow a minute later.'

However, just as I was about to complete the act of abandonment and treachery, I felt someone tugging on my sleeve.

It was the old lady who had told me to get a proper job.

'Can we have breakfast, please?' she said, almost insisting.

'Breakfast? Why do you want breakfast? I'll go get you all a cup of tea if you just wait at your tables.'

'But we haven't had breakfast,' she replied, disappointed in the level of care at the care home.

'You must have had breakfast,' I said, wondering why Matt looked distinctly void of any presence with reality.

'No,' she replied. 'They put the food on the table, but nobody helps us.'

Now that didn't surprise me.

'OK,' I said, closing my eyes and seeking an inner strength and moral fibre somewhere deep inside my lack of conscience. 'Why don't you sit down, and I'll get you all some breakfast?'

Her eyes lit up as if I were her long-lost son, and I walked over to the burger bar.

I stood in the queue for five minutes and then placed my order. '12 double cheeseburger meals, please, with fries and vanilla shakes. And four coffees please.'

It was edging me towards my credit limit as I took the receipt and folded it into my wallet. This would be evidence at my trial: that I was not a total heartless kidnapper and I had fed the hostages before we made our escape.

With four or five trips to their tables, I had the ladies scoffing what was in front of them like they hadn't eaten for months, which might have been the case. I had to take the wrappers off the burgers, and shove a few straws in their mouths, and there were a few who could be classified as dazed and confused, but they all munched like savages with cheese, meat, fries, and milkshake dripping out the side of their mouths like toddlers at a tea party.

Of course, Matt, having absolutely no social conscience compared to my 1%, had left me to my own devices. I assumed he had made his own way back to Danny and Samira, as I made the lame excuse to the ladies that I had to go to the toilet.

That was when desperation took hold, and I ran back to the transport, balancing four coffees. 'Go, go, go!' I screamed.

Danny took his time as he put it into reverse, and we dawdled out of the car park.

'Thanks a lot,' I said to Matt, as I sat next to him so I could firmly squeeze his burnt hand.

Although normally Matt would be unmoved by anything I complained about, there was definitely something that was beyond his usual lack of comprehension and understanding. He was distant, not there, as I tried to grab hold of his burnt hand. But in his other hand, he was holding something.

'What's that?'

'It's a sugar sachet,' he replied, as if it were a rare and precious artefact.

'I thought you didn't have sugar,' I said, handing coffee to Samira behind me.

'I don't,' he said mysteriously.

'Fair enough.'

'But look,' he said, holding the sugar sachet in front of my face.

And there, printed on the white sugar sachet, was the iconic graphic of Che Guevara.

And what special meaning did this have for Matt?

'The world's crazy,' he said, like it was a revelation that

had passed him by, whilst the rest of us knew it from the day we were born. 'I wonder what Che would have said, if he knew that a second before he was shot in a Bolivian jungle, his face would end up on a sugar sachet in a service station off the M5.'

'I don't know,' I said, struggling to find any logic to Matt's pseudo-revelation. 'Eh, something like, "Is that one lump or two?"'

'It's a sugar sachet,' corrected Matt. 'A great historical figure has been commodified into a sugar sachet.'

'Well, I'm sure we did some hedging on Cuban sugar crops last year, so he's not a complete waste of space.'

'But we are,' said Matt uncharacteristically.

'Please don't tell me you want to start a revolution on the Shetland Islands.'

Matt ignored me, like he had far more profound thoughts on his mind.

I sipped my coffee and asked if I could use the sugar, but Matt jealously kept it and slid it into his pocket.

'I think I need to inflate,' he said.

'Listen, mate, blow yourself up, just as long as you don't go crazy on us.'

And that was the last thing I said, but it may have accidentally planted a seed in Matt's deteriorating brain that was going to have ramifications further up the road.

# CHAPTER THREE
## BASILDON

We were now further up the road – or the motorway, to be precise – and I was implementing my personal survival plan, which consisted of befriending Danny so that he thinks that it's only worth causing me serious injury rather than extermination by letting me live once he retrieves the £250k.

Selfish, I know, but that's us city boys for you!

Which meant that once we had got close to Bristol, and had planned to drive up the M5 towards Birmingham, I was doing my best to ingratiate myself with Danny. Admittedly, it was a stifled conversation, with hints and minor revelations I shared with you earlier on, but I still believed I was making progress by drawing a human face that deserved some kind of chance in this rotten, corrupt world we lived in.

But if I thought everything was now going to plan, I should have realised that nothing, zilch, zero, nada, was *ever* going to go to plan.

And that was because I'd had a text from my sister that put a spanner in the works.

It was genuinely out of the blue, an emergency, and not the kind of thing I could ignore, unless Danny put his foot down – and I don't just mean on the accelerator – and stopped me from taking a diversion. But he was generous, understanding, and apparently it also fitted in with an idea he had to solve the problem of the "conspicuous" vehicle.

I was OK with that.

What I didn't like, but would have to face up to, started with having to go back home, and that meant driving along the M4, then northbound around the M25, until we got to where I was born and bred: Basildon.

To be honest with you, I'd rather not have to say anything about Basildon, partly out of respect for the people who have to live there. And as much as I hate the place, hating it feels like I'm hating something about myself, which I probably am.

But for those of you who don't know, and for those of you who do know, but just want to see it confirmed in black and white, Basildon is a soulless Essex new town, a post-war, town-planners cock-up that sucks the life out of any semblance of organic matter and leaves dry husks of humanity wandering aimlessly across the empty green spaces, overshadowed by three-storey flats and faceless terrace houses. Yet somehow, through the minefield of social deprivation, there emerged one cultural highlight: the birthplace of '80s synthesised pop, the monotone of spaces in between the music representing the chasms that ripped through the community that should have existed after the planners had built their vision of a village utopia.

No community.

Just a simulation of purgatory.

Which perhaps explains why I've turned out the way I have, fighting for my life all the time in the city, taking part in the greedy sugar mountain.

You see, in part, I blame Basildon for the way I've turned out, rather than just my parents. Well, I don't blame my mum, who I was rushing to get to, but certainly my dad, who has a lot to account for regarding himself and the hapless son and daughter he left behind.

More on that later.

In order to see my mum, I was dropped off at Basildon bus station and told I had until 7:00 p.m. to get back for my pick-up. If I weren't there, if I had been lying and trying to escape and go on the run, I was reliably informed that wherever I thought was safe, wasn't, and that I would definitely be killed, my eyes pecked out by seagulls, and my body turned into fish bait.

Nice.

This cannot be said for Basildon bus station. If there is one place on earth – or in this instance, the country – that sums up the state of things and the deployable state of things, it is Basildon bus station.

"Poverty in transit" is about the best way to describe it. I know that sounds awful, unfair, derogatory, and insensitive, but trust me, most of us are probably only one step away from the poverty terminus. I don't in any way feel superior to the people who roam the bus bays and travel idle distances from a run-down shopping mall to home and back again.

The thing is, that was me 10 years ago, drugged up to my eyeballs and nicking what I could to feed the habit. Because, to some extent, that's what places like Basildon do to you: they are built to give hope and only succeed in creating despair.

I have my probation officer to thank for pulling me out of the hopelessness. He kept me on the straight and narrow, and as crazy as this sounds, places like the capital have the capacity to look beyond the stains that mark you. I was grateful at first, but I suppose old habits die hard, and opportunities led to going back to things that gave me just that little bit more reward, just that little bit more that I thought I deserved.

So in some ways, I haven't fully learnt my lesson. I've got unemployment, the high risk of sustained unemployment, a Dublin drug gang that wants to do me serious harm, and the risk I could end up back in prison.

I was back feeling totally sorry for myself, until I heard my name shouted down half a dozen bus bays.

What could I do?

It was Trevor, who was somehow still alive. Trevor, who hobbled his drug-addled pins on busted trainers, his filthy face and broken teeth lit up with the potential to fuel his daily requirements.

'Jamie,' he said, shaking his head as he too struggled to comprehend how I was standing waiting for a bus to go to Basildon Hospital. 'Jamie, man, how you doing?'

'All right,' I replied sheepishly, wondering if I could just flash up a short summary of why I happened to know a well-known local drug addict.

'Man,' he said, nodding in approval. 'You're looking good.'

'Thanks.'

'Yeah, heh, things are good,' he said unconvincingly. 'Yeah, you know, I'm doing all right.'

'Yeah,' I replied, as unconvincingly as Trevor's optimism.

Which, for all of Trevor's spaced-out contact with reality, he detected as condescending.

So he quickly got to the point.

'Heh, man, you know, you couldn't lend me a tenner? You know I'll pay you back. I always pay you back, you know that, Jamie.'

'Cash?' I said, shrugging my shoulders. 'Sorry, but I don't have cash on me.'

'Heh, yeah, I know, it's like a cashless society and all that. But, yeah, heh, man, you know, if you want, you know, we can get some money.'

'Sorry, but the bus…' I said, relieved there was one just pulling into the bay.

'Oh, man, yeah, you've got to get the bus.'

I nodded.

'Listen, I'll come with you if you want.'

'No mate, I've got to see my mum. She's in hospital.'

'Oh, your mum, she's in hospital. That's not good.'

'It's OK,' I said as the bus door opened and people started shuffling onto the double-decker.

'Heh, Jamie, you know, I'll wait here, you know, and then we can get some things, you know.'

I smiled and got onto the bus, avoiding looking out of the window in case I caught the eye of the drug-ravaged, eye-popping casualty who was desperate for me to fuel his fix.

Not that I had any right to feel better than Trevor. After all, that was me, or that could have been me. I just count myself lucky that at the right time and place, I somehow made the right decision to get out of the hellhole I was in (even if it was during a six-month jail sentence shortened to three months due to good behaviour). Even in the dire circumstances I now found myself in, I still counted myself lucky to have escaped the treadmill of hopelessness. I knew only too well the consequences of missing that opportunity to take the right turn.

So why did I do it? Why did I turn 10 good years of safety

and security on its head, and why did I risk it all for some skiing trips and a squash racket?

That's a good question, and one that I don't have a simple answer to just yet, but I had certainly made the mistake of letting myself get sucked into scheming and defrauding with Matt. And as the bus pulled off on its 15-minute journey to Basildon Hospital, I had to accept that maybe these things were genetic, built-in, inherited.

And that is all down to my dad.

No one knows where he is because he simply walked out of the house one day and never came back. He left my mum, me, and my sister with his last words to us something along the lines of, "I'm just going to the shops."

What we didn't know back then, but found out when the police came to visit, was that he had been a bit of an embezzler, surreptitiously removing small amounts of cash, and then rather larger amounts of cash, from his employer – an insurance broker in the city.

Sound familiar?

I know.

But, heh, what can I say?

It kind of hangs around in the air, that kind of thing, the knowledge of what your dad got up to. As much as I curse him for it, which was mainly for abandoning my mum, me, and my sister to impoverishment, I think it leaves a subconscious stain, a little seed that is planted, that maybe if my dad did it, then maybe it's not such a bad thing after all.

Sounds crazy, but there was probably no need for me to take advantage of the discrepancies and create more discrepancies at my comfy city job. In most people's eyes, I had it made, and yet I just couldn't help myself indulging in a bit of risk-taking. There must be a good reason for it, and I needed to find out. I needed to ask myself why and come up with a rational reason – at least before my eyes are pecked out, and my balls severed from my nether regions and served up as a delicacy in some five-star Michelin BS restaurant. By the way, if you think you've had them, you haven't, because the last time I looked, they were still attached.

Anyway, the one thing my sister and I never spoke about was our dad; he was persona non grata, he didn't exist.

I smiled weakly as Brenda met me off the bus. She was five years younger than me, a bit rotund, but also a saint, or an angel, because she was a nurse at the hospital.

'You made it, then,' she said, her disappointment in me established many years ago.

I shrugged.

I didn't want to get into an argument, and I could tell straight away that Brenda had something serious to tell me before I got to see our mum.

'Come on,' she said, leading the way through the front entrance. 'I'll get you a coffee.'

We walked through a maze of corridors, the nauseating hospital smell only making the passageways feel like they were specifically designed as entry points to suffering.

We then sat down at a Formica table, sipping from a paper cup of diluted coffee beans.

Brenda broke the news to me the only way she knows how. Directly. 'Mum's going to die.'

'What do you mean?' I said, thinking that there is obviously only one certainty in life, and that surely didn't mean mum was going to die now that I had managed to visit.

'I mean, Jamie,' she replied, using her professional practice stare, 'that mum has pancreatic cancer.'

'Cancer?' I said, because that's what people say when they are told someone has cancer.

All Brenda did was nod, looking for any reaction in me, such as a tear, shock, horror, or sadness. But it was too early for any of that; I was assimilating, wondering how I should say anything that sounded reasonably engaged with the fate of Mum.

'Are they treating her?' I asked, hoping this was why she was in the hospital.

'No,' said Brenda, shaking her head. 'It's too late for that.'

That's when it hit me. Brenda, my sister, had just told me that my mum was going to die, sooner rather than later.

'It's not long,' she said, reaching out to hold my hand across the table. 'I'm afraid she's only got a few weeks left.'

'A few weeks!' I blurted out, causing people around us to look up who knew only too well that's what happens in hospital cafeterias.

I was struggling now, struggling to understand how my mum, our mum, can just be told that the lights are going out; how the gods have decided to move the mortality finishing line forward, and she is going to be out for a duck without having a chance to bat.

'I know it's difficult,' Brenda said, as I let her hold my hand. 'It's a bit of a shock. But I didn't want to tell you over the phone or by text.'

That made sense, amongst all the things that didn't make sense. Like, why do people die? Why should any of us have to die, especially our mums?

I tried my best to gather my thoughts, as I felt the sudden rush of emotions appropriate for such a shock well up inside, from the belly to the heart, from the heart to the head, which was beginning to turn into mush.

'So there's nothing they can do?' I asked, wondering if this was the moment I should think about crowdfunding and American healthcare.

But Brenda just wisely, knowingly, slowly shook her head.

'Christ,' I said, sitting back in my chair, reeling from the unmitigated trauma.

We both sat in silence for a few minutes, watching people put money into the vending machine and look disappointed with the healthy food options they had to pick from.

That's when I had to ask myself the question: so, Jamie, how do you feel about Mum dying?

That's a good question, because while I knew I was upset, I didn't really know how I was feeling. It was raw, hard, and harsh, but I did wonder if I was genuinely feeling upset. I mean, should I be thinking like this? But the thought did occur to me, because, as well as disassociating emotionally from my dad, I hadn't really gotten along with my mum.

She liked Brenda, but perhaps she saw too much of Dad in me? Perhaps I reminded her of the rascal who ran off without a goodbye, a letter, a telegram, a memo, email, phone call, or text, or any other type of messaging device to give a good reason.

And in truth, that's what I had done.

I lived on the streets, got wasted, lived in other people's houses, and then when I got straightened out, I was living in my own flat and keeping well away from everything that had the word Basildon in it.

Still, I was following the advice of my probation officer to avoid the drug-fuelled environment and keep my distance, but it was also convenient, staying away and maintaining my detachment.

In fact, I hadn't spoken to Mum or Brenda since last Christmas.

'Hey,' said Brenda. 'Are you all right?'

'Yeah,' I replied, with a deep sigh.

'She's expecting you,' she said, as if she was reminding me that I wasn't a good son.

'What's she like?'

'What do you think she's like, Jamie? She's dying!' said Brenda angrily.

That was dumb.

'I mean, is she dosed up on the morph and everything?'

'Why, do you want some?'

'No,' I said, realising how prickly Brenda had always been towards me and my recalcitrance.

'You need to talk to her,' Brenda urged.

'Yeah, I know.'

But what do you say to someone who's dying?

'Are they going to move her?' I asked. 'To a hospice?'

Brenda laughed like I had made a sick joke. 'There aren't any places at a hospice. Well, none that don't involve travelling halfway across the country. And I'm not doing that. She's my mum, she's got to stay here, even if they are trying to throw her out so they can have her bed.'

'Wouldn't she be better at home?'

‘No, Jamie, she wouldn’t be better at home, because then I wouldn’t be able to work and I’d have to look after her.’

‘What do you mean?’

‘I mean, Jamie, that there are no nurses. I’m the one looking after her on the ward, and in between that, I’m having to do my shifts.’

‘You’re joking!’

‘Have you seen any nurses, Jamie?’

‘No.’

‘That’s because there aren’t any. Either that or they’re stuck in passport control.’

I was angry now, like Brenda. It didn’t surprise me that the NHS was DIY.

‘Come on,’ she said, standing up. ‘You need to go and say your goodbyes.’

# CHAPTER FOUR

## DANNY BOY'S UK TOURS LTD.

I could bore you with what it's like to visit your mum when she's dying, but I suspect a few of you might already know what that feels like, and for those of you who don't know, trust me, it feels and sounds like:

Ahh…

After that?

Well, what can I say? Other than that it gets you thinking about your own mortality.

The thought occurred to me that when you're young, you just want to die, and when you're old, you just want to live.

Anyway, as Brenda waited for me to get the bus back to the bus station, she knew something was up with me – and not just because I'd spent a couple of hours with our dying mum.

'I can tell, you know,' she said, already replacing Mum as the surrogate mother.

'Can you?' I asked, lacking the energy to pretend there was nothing wrong.

'Whatever it is, Jamie, be careful.'

'Don't worry,' I said. 'It will get it sorted.'

Brenda raised her left eyebrow because that was what I always used to say when I was drugging myself up and doing the maximum amount of thieving to maintain my supply.

Back on the bus, I pushed all thoughts of my mum to one side. I had to refocus.

First question, should I do a runner?

No, too dangerous. No way to live.

And there was no way I was going back on the streets.

Second question, was there anything I could do to mitigate the threat of serious injury or death before we got to see Samira's gran? Befriend Danny seemed to be the recurring mantra in my head.

I jumped off the bus and then walked around the corner and waited to be picked up by Danny in the North Devon NHS Community Trust Transport van. I had to accept that, for now at least, I should go along with this road trip up to the Shetlands. After all, what else was there to do, given I was now an ex-employee of a highly lucrative city firm? Normally, about this time, I would be with Matt and other assorted city folk, downing pints and talking bollocks in the nearest pub. All that was gone now, and as much as I knew I was going to miss it, there was also another feeling inside of me, one that made me think it was all a bit of a relief.

The thing is, there is so much pretence, game-playing, one-upmanship in the world of city finance, that there is never a second that doesn't contain the need to be questioning why a certain person is talking to you, what is the veracity of what they are saying, and will they stab you in the back at the next team meeting. It sounds like a cliché, but the city is not only the fat belly of greed and selfishness, it is the heart of heartlessness, the corporate paradigm embossed, embedded, and imprinted into everyone who partakes in the orgy of mind-numbing self-aggrandisement.

In a way, I think I was beginning to feel relieved that it was probably all over, even if my fate was rather unknown.

Perhaps things weren't so bad after all. Which was a stupid thing to say, really, as I watched the headlights of a vehicle coming towards me and then pulled up where I was standing at the side of the road.

At first, I thought I was going to have to give directions, until Danny stuck his head out of the window just as he did outside the Pink House

'What do you think?' he shouted down at me.

What he meant was, what did I think of the paint job that had replaced the North Devon NHS Community Trust Transport logo with: Danny Boy's UK Tours Ltd. Lands' End to John O'Groats. I suppose the only thought I had, which reflects how pedantic I can be, was the accuracy of the geography, because, of course, we all know that we were actually travelling from Ilfracombe to the Shetland Islands.

'Inspired,' I mused, looking along the length of the paint job that had been coloured in emerald green.

'I have a mate who did that for me,' Danny said, winking. 'Plus, I got them number plates changed so we don't keep springing up on them CCTV cameras.'

'Well, none of us would want that,' I said, seeking to be compliant with the Danny Boy's UK Tours Ltd. team perspective.

'OK, how's your mum?' he asked, keeping a steely eye on me to make sure I hadn't been lying.

'She'll be dead in a couple of weeks,' I replied, full of deadpan fatalism that was the god's honest truth.

'Well, if I were a religious man, I'd have been praying for her.'

‘Thanks,’ I replied, surprised that Danny had summoned a bit of understanding.

Then he twitched his head to indicate I should come closer, so he could say something discreetly to me. ‘I think there’s something wrong with your friend there. He keeps talking gibberish.’

‘You mean Matt?’ I asked, peering through the window to see him staring off into space.

‘I think he’s not right in the head.’

‘That’s normal,’ I assured him, because Matt had never, ever, been right in the head.

‘Well, that may be normal for you. Do you know he says he’s found Che Guevara living in a service station and thinks he’s coming to get him because he’s ripped him off over a deal for a cheese plant.’

That still sounded like Matt to me. However, Danny was looking well pissed.

‘Now, you may get the privilege to know me a bit better, if you live,’ Danny continued. ‘But I personally find his references to a great revolutionary like Che a bit of a bloody insult – apart from the fact that it is my understanding that Che Guevara was assassinated in the Bolivian jungle. So, unless Che has come back from the dead, you need to bring your friend down to earth before I turn him into fish bait. Find out what’s wrong with him, because the last thing I need is a hallucinating eejit sitting in me transport talking gobbledegook.’

I nodded, providing assurance that I would attend to my friend.

I sat next to Matt, wondering if his wound had poisoned his

blood and was causing the emergence of paranoid delusions, whilst he was quietly mumbling to himself about cigars, bananas, and the CIA. I also tried to say something pleasant to Samira, but she remained impassive and uninterested on the back seat.

'We've been fed and watered, Jamie boy!' shouted Danny, as he started the engine. 'Let's get out of this godforsaken place before we all lose the will to live.'

'You have my vote,' I replied, smiling at Samira, who scowled at my bonhomie with my new friend, Danny.

I shrugged, as if to let her know she was only jealous, as I thought about the deals I would be doing with Danny to ensure he only bruised me rather than slashed my throat.

And that would have been that, a good end to a very difficult day, were it not for the sudden bump, crunch, and expletive from Danny, as we pulled up sharply.

It didn't sound good.

It's the kind of noise you hear when something has crashed into something. I always think a car crash should be loud and noisy, but it's not. Instead, the sound is clipped, punctured, and hollow. However, as I looked in front of us and to the side, as did Samira, there was no other car or vehicle.

We both moved swiftly towards Danny, who was a bit frozen, dazed and confused.

'What is it?' asked Samira, as we peered into the darkness, the road empty and blank housing either side of us.

Danny raised his arms, indicating he had no idea how to explain.

'Did we hit something?' I asked, checking on Matt, who was definitely oblivious to the events going on around him.

'This guy,' said Danny, struggling to find the words. 'He just stepped out in front of me.'

'You ran over somebody!' screamed Samira, as if this were worse than all the crimes someone like Danny committed on a daily basis.

Danny grimaced, coming to his senses and realising he was not meant to be so shocked by such an incident. 'OK,' he said, seeking to correct Samira in case she thought he was a murderous driver as well as just generally murderous. 'You need to know, he just walked out in front of the vehicle. He was standing there on the edge of the kerb, and he looked at me, and then he just walked out, like he wanted me to run him over.'

'Where is he?' I asked, looking onto the road, which was just bare tarmac.

'I don't know,' replied Danny. 'But you heard me hit him, so you go out there and see where he is.'

*Not again*, I thought to myself, *having to sort things out in the cold and the dark.*

'Both of you,' Danny added, putting his hands back on the steering wheel and sighing heavily.

I suppose I could have said I needed to keep an eye on Matt, but ultimately, we were always under instruction.

'You first,' I said, inviting Samira to do the honours.

She yanked open the door and jumped down the few steps onto the road. As I followed, she stood in front of the vehicle and pointed at the floor.

There was a body, lying motionless, lit by the blazing headlights.

'Turn them off!' Samira shouted at Danny. 'Turn off the headlights!'

Which I suppose made sense, because the last thing we needed was to be all lit up standing over a dead guy – because from where I was standing, he definitely looked dead.

Then the worst-case scenario kicked in.

Unfortunately, I knew who it was and why he had done it.

It was Trevor, staring up into the night sky above, his frail and drug-addled body pulverised by the front end of Danny Boy's UK Tours Ltd. vehicle.

As we both looked at him, I had to ask the question, 'Is he dead?'

'How do I know?' Samira hissed, which was indicative that there was no way she was going to get up close and personal to check.

At this point, it is worth revealing that I had never been confronted with a dead person, not that I knew that Trevor was dead, but he did look like it, all prone and not of this world, which, I might add, was also his general state of being.

I knelt down by his side and looked vaguely at his face. If he were dead, he seemed at peace.

'See if he's breathing,' Samira said unhelpfully, as she left to inform Danny that he could add another notch to his belt.

'Trevor,' I whispered, 'what's it like in Heaven?'

But that was as much as I was going to do.

You see, the thing about Trevor is he had a modus operandi that went back years to when I knew him, and it went something like the following: "Desperate times call for desperate measures, and in times of desperation you must put your life on the line to meet the needs of family", which in the case of Trevor was a wife and three kids, at the last count anyway. As bizarre as this may sound, Trevor had a rolling programme of traffic accidents so he could make dubious claims to the Criminal Injuries Board for compensation or con the insurers. Of course, this did mean walking in front of cars, making sure to avoid trucks and buses, as they would more than likely prove fatal.

I never believed he would do it until one day, sitting in A&E on the off chance I might scam some kaolin and morphine for my excruciating constipation, Trevor rolled in on a wheelchair having successfully been run over. He was ecstatic, and calculated he'd be getting paid within six to 12 months, and believe it or not, I heard from Trevor while I was in prison that he had got the money out of the CIB and was on one serious bender.

'Danny said to get him in,' Samira told me, leaning over my shoulder.

'But he's dead,' I replied.

'How do you know?'

I shrugged. 'He looks dead, don't you think?'

Samira pushed me over and did a couple of health checks as first responder and declared it was all over.

'We need to get him on board and get out of here,' she said, picking up his legs and leaving me with the head and shoulders.

She had a point. But as I pushed my arms under his and lifted, there was a sudden gush of air from Trevor.

'Christ!' I said, thinking he must still be alive. 'Did you hear that?'

'It's nothing,' Samira replied. 'Just the gas left in his lungs.'

'Oh, so you're sure he's dead?'

'Probably,' she said, which was mildly reassuring in the

wrong kind of way.

We then did a 360-degree turn so I could drag his body in headfirst.

Danny told us to leave him in the back seat. He then started the engine, put his foot down on the pedal, and cursed a lot.

# CHAPTER FIVE

## TOXICITY

'Sepsis,' said Samira as we sped along the M25.

'Septic,' I said back, thinking that summed up Matt quite well.

'No, *sepsis*,' she said, looking into Matt's eyes.

'That's blood poisoning, isn't it?'

'Something like that,' she replied, avoiding a more precise first responder's definition.

Samira then put her hand on Matt's forehead, as I glanced over at Trevor lying across the back seats, praying for the resurrection of junkies.

'He's got a temperature and a fever,' she announced, scrutinising Matt as if she had just discovered alien life.

I breathed in deeply, sighing at the prospect of two problems that needed a resolution.

'What's his hand look like?' I asked, sitting across from Matt with Samira sitting next to him for the first time since we hit the road.

She lifted his hand so we could see it more clearly in the flickering neon lights. The cling film had holes in it, and there appeared to be some kind of seepage.

I offered my own highly qualified medical opinion: 'Gross.'

For the first time since the Pink House, Samira looked as

though she was genuinely concerned for the well-being of her not-to-be-married fiancé.

'Matt,' she said, placing his hand carefully down by his side. 'How are you feeling?'

But all Matt could do was shiver, his body contaminated with an all-consuming fever.

'I don't think we can take him to A&E,' I said, trying to think through what would be worse: explaining to Danny we needed to stop off at another hospital, or explaining to a doctor how Matt got his hand stuck in a toaster.

For a minute or two, Samira ignored me, as she seemed deep in thought, peering into Matt's eyes, and perhaps hoping he would snap out of his state of delirium and solve the problem so we could focus on a dead junkie. Because the latter was preoccupying my own thoughts, as much as having to think that Matt would need some kind of medical intervention.

She then indicated we should sit away from Matt so we could talk, and we sat two seats away from him and two seats away from Trevor.

I waited for Samira to say something, reflecting on how strange life can be because I had waited for this moment for a long time, although without a dead junkie and a toxic Matt between us.

'I think he's going to need some antibiotics,' said Samira, who looked straight ahead, avoiding eye contact.

Now, as much as I have tried every kind of illegal drug and domestic chemical thrown in, I find it difficult to acquire the more sensible substances that make people better; pharmacists always view me with acute suspicion, even if I am just trying to buy haemorrhoid cream. I also assumed we were not going to have an awkward conversation with Danny just yet, because his solution might end up being terminal for Matt.

So I waited for Samira to advise on how best to source the medication.

'We can try a pharmacy,' she said, pulling a face that showed that this would prove problematic.

'Can they do that?' I asked, feeling a sense of relief that meant I was probably out of the loop on the requesting of prescription drugs.

Samira shrugged.

'It's the best we can do. He should go to A&E so they can assess that burn, but it's better than nothing.'

I then tried to envisage talking to a pharmacist with Matt feverishly deluded.

'Are you sure they'd give us antibiotics for sepsis?'

'I don't know, but we – you – will need to ask. We need to think of something that needs treating, so they can give you some antibiotics. It will probably only be penicillin, but it will be better than nothing.'

'You said we, and then you said me. You do realise that pharmacists won't even give me paracetamol without a long checklist. Plus, I can't think what ailment would prompt a pharmacist to prescribe antibiotics – they're only going to tell me to go to a doctor.'

'Jamie, what's wrong with you?' she said, raising her voice, unimpressed with my reluctance to face the scrutiny of the chemist.

'What's wrong with *me*?' I asked exasperated, ready to explain that Matt was her fiancé while he was merely a friend to me. 'Why do I have to do it?'

'Because you're good at lying,' she said irritably, looking through me all the way to the back of my head. 'And I suggest you don't test me on what's wrong with you.'

'Ouch,' I said sarcastically.

'Good,' she said, pleased with her succinct diagnosis. 'Because I hope it hurts.'

That was it, I decided, having to put up with everything for the last two days, and which any reasonable, rational person would have walked away from right at the beginning.

'You know,' I said, building up a head of steam. 'I don't know why you hate me, Samira – even if I did dump you and was a passenger in Matt's car when he crashed and lost the coke.'

Samira offered a barely restrained, withering glance. However, I was just starting.

'But I would have thought that at a minimum you would think we needed to be more of a team, given the situation we are in, and you had a bit more sympathy for me, given that I've just found out my mum is going to die and I've just lost an old friend.'

I thought that would make Samira feel completely rotten inside, and we could begin reassessing our failed relationship. Instead, she focused on the one thing I should have kept quiet about.

'What old friend?' she asked, perhaps because she knew Matt was my only friend.

I tried to nonchalantly ignore her question and to get her focused on the sympathy she should be applying to my impending bereavement. 'My mum, I mean,' I said awkwardly.

'Yes, I'm sorry for your loss, when it comes,' she said, suspiciously. 'But who else has died, Jamie?'

'Who else?' I replied, uncomfortably.

'Yes, who else?'

What could I say? So I just turned my head towards Trevor.

'You know him?' she said, so loud that Matt mumbled and Danny intervened.

'Hey! You two, move apart!' he said, no doubt concerned we might be plotting his downfall.

If only…

'I don't believe you,' Samira said, looking back at Trevor.

'Heh! Come on!' said Danny, who swerved across two lanes as he craned his neck to make sure we moved apart.

Samira jumped forcefully out of her seat and sat behind Matt, whilst Danny regained control of the vehicle. However, knowing Samira as I do, she wouldn't let up until she had gotten some kind of truth out of me. Once Danny was focused on driving, Samira instigated her whispering interrogation.

I did my best to explain, in as few words as possible, the origins of my relationship with Trevor, my misspent youth, and the peculiar rolling programme of death-defying income stream Trevor had employed up to his eventual demise.

Samira's response was to slowly shake her head in disbelief, as she didn't know where to start, shocked by my revelations regarding my former life, a former life, I might add, that I had kept discreet while we were going out together.

'You're a crook.'

'Pardon?' I said, hoping she had used the word "cook," even if my skill set was in financial reconciliation.

'You heard,' she said emphatically. Which I thought

was a bit rich coming from somebody who had arranged a significant coke deal and scammed 50% of the investment.

I was then going to suggest that if I were a crook, it made us vaguely compatible, integrating our sinful ways, but there was little point in stirring a stew that had far too many bad ingredients. Plus, I was beginning to think that Samira had demonstrated over the last few days a side to herself that was close to psychopathic, sociopathic, and morally vacant.

Then Matt offered his personal take on things. 'Bananas!'

At last, Matt was right about something. So we both told Matt to shut up and retreated to our own thoughts on everything.

And that was when I thought I did have a conscience; that I was the only one on Danny Boy's UK Tours Ltd. who had a grain of humanity left in them; that it was up to me to do something for Trevor, whose last insane act was to walk in front of us and get himself deliberately run over.

I mean, after all, he had a wife and three kids. And they should know that, in the end, at the final curtain, we, or probably I, did our best to ensure Trevor had a final resting place with some degree of dignity attached. But that was highly unlikely. He probably didn't deserve the kind of burial he was going to get, if Danny had any thoughts on burial, that is.

Not that I knew what we were going to do with Trevor, but I thought that at some point, and ASAP, we needed to do something with his body. Because, well, they tend to rot... Get smelly. I was sure of that, though I had no idea how long a body could remain intact before all the bits start falling off. No doubt this was Danny's specialist area, so I was calculating that we had to do something with Trevor tonight.

Which got me thinking about a eulogy: Here lies Trevor, not so clever.

Was I being cruel? Yes.

I was like Trevor, once. What right did I have to think I was somehow superior? I just got lucky. I had the luck that someone thought I had the brains to pull myself out of the cesspit and make something of my life.

Only I was not very good at keeping on the straight and narrow.

Mum knew that about me.

Brenda knew that about me.

They both said I took after my dad.

And where was he?

Still, none of those things addressed the issue of poor Trevor. I would message his wife, if I knew her contact details, and tell her that her husband was going on a trip, and he'd be away for a week or two, but he was going to straighten himself out and come back a better man. He'd be off the junk, he'd have some money in his pocket, and he was going to give his family whatever they wanted instead of putting all the welfare benefits into his drug-addled arms, feet, and legs.

I kept these good thoughts in my head as I drifted off to the slow slumber of the wheels turning over and over on the motorway tarmac. I deserved sleep, I said to myself, dreaming that I was trying to get to sleep whilst I was actually sleeping.

And how did I know that?

Well, because I was rudely awoken by Danny prodding me in the stomach.

We had come to a stop in a budget hotel car park, and I

was instructed to book two double rooms.

'Where are we?' I asked.

'Coventry,' Danny replied before he sat back down in his driver's chair and put his feet up on the dashboard.

'And who's paying?' I asked optimistically as I scrolled through their online booking app.

'I think you know the answer to that one,' he said.

I looked at Samira, hoping she might come to my aid in a time of need – also known as the financially distressed – but she turned her head away.

'You know, if I have to pay for everything, I'm going to end up going over my credit limit,' I announced to one and all.

Unfortunately, my attempt at achieving equity was answered by Matt, who stood up and shouted, 'No more cigars, I only want bananas!'

'I think that answers your question,' said Samira, with a sardonic grin.

As I carried on with the booking, I thought about keeping a record of my expenses, and if I was still alive by the end of all this, presenting an invoice to the Dublin gang with a shortened due date.

With the online booking done, I stepped outside.

The car park was half full as I listened to the distant sound of other cars, trucks, and lorries heading along the motorway in both directions. As is the case with all budget hotels of a certain well-known franchise, it was on the outskirts of Coventry – and probably no bad thing considering the collateral damage we had lying on the back seats. Out of sight and away from prying eyes seemed to be in all our interests.

The hotel was composed of low-level units, and a terrace that disappeared into the misty night, as I dutifully plodded over to the reception to confirm our arrival. The doors slid open, and I was greeted by an all too familiar empty desk of self-help check-in portals. I was useless when it came to these kinds of machines, because they never knew who I was, never had a record of my booking, and never took me out for dinner.

Instead, I pressed the buzzer and waited for a human to come forth and reveal themselves.

This was a long wait, or at least what felt like a long wait, because I had read through all the pamphlets promoting all the exciting things you can do in and around Coventry, which isn't much, by the way. Which also means my patience was tested by five minutes of waiting before I saw signs of life emerge through the "Staff Only" door.

'Good evening, sir. How can I help?'

I didn't want to say, because it seemed obvious to me that there was only one thing they could possibly help me with.

The guy was dressed in a purple uniform and had a strip of coleslaw hanging from the side of his mouth. That was when I wished I had more faith in self-help check-in portals to confirm our beds for the night.

The thing is, I was grumpy. About everything. And felt entitled to be pissed off, having spent over £200 on two rooms whilst wondering who I might end up sharing a bed with.

Anyway, I think he could tell I wasn't someone to idle chitchat with as he booked me in quickly and directed me to rooms 101 and 102, which apparently were right at the bottom of the car park, and the last two units, if I turned left out the door and kept walking to the end.

*Sleep, please*, was the next immediate thought as I stepped through the sliding doors and into three people whom I wished I didn't know.

'Are we done, then?' asked Danny, who looked as weary and tired as I felt.

'Kind of,' I said, as I hesitated to ask two fundamental questions before we retired.

Fortunately, Danny didn't stab me and merely raised an eyebrow, which I took to mean I could seek further clarification on the impending arrangements.

However, I thought it best if I start with the dead people.

'What are we going to do with the body?' I asked, hoping we could also move further away from the reception area and converse in the shadows.

'What do you suggest?' said Danny, as I noticed that Samira was propping up the feverish and delirious Matt.

'I don't know, it's not my area of expertise.'

'So you think I should know how to deal with a dead body?'

I shrugged. It seemed obvious to me – the elephant in the car park, so to speak.

'Don't you worry, Jamie,' said Danny, who was suspiciously conciliatory. 'Your junkie friend Trevor doesn't need a bed for the night.'

I looked at Samira. 'You told him?'

'Why shouldn't she?' said Danny, warming to this minor revelation. 'Is this just a junkie thing or specific to people from Basildon, jumping in front of vehicles to earn a little bit extra?'

'I don't think it's specific to Basildon,' I said authoritatively.

'No, well, you English seem to think us Irish are stupid, but I've never seen a junkie in Dublin do such a thing.'

I nodded, wisely. 'Probably very specific.'

'To our Trevor, you mean?'

'Yeah.'

We all drew in a deep breath, sighing at the absurdity of someone else's life.

But I didn't have the matter fully resolved.

'I just want to say,' I said, holding up my arms, 'that Trevor has a wife and kids. We should try to think about that before we… You know.'

'And what do you suggest?' asked Danny, who was showing signs of increasing impatience. 'That we return him first-class by parcel post?'

'No,' I said sheepishly, realising that wherever we dumped his body, I would have to write something anonymously to the wife and kids. 'I was just wondering how long it takes before the body starts to rot.'

Danny then stepped forward and slapped me hard on the shoulder.

'Don't you worry, Jamie,' he said, cruelly winking at me. 'Apparently, I'm an expert in these kinds of things. I am more than happy to advise you that a dead body can be kept for at least 24 to 48 hours. That is before it gets really smelly, and the guts start running out of its bottom.'

I nodded. 'Thanks, that's good to know.'

'OK then,' said Danny, keeping his hand firmly rooted on my shoulder. 'If we're done with talking about a man who was always destined for a Tinder date in Heaven, I would like the key to my room, please.'

Which brought us around to the second fundamental question.

And Danny could see it in my eyes as he grinned and penetrated my nervousness. 'Two rooms, Jamie, I think, is what may be preoccupying you,' said Danny, correctly reading my mind.

I shrugged, as if it might be.

'Don't you worry, because you'll be sleeping with your psychotic friend while Samira and I will be cosying up to each other in the room next to you.'

'Eh?' I managed to utter, looking at Samira to make sure she was agreeable.

'Oh, are you a gallant knight, Jamie?' said Danny, reading my thoughts. 'You don't have to worry, because ladies' private parts have never interested me.'

I tried not to look relieved, but I was.

'That's not a good look, Jamie,' said Danny, who eased off the firm grip on my shoulder. 'Just because I'm a gay man doesn't mean I couldn't, but I also understand that you and Samira have been romantically involved. So out of respect for your emotional well-being, I can assure you that our sleeping arrangements will be strictly platonic. Of course, what goes on in your own room with a vulnerable adult is entirely up to you.'

I sighed.

And handed Danny his key.

# CHAPTER SIX

## GHOST TOWN

It may not come as a surprise to any of you that a good piece of general advice is to never share a double room with someone who is insane. Not that it was Matt's fault, as such. Though he did deserve to have his hand evenly toasted because he was a prolapsed anus eejit, his gibbering was off the scale! His feverish mutterings were interspersed with cries of anguish, fear, and acute paranoia, all referenced by his deluded belief that he was somehow connected to Che Guevara, or he was Che Guevara, and he was being chased by the CIA, or oversized cigars that could be painfully inserted, or rampant bananas that apparently *had* been painfully inserted.

In the end, I took refuge in the bathroom and curled up as best I could in the cold ceramic tub. As the restless hours passed, I cursed Samira, cursed my mum because she was dying, and tried to curse Danny, but thought better of it in case he could read my mind through hotel walls. I cursed Trevor for being such a dick, cursed Bridges for finding out I was just a thief all along and sacking me, cursed the Dublin gang, Damien Hirst, hoovers, seagulls, and fish that swam in the sea, the North Devon NHS Community Trust, abandoned big cats, and care homes that failed to check on the credentials of dubious-looking volunteers.

By the time all the cursing was over, I was determined

to be first in the queue for a lorry-load of good English breakfast. I left Matt to his sleepy delusions and helped myself to a large plate of bacon, fried egg, sausages, black pudding, mushrooms, baked beans, fried bread, hash browns, and four pieces of toast.

Then, just as I was contemplating another plateful, Danny and Samira appeared, looking suspiciously like a couple who had enjoyed the night together. I didn't know what made me sicker: overloading my stomach with animal fat or the sight of the happy couple scrutinising the buffet. Convinced that Samira had applied the inappropriate use of conversion therapy, I scowled and drank my coffee as the two love birds sat opposite me, full of the satisfaction that comes with not having to suffer sleeping with a psychotic neanderthal.

'You look rough,' Samira commented, tucking into a bowl of fruit and berries.

'Yeah, there's a good reason for that,' I said, trying to work out if Samira could really have managed to indulge Danny in the highways and byways of heterosexual activities.

Then Danny proved he did have mind-reading powers. 'I think your ex thinks we might have rubbed our private parts together.'

'No!' I asserted, barely disguising the thought bubble that appeared above my head. 'I had to sleep in the bath because of you-know-who.'

'Sounds rough,' said Samira, unsympathetically.

'Exactly,' I replied, moving my neck sideways as the bones in my upper spine cracked.

'Well, we need to find a cure for that eejit,' said Danny, who was tucking into the breakfast of his historical oppressors.

I was about to offer my own prescription on how to cure Matt Chubb of all the things that ailed him, which are many and go way beyond his current psychotic episode, when I realised that the two smiles confronting me had a plan in mind that involved "errand boy". Also known as *El Self.*

'Really?' I asked despairingly.

'Yes, really,' they replied collectively.

Apparently, so Samira argued, I had the experience and the skillset to negotiate my way into acquiring bacteria-eating medication, also known as antibiotics, because of my previous history as a junkie. I did vigorously remind her that because of my history, pharmacies and pharmacists were reluctant to do any kind of transaction, as they seemed to have a sixth sense about me, which meant even simple things such as paracetamol were reluctantly handed over. In fact, I should be the last person to request things that were made up of chemical substances.

However, it was Danny who was insistent that I go into town and hunt for a cure for the hapless, deluded psychotic, or else I would find out that cruelty was just a sharp knife away from being applied indiscriminately. All of which was harsh and unfair, as well as profoundly unrealistic, because I had no faith whatsoever in achieving the mission I had been set.

Still, yet again, I was in no position to argue and had to assume that Danny would always want Samira near him because she was the one who knew how to get the money

And so, without revealing the many expletives that exploded in my head, I was dispatched with a fake diagnosis to find a pharmacy and acquire the antibiotics that may or may not bring Matt back down to earth. I actually found the morning walk relatively refreshing, as I Google-mapped my way into the centre of Coventry, to look for a pharmacy willing to hand over some meds.

That was when I discovered Coventry was just as bad, if not worse, than Basildon. That, folks, is really saying something!

What once must have been a thriving shopping centre looked like a ghost town. The place was littered with empty shop units, boarded-up windows, and tired brand signs smeared with the dirt and rust of retail casualties. The City Arcade was no fun. Like faded imagery from a generic movie called *The Apocalypse*, the sad entrails of the city centre had been gutted and left to rot in the stinking fume.

As I walked along the cracked pavements, around random overflowing rubbish bins, past battered bus shelters, I watched the struggling citizens wheel their trollies, no doubt looking for something to buy that was cheap enough to keep them going.

I suppose you kind of saw the same thing in London, but the shallow callousness, the empty soullessness, of small cities and towns was like a cold shower of minor revelation. It's not until you saw it that you realised the landscape had changed. The Forum was no longer functioning; it was nowhere to be seen. The essence of a marketplace had probably been relocated to an out-of-town shopping mall that had as much heart as a pacemaker.

As I wondered what it would take to retrain as a town planner, I struck gold with a pharmacy whose name had something to do with things you put on your feet when it's raining.

I navigated my way through shelves of men's and women's toiletries, and vitamins and baby food, and waited in line at the prescriptions desk. I began to run over in my head the instructions I had been given by Samira, the fully qualified First Responder, when I noticed the strangest and most innocuous-looking creature sitting patiently in a chair next to the dispensary, who I assumed was waiting for her medication.

She was an impish-looking teenager, with dank brown hair down to her shoulders, a mildly pimpled face, and her shoulders hunched over as she scrolled skilfully through her phone one-handed. I wouldn't have thought anything of her, had she not suddenly looked up and directly at me as if I were someone she had been waiting for.

It was an odd feeling, almost unnerving, as I noticed a twitch to the right side of her face and her right eye. Had the queue not moved forward, I probably would have continued returning her stare.

I resorted to scrolling through my own phone, checking to see if Brenda had communicated some fateful news about my mum, hoping against hope that Bridges had forgiven me and retracted my termination of employment, and idly filtered various social media, acutely aware that I was banned by the Boss Man from posting anything.

It seemed to take an eternity before I was at last at the front of the queue. However, the words that came out were not the ones I had rehearsed so assiduously.

'Pee,' I said, as if that constituted all the young female pharmacist needed to know.

Quite legitimately, she remained passively unmoved by my lack of clarity.

'Sorry,' I said, gathering my thoughts and glancing over at the impish teenager, who I decided was putting me off from being explicit. 'I haven't been able to go, so can I have some antibiotics?'

The woman pulled a face, one which was familiar to me from all those years ago, trying to scam pharmacists of anything that had mind-numbing qualities.

'Are you having trouble urinating?' she asked quizzically.

'Yes, exactly,' I replied unconvincingly. 'I've been drinking cherry aid, and I still can't go. I'm sure I've got an infection.'

'OK,' she said, looking as confused as I was. 'But why have you been drinking cherry aid?'

Cherry aid? Yes, why have I been drinking cherry aid? What an excellent question.

I had no idea why I said I was drinking cherry aid.

'Cranberry juice!' I said. 'I've been drinking cranberry juice, but I still can't go – and it's very painful when I try.'

'Well, you will need to go and see your doctor.'

I wasn't expecting that.

'Can't you prescribe me antibiotics?'

'No,' she said, shaking her head. 'We would only prescribe those for women who have a UTI. If you do have a urinary infection, you really should get an appointment with your GP. I am sure they would be able to help you.'

That was not what I wanted to hear.

'OK,' I said, leaning forward on the counter. 'But the thing is, I am on holiday, and so I was hoping I'd be able to get something for my… Problem.'

She raised her eyebrows, just the way all pharmacists used to raise their eyebrows when I had bargained my way down to cough mixtures instead of opioids.

It was then that I decided to get desperate as I recalled the list of things Samira had said a pharmacy *could* prescribe.

'What about an ear infection?'

'Are you now saying that it's not a urinary infection you have but an ear infection?'

'Both,' I replied confidently.

'Well, again, I think you should go and see your doctor.'

Right, that's it! 'Sinusitis,' I said.

She began to shake her head.

'Shingles?' I asked hopefully.

And then, I could tell, in her face, she was going to call security.

I hate pharmacies. They make you wait and wait and wait, and then tell you they can't give you what you want.

Well, at least that's been my experience as a professional junkie.

But I felt compelled to buy something, anything, to prove to Samira and Danny that I had gone to a pharmacy. Non-controlled substances were reluctantly handed over as I noticed the impish teenager had vacated her seat.

I trudged back to the hotel, with a vague belief in the transformative qualities of the air in a budget hotel room to make Matt better. I found Danny in the vehicle, checking that Trevor was still there and metamorphosing, asked where Samira was, whilst acknowledging I had gotten something from the pharmacy. We both then headed back to my room, with Matt shivering quietly in his bed.

I held out the bag for Samaira to open, with the one thing I did get the pharmacist to give me.

'You got them,' she said, almost impressed with my capacity and capability to achieve the objectives of my mission.

I didn't want to initially disappoint her, so I kept quiet as I glanced at Matt and waited for her to open the bag.

'A nasal spray,' she said, confused, and then angry, and then forming a highly disappointed shrug.

'They wouldn't do it,' I said, whilst wondering if we should ask Danny to put Matt out of his misery.

'And you told them you had a UTI?'

I nodded, because it was true, even if I had no witnesses to back me up.

'Well, you know where you can put that!'

'I'll happily shove it up his arse, if that's what you mean.'

'No, Jamie, it belongs up yours, you useless… Something or other.'

'OK, enough,' intervened Danny. 'We need to get going.'

Fortunately, we didn't have anything to pack as I had worked out it was Wednesday, and we were still some way off from getting to Mavis Grind by Friday.

So, I had to ask Danny if there would be any serious consequences if we weren't on Shetland by the agreed day, and he heartlessly informed me that the only consequences for anything going wrong would be allocated to Matt and me.

*Nothing changes,* I thought, as Samira and I helped Matt across the car park to Danny Boy's UK Tours Ltd.

As I held Matt, preventing him from falling flat on his face, I heard a very long sentence of expletives from Danny inside the vehicle. Samira left me with my hands on Matt's arse, so I pushed him in to see what all the fuss was about.

That's when I discovered the impish-looking teenager

from the pharmacy sitting on the back seat.

I should have kept quiet, but I said over Danny's shoulder, aiming at the inquisitive intruder, 'Oh, it's you!'

'What the—' Danny tried to say, but was clearly struggling to finish the sentence.

'Who are you?' Samira asked.

I sat Matt down on the nearest seat as I felt a keen sense of Danny's rage and confusion visibly focus on me.

'Did you lock the vehicle?' I asked sheepishly, in an attempt to deflect any accusation that I was responsible for our uninvited guest.

'No,' he said, as the teenage imp kept her eyes firmly fixed on us all. 'Anyway, how come you seem to know who she is?'

'I noticed her in the pharmacy,' I said, which was the gods-honest truth. 'Perhaps she followed me.'

Danny wanted to blame me, of course, but perhaps realised there was a dual culpability here. However, the blame game could come later. The key issue was having a teenage imp sitting next to Trevor. It wasn't a good thing for her or for us.

As Danny strained to find the words that could begin to address the problem, she piped up.

'I want a ticket,' she said, with an aggressively fixed stare. 'For the tour.'

'No,' said Danny, shaking his head. 'There are no tickets. There is no tour. You need to get off my coach. Now!'

'What about him?' she asked, using her eyes to force us to look down at Trevor's body, which occupied the rest of the back seats. 'Has he got a ticket?'

That's when Danny, Samira, and I looked at each other, and

for the very first time, I felt a sense of collective responsibility to address the problem confronting us all.

'That's an accident,' I said, a bit like parents who seek an excuse for their own poor behaviour in front of their children.

'You mean, he died in an accident?'

'Yeah, he got run over… By accident,' I said.

'So why is he here, in this van?' she asked, which probably wasn't an unreasonable question.

Danny took it personally that his vehicle repurposing was not being given the recognition it deserved. 'This is a coach,' he said, like some mildly abused business owner. 'Exclusive tour. Ticket holders only!'

She shrugged. 'OK, then, I still want a ticket. It looks like you've got room for one more.'

'There are no tickets,' chipped in Samira. 'They've all gone.'

'Then I'll tell.'

'Tell what?' asked Danny.

'I'll tell the police that you ran over a guy, and you haven't reported it.'

Awkward.

'How do you know we haven't reported it?' said Samira.

'Because he's still here. In your van.'

Then Danny, out of desperation, appealed to us both. 'Why does she keep calling it a van?'

'Well,' I began, getting back to the point the little imp was making, 'we're taking him to see his mum.'

'It's what he wanted,' offered Samira.

'His dying wish,' I added, for completion.

'But he's all smelly,' she said, as if we should give him a

good bath before we showed his mum her dead son.

'I can't smell him,' Danny said, who I was sure had assured us that the rot wouldn't set in for 24 to 48 hours.

'Which is why we're in a hurry,' I said, knowing that Trevor did generally smell, even as a junkie. 'And you are getting in the way of his dying wish… To see his mum.'

'Before he's buried,' Samira added, expanding the absurdity.

'Or cremated,' I said, remembering a drug-addled conversation with Trevor once about where we would want our ashes to be scattered. I chose the sea, and Trevor insisted in his back garden next to the goldfish pond.

'I'm not stopping you,' the imp said defiantly, taking her phone out of her pocket and starting to scroll.

'Yes, you are,' said Samira, in a voice that reminded me of my mother when she wanted me to do something I had no choice over. 'You're asking for something that can't happen. Trust me, you do not want to get involved with us. It's very… Dangerous.'

'Did you kill him?' she asked, casually glancing up from her phone.

'No, it was an accident!' I said, again seeking to establish some kind of objectivity. 'He had this thing about stepping in front of vehicles. Only, you know, it was bound to go wrong… Eventually.'

'He sounds like an idiot,' she said, which was closer to the truth.

'Well, he might not have had all his wires connected, but he deserves some respect,' I hissed, which was kind of what I thought.

'I respect him. I think he looks cool,' she said, standing up to take a selfie with Trevor.

'What are you *doing*?' said Danny, who I suspect had been calculating various unpalatable scenarios for the imp.

'Snapchat.'

'Oh no you're not!' he said, as he lurched forward and grabbed her phone.

There was a moment of pure fury in the eyes of the teenage imp before she realised that whatever she thought should happen, was not a runner.

'Right,' said Danny, standing over her. 'You need to get off my coach and forget everything you've seen here.'

She sat down, biting her lip, her eyes darting around like a caged animal. 'I've got antibiotics.'

'No,' said Danny, as he walked away with her phone.

Now this was a dilemma. Whilst Danny was right to put his foot down, whatever was going on with this kid, she certainly had something to trade.

Samira was of the same mindset.

'Show me,' she said, sitting down in the seat next to the imp. Who then handed over a sheet of tablets to Samira.

'What are these for?' she asked.

'Tuberculosis.'

'You've got tuberculosis?' Samira asked in a tone that suggested mild shock with a hint of disbelief.

She nodded, as if it didn't really matter to her.

As I looked at Samira, we had the same thought: *better than nothing*.

'You don't mind if we use some of these for our friend?' asked Samira.

The girl shrugged again, which confirmed she was OK with it.

Then we both looked at Danny. He started shaking his head and then walked back to her, his face stern and strict.

'OK,' he said. 'Why do you want to come with us?'

'Because I hate it here.'

'What about school?' asked Samira. 'Your parents?'

'I don't go to school,' she replied. 'And I don't have parents.'

Danny carried on looking at the imp, as if he were keen to ascertain the truth just by staring. 'Where do you think you are going to go with us?'

'John O'Groats,' she replied, which was pretty much our formal destination blazoned on the side of our vehicle.

'You're a sad little waif, aren't yer?' said Danny, who I hoped had a soft touch about him. 'OK, you can come for a bit of a ride, seeing as you're at a loose end, but you follow the rules that I'm about to tell yer. There's no phone while you're with us. Anything you see or hear is between you and me. If anything you see or hear goes anywhere else, I will find you, and I will cut out your tongue, cut out your eyes, and chop your fingers off.'

'OK,' she replied, as if such dire consequences were nothing to worry about.

'What's your name?' I asked.

'Janet.'

# CHAPTER SEVEN

## JANET

As we got back on the road, along the M6 towards Manchester, I really had no idea why Danny had agreed to let Janet "come for a bit of a ride". It seemed exceedingly reckless, and not just for us. If she were to wander off to the nearest police station, Danny would no doubt do all that he had threatened to do to her. It was a risky day trip she had signed up to, assuming it only takes us a day to get to Scotland, where I suspect Danny will then throw her off his precious repurposed van, I mean coach, of course.

Still, Janet seemed happy enough, even without her precious phone, looking out of the window and watching the traffic pass us by – and I mean all the traffic, because we were not exactly the fastest wheels in motion. We did suggest that Janet should perhaps occupy a few seats forward from my old mate Trevor, but the body of Trevor, pale and grey-skinned, seemed to be part of the attraction of coming with us.

It is tempting to say at this point: teenagers! But that's not something I am going to say, even though I have just said it.

The fact is, Janet was a teenager, something we had all been through and should be able to relate to, excluding obscure subculture references. Lost and neglected was the unsaid collective thought we had of Janet. At least, so she appeared to be whilst riddled with Victorian disease. Given what Coventry had to offer, which was a vacuous dead zone in the centre of a wasteland, who wouldn't swap it for a ride on a coach with a dead junkie, a septic deluded Che Guevara, a disappointed personal trainer, a Dublin gangster, and an unemployable reconciliation clerk?

As we trundled along, Samira managed to persuade Matt that the pills she had in her hand were not cyanide but would help him get better, which, I might add, we had no medical proof of one way or the other. Like a man who had no idea where he was, who he was, or where he should be going, he swallowed.

However, once Matt was left to his feverish torpor, and Danny had his eyes yet again firmly fixed ahead of him, both Samira and I could feel the keen presence of Janet. It was frustrating, because this was as good a time as any to try to get some kind of sensible conversation going with Samira, but the last thing I needed was the teenage waif overhearing.

I did wonder if that was why Danny had let Janet come on board, serving as an obstacle to more effective communication and potential solutions to impending issues such as life or death. I was sure by now that Samira had concocted something that had given us time, but not the get-out clause we needed to pay off the Dublin gang. All I needed was Samira to confirm that we were in a "holding pattern", and then we could get down to some serious planning for a way out of this. But if her gran did have a bag full of cash to the tune of £250k, then all the better. I just didn't see how, once the money was handed over, we would then be left to wander off into the sunset.

It would have to wait, I decided, as I moved a few seats

down and formally introduced myself to Janet.

'Why did you follow me?' I asked, as she continued to stare out of the window.

She shrugged.

I wasn't going to get an answer.

'And how did you know it was me travelling in this vehicle?'

This time, she did answer. 'I saw you in the van, and I remembered that you said you were on holiday when you were talking to the pharmacist.'

'So you put two and two together.'

She smiled.

I knew I was going to regret trying to talk to her, but Janet intrigued me. Perhaps she reminded me of myself when I was her age.

'I was like Trevor, once,' I said, nodding in the direction of the prone festering corpse next to her.

'You mean, dead?' she asked, keeping her impish little face as deadpan as possible.

'No, I mean, I was a junkie,' I said, although there were a few near-death experiences along the way. 'I mean, I did do some daft things that nearly got me killed.'

She wasn't impressed.

'Aren't you worried that you're getting into something that is a bit out of your depth?' I said paternally.

She looked me straight in the face. 'How can going on holiday to John O'Groats get me killed?'

She had me there.

'It won't,' I said, flapping.

'So what are you guys up to?'

'We're not up to anything,' I replied, fully regretting my attempt to be kind and sociable.

'I don't believe you,' Janet said, pulling her jacket tighter by shoving her hands in her pockets. 'You must be up to something, or else you wouldn't be hanging on to a dead guy.'

Annoying, but it was painfully obvious.

'Well, OK, there is, probably, more going on than just a holiday. Which means, if you're sensible, that you just get off the next time we stop, and like Danny says, forget about us and go back home, or go and do whatever it is you do.'

'I don't want to do that,' she said defiantly.

'Why not?'

'Because I don't want to go back to Coventry.'

'Why, what's wrong with Coventry?'

Janet raised her eyebrows, and I knew I had already answered my own question.

'OK, so there's not a lot going for Coventry. I can see that having been there for five minutes. Shouldn't you be at school, though? Or college, or something like that?'

That made Janet angry. She gave me the hardest stare I'd had since Samira started staring at me.

'I don't go to school, and I don't go to college,' she said categorically. 'No one wants me, and no one likes me. You don't care about me, and I don't care about you, so don't pretend that you're going to be my friend or anything else because everyone is fake.'

I was being naive.

God knows what kind of life the poor kid was having to put up with, and it was probably none of my business, but I also didn't want the kid to get hurt just because anything was better than what she had to live with back in Coventry.

'Look,' I said, trying to use a tone that said I was levelling with her. 'I think you'll be OK to come along with us for a bit, but we're not going to John O'Groats, if that's where you really want to go.'

She frowned, and probably not because her unofficial ticket didn't take her all the way.

'But we are going up to Scotland,' I explained, trying to mitigate her frustration. 'So that's probably where you can then make your own way.'

'I don't care what you say,' she said, all surly. 'You're not in charge.'

True, I wasn't in charge. I felt like saying, so on your head be it! I could also have said, I've tried to warn you, but it's all going to be too late, because I'm not going to do anything to help you if Danny puts a knife across your throat because you're a pain in the arse, you little brat!

'Nice chatting,' I mused, and wobbled my way up to sit behind Danny.

Just as I was about to open my mouth, Danny dealt with it.

'Don't waste your time,' he said, moving between lanes. 'They don't understand you, and they don't want to know. They think they know it all, so it's best to leave it at that.'

I was going to say that I was sure I wasn't like that as a teenager, when in fact I probably was exactly like that as a teenager.

'OK,' I said. 'But we really shouldn't have her with us for too long.'

'Are you telling me what to do now, Jamie?'

'No,' I assured him. 'But—'

'But what, Jamie?'

'But it doesn't seem sensible.'

'How do you know what's sensible and what isn't?'

'Well, in this case, I think it would be sensible to drop her off somewhere.'

'Then what?' What do you think happens?'

'She goes home.'

'And do you think she's got a home to go to?'

'I don't know.'

'No, exactly, Jamie, you don't know. She's already seen enough, so I think we keep her with us.'

I glanced back at Janet.

She must have had major antenna attached to her ears because she smiled at me, confirming that I wasn't in charge and Danny was, and she had got what she wanted, however bizarre that wish may have been.

'How's yer man back there?' said Danny.

'Which one, Matt or Trevor?'

'The eejit whose got a face like a prolapsed anus.'

'Same as,' I replied, looking unsympathetically at the agitated Matt.

'Let's get him to the doctor,' said Danny.

*Wow*, I thought to myself, *Danny must have a heart in that toughened gangster skin of his.*

Little did I know what Danny's definition of a doctor meant.

# CHAPTER EIGHT

## DR Q, AKA "THE PENGUIN"

No one else, apart from Danny, knew what was happening as he parked up in front of a row of terraces on the outskirts of Manchester. We were all instructed to wait whilst Danny knocked on the door of number 32.

'What do you think?' I asked Samira, as we watched Danny laugh and joke with someone who stood inside the front door.

'Perhaps he's talking to a friend,' she said uncertainly.

'Not a doctor?'

'I don't know, Jamie, do I?' replied Samira hastily.

I felt like a child, being told to wait in the car whilst the parents sorted out something that we were never going to be told about.

Then Danny returned and announced that we were to "take a break" and go inside.

'Does the doctor live there?' I asked, wondering if this particular practitioner was a bit down on his luck, having surveyed the crumbling street and boarded windows of the less-than-salubrious neighbourhood.

'You'll meet him,' he said. 'Come with me, but leave the junkie – we'll sort him out later.'

What Danny meant by that, regarding poor Trevor, was only going to become apparent later, as we dutifully trundled out of the vehicle and into the humble abode of Dr Q, AKA "The Penguin".

Now, you may be wondering what all of this has to do with getting to the Shetlands to have tea and cakes with Mavis Grind.

Not a lot, actually, at the moment, although all will become clear. Possibly...

Our road trip was under Danny's command and control, and, as we were gradually to find out during the rest of the day, there was a plan, and we all had a key role to play in it.

We all strolled into a tiny living room that faced the rubbish-strewn street, with Danny occupying prime seating on a comfy leather chair, and Samira, Matt, Janet, and I squeezed onto a two-seater sofa. Standing in the centre of the room in front of a gas heater, warming his hands behind his back, was the man who called himself Dr Q.

He looked like he was in his 50's, with his stomach protruding a sizable middle-age spread, his hair reduced to a few redundant strands, and a pugnacious face that smiled benignly, but held back a potentially sinister thought process that would probably only come out at night or in the small wee hours.

But what he didn't look like was a doctor, even though Danny had insisted.

It was Samira who was prepared to ask the most obvious question. 'Are you a doctor?'

'Nah,' Dr Q said disparagingly. 'It's just what they like to call me around here.'

I also left it to Samira to give Danny one of those disappointed looks.

'Why are we here then, Danny?' asked Samira, who had now translated her disappointment into incredulity.

But it was Dr Q who intervened on Danny's behalf. 'Hasn't he told you?'

We all shook our heads, even Matt, who seemed to have regained a mild degree of consciousness.

'OK,' Dr Q began. 'I'll leave it to Danny to explain things. Would you all like something to eat?'

'Yes,' said Janet, who looked like she was suffering from mobile phone withdrawal, her hands and thumbs waving in the air like she was using a gaming controller.

'You lot sit there, and I'll make you some sandwiches,' said Dr Q, pulling up his trousers over his expansive waist, and shifting what looked like a dodgy right leg behind him.

Then, for the first time since we had started on this bizarre odyssey, I saw a slight awkwardness, a pensive pause, as Danny gathered his thoughts and prepared us for the breaking news.

'I suppose you all want to know why you're here,' he said, closing one eye and keeping the other firmly fixed on us.

'That would help,' said Samira, who sounded as if she had yet again been let down by the male species.

'OK,' said Danny, preparing himself. 'There's a small mission we need to fulfil.'

It was Samira who leaned forward from being wedged onto the sofa. 'We are already on a mission.'

'Well, if you don't mind, it's me who determines the flight plan,' he replied, scowling. 'And this was always going to be a stop off. That means that while we're here, there's a job we have to do.'

'Well, it can't be window cleaning,' I said, 'because I don't see any windows in the houses around here.'

'Shut up, Jamie!' said Samira, who never, ever, liked my sense of humour.

'But what about Matt? You said we were taking him to see a doctor.'

'Don't you worry,' said Danny confidently. 'I think our Dr Q here can sort something out for him.'

Samira rolled her eyes as I pressed Danny on what this mission was going to be.

'I'll tell you the details later,' he said. 'But we'll be staying here for the rest of the day, until it gets dark.'

With Danny having laid down the law, we remained seated like four naughty children who had been caught playing truant and were waiting to see what the punishment might be. We were all restless, for one reason or another.

Janet asked Danny if she could have her phone back because she was bored.

Request denied.

Samira wanted to know if we would still get to see her gran by Friday. Danny said it was *his* schedule and timing, and Samira just needed to worry about the money being there when we arrived.

Matt wanted to go to the toilet, which was an improvement on bananas and rampant cigars.

Request denied temporarily.

Lastly, I was desperate to know exactly what this mission was that we had been signed up to without prior consultation.

Request firmly denied.

Our frustration was relieved by the return of Dr Q, who brought with him two large plates full of white bread sandwiches.

'Right,' he said, placing them on top of piles of glossy magazines that populated a glass coffee table. 'There's fish paste or chicken and liver pâté.'

It would have been rude to decline such hospitality, but at the same time, there was little enthusiasm to start scoffing up what was in front of us.

'Are none of you hungry?' he asked innocently.

'I am,' Matt replied, whose rationality was a sign he may be coming round from his toxic psychosis. He stretched out his healthy left hand and forced half a sandwich into his mouth in one go.

'Do you have a drink?' asked Janet.

'I've got orange squash,' said Dr Q, who I think in that moment realised Janet was the child among us.

'Have you got any milk?'

'Sure.'

'Excuse me,' said Samira, who I suspected was going to decline feasting on the miracle of the five loaves and two fish. 'Why do they call you Dr Q?'

The rotund belly and red blotchy face chuckled to himself, before revealing his community function. 'Q stands for quack, and I supply the tranq dope to people around here.'

'You're a drug dealer, and not a doctor,' said Samira disapprovingly.

'Trust me, for most people around here, what I give them is as close to a doctor as they're ever going to get.'

'Which makes you a bit of a quack,' I added helpfully.

'What is tranq dope?' asked Samira.

'Xylazine,' replied Danny, who peeled open a sandwich to view its contents and then left it on the pile. 'They use it on animals.'

'It's not approved for use in humans?' I asked.

Dr Q ignored me. 'What's wrong with the famished one? He looks a bit pale and injured.'

Samira spoke on Matt's behalf.

'He's had an accident; burnt his hand, and it's got infected. He's got a fever, and he's a bit deluded.'

'Give him these,' said Dr Q as he pulled out some tablets from his pocket. 'It will calm him down.'

'What else will it do to him?' asked Samira, examining the large pills.

'He'll be OK, as long as he sticks to those, but if you cut it with heroin, coke, fentanyl, and inject it, then you're going to end up looking like a zombie.'

'Interesting,' I pondered, feeling the urge of my junkie days shoot through me.

'It's only the headcases who do that,' said Dr Q reassuringly. 'There's a guy who's just had his leg amputated because he was cutting it and then injecting. Not a pretty sight; covered in skin ulcers. That's why it's known as the flesh-eating zombie drug.'

We all looked at Matt, who seemed oblivious to what might be coming his way, but then he was not a real junkie: that honour rested with Trevor, who was definitely on his way to being zombified.

'Come on, I'll get you that milk,' said Dr Q to Janet.

'I'll have some as well,' I said immediately. Not that I wanted milk, but I had a vague premonition that Dr Q might assume that Janet was potentially payment for his hospitality.

We followed Dr Q out of his living room and along the corridor into the kitchen at the back of the house. I was about to make small talk when I realised that Janet was no longer behind me. As Dr Q held out two glasses of milk, he rapidly grew anxious.

'Where's she gone?'

I backtracked to see another door in the corridor half open. As I pushed it, there was Janet, standing in the centre of the room, surrounded by wall-to-wall glass cases, each one containing a *Batman* magazine.

I thought Dr Q would go ballistic, messing with what was obviously a treasured collection of comic books, but I think he was pleased he could show it off.

'I'm a fan,' he explained to both of us.

I was about to compliment him on a fine method of storage and display when I noticed, leaning in the corner, a full-sized coffin standing on its end.

'Do you like *Batman*?' Dr Q asked Janet, who was studying the comic book graphics.

Of course, nothing impressed her, but she didn't say she did not like *Batman*. Which, for an aficionado like Dr Q, was an open invitation.

'Did you know that *Batman* was created by the artist Bob Kane and writer Bill Finger and debuted in the 27th issue of the comic book *Detective Comics* on 30 March 1939?' he asked, pointing at the prized issue behind the glass. 'That is the first *Batman* story, *The Case of the Chemical Syndicate,* although it largely duplicated the plot of the story *Partners of Peril* in *The Shadow*, issue 113. It wasn't until 1940 that *Batman* had his own title in *Detective Comics*, and by that time, *Detective Comics* was the top-selling and most influential publisher in the industry. *Batman* and the company's other major hero,

*Superman*, were the cornerstones of the company's success.'

Then Janet, who now seemed genuinely interested, asked a question. 'So why do you like *Batman*?'

'He was the antidote to *Superman* because he does not possess any superpowers. Instead, he relies on his intellect, fighting skills, and wealth. It wasn't until a bit later,' Dr Q said, whilst stretching to point out another prized and preserved comic book, 'that he was the fully matured *Batman*, when he gets his utility belt in *Detective Comics*, issue 29, July 1939. In fact, you don't get the character's origin until issue 33, November 1939, in a two-page story about the death of his parents.'

It was this last remark that made Janet blush.

We both took it as a sign that this had far greater meaning.

'Anyway,' said Dr Q, moving swiftly on, 'most of the comics are war and pre-war, and by then they'd kind of softened him, you know, by adding things like *Robin*'s character. I don't think they wanted *Batman* running around like a crazed vigilante exterminating all of them baddies, but the real *Batman*, the true *Batman*, lives in a bleak and menacing world.'

'Just like life, then,' I mused, gazing over the plethora of *Batman* front covers.

Then I heard Janet ask another question. 'Is that you?'

She was pointing at a photo of Dr Q wearing a monocle, top hat, morning suit, and carrying an umbrella.

'My favourite villain,' he said. '*The Penguin*.'

'Is that why you are called Dr Q?' I asked, even if he had previously stated it was due to his rather dubious community service.

'*Quack, quack*,' he said, mimicking *The Penguin*.

'But that's a duck noise,' said Janet.

'*Quack*,' said Dr Q, his feelings mockingly hurt.

Which left only one more thing. So, I had to ask a question of my own. 'What's in the coffin?'

'Nothing,' said Dr Q, smiling benignly. 'Yet.'

# CHAPTER NINE

## THE ZOMBIE CITY PALLBEARERS PLAN

This is a disclaimer: everything you are about to read may be true, partially true, or seriously made up. But what is true, and I kid you not, is that Danny, Samira, Matt, Janet, and me were going to be pallbearers at the Zombie City Nightmare Apocalypse!

And it all starts with Dr Q.

Believe it or not (and I initially found it hard to believe as I chomped my way through chicken and liver pâté white bread sandwiches) Dr Q was once a child with a mummy and daddy, and in fact not necessarily destined to be the official supplier of highly destructive community tranq dope. He had, apparently, a love of animals, which he had acquired and demonstrated from an early age. And he loved nothing more than spending the whole of the school summer holidays staying on a farm just outside Dublin. These were his mother's relatives, who were also related to Danny's relatives, and one way or another, this made Danny and Dr Q related.

Hence, the reason we were sitting in Dr Q's living room listening to his long and convoluted explanation for why we were being press-ganged into participating in a hairbrained scheme to rob the Zombie Motorcycle Club, known as ZMC, of their highly valuable tranq dope stash.

I digress, or should I say Dr Q continued to digress, as he

revealed how much he loved both his parents, being an only child, and was supported in anything and everything he ever wanted to do. Yes, I know, unusual as far as I was concerned, or indeed you may be concerned, that there was somewhere in the universe evidence of good parenting.

Dr Q drew the dots to reveal that his joyous times on the Emerald Isle, staying on a farm and learning everything he could about domesticated animals, led him to the inevitable conclusion that his life was destined to be involved with animals as a vet. Therefore, Dr Q was a diligent student, studied hard, and was one of the few, if perhaps the only resident in this part of Manchester, who went on to attend university and vet school. He loved it, he said, and was on an accelerated upward curve, sailing through the learning, a distinctive undergraduate always attaining distinction.

That was until tragedy struck.

I swapped the chicken and liver pâté white bread sandwiches for the few remaining fish paste white bread sandwiches, and waited with a mouthful of fish paste for the traumatic events to be revealed.

Dr Q's parents, whom he loved dearly, were both tragically killed in a road traffic accident. A cow, he said, or perhaps a herd of cows, had broken out of their field and were rushing to cross over to pastures green. This is what caused Mr and Mrs Quack to steer across the road and into an oncoming HGV that was taking an illegal shortcut through the country lanes. As is the way with these kinds of things, so Dr Q said, it was an accumulation of factors that led to the tragic accident.

Then a tear appeared on his cheek.

'I feel no miracles, mercy, redemption, Heaven or Hell,'

said Dr Q, wiping away his tear. 'That's an indirect quote from *Batman: Absolution*, January 2003, DeMatteis and Ashmore.'

The tragedy, so Dr Q explained, was devastating for him, leading to a self-destructive spiral of excess and toxic indulgences, all culminating in his expulsion from the vet school.

'That's not fair,' chipped in Janet.

I noticed Dr Q glance at Danny, who seemed to indicate that it was probably not best to expand, but Dr Q was on a cathartic roll, as if it were rare that he got the chance to elucidate on his post-traumatic stress disorder.

'The accusations were false,' he said determinedly. 'But there was some truth in the attachment I had to Dolly.'

'Was that your girlfriend?' asked Janet innocently.

'It may have been portrayed in that way, but rest assured, my association with' – he paused as he drew in a deep breath – 'with Dolly, who happened to be a sheep, was purely platonic.'

I watched Danny wince, whilst we all nodded sympathetically.

Matt had seemingly just twigged that he was listening to a strange-looking man who looked a bit like a penguin. 'Did I just hear right?' Matt, who was beginning to sound vaguely coherent, whispered in my ear. 'Did this guy just tell us he's a sheep-shagger?'

I pretended not to hear, encouraging Dr Q to continue, but Danny had decided we had heard enough from his distant, or very distant, cousin.

'All right, that'll do, because you all need to know what the plan is.'

'A plan to do what?' asked Samira, still annoyed at the diversion to our itinerary.

Danny nodded at Dr Q to not pick up from where he left off, but to move rapidly on to the mission that lay ahead of us.

And so it was revealed that the supply of tranq dope was in the hands of the notorious local biker gang called the ZMC. I had noticed their brand graffitied over a number of hoardings and billboards on our way into the housing estate.

They were Hells Angels who had acquired a more menacing, if anything can be more menacing, approach to their illegal activities once they had become the main suppliers of Xylazine.

ZMC were not to be messed with, not least because there were one or two of them who had developed the kind of skin ulcers that gave the combination usage of Xylazine, heroin, and fentanyl its zombie branding. Rather than hand themselves in to the nearest addiction clinic, they had taken pride in their evolution, so that the ZMC now distinguished itself from the Hells Angels, and could prove their difference with their authentic zombie characteristics.

Having listened with a mild degree of scepticism to Dr Q's explanation of the vertical supply chain of Xylazine, he then pulled from his pocket a crumpled flyer that he handed to me.

I then read out loud, so everyone was suitably informed.

At the top of the flyer was the headline: Nightmare Apocalypse! Underneath it, a type of sub-heading that overlaid various gruesome ghouls, monsters, vampires, and zombies, and then came the publicity:

'"Fancy an experience like no other? Zombie City, Nightmare Apocalypse is back! The immersive, horrifying experience is taking over the old Knights of the Roundtable Theme Park!

'"Real-life actors are on site to scare you senseless as you walk through the world's longest horror attraction. An immersive experience featuring zombies hungry for human flesh and people acting as military personnel hunting you through the abandoned site. Will you make it out alive?

'"Complete with delicious food and drink, this is not to be missed!"'

'Food,' said Matt, as if that was the only thought he was capable of.

'Zombies!' said Janet excitedly.

However, I was far less excited because I was trying to connect the dots and assimilate how such an event had any relevance to "the mission".

Regrettably, Dr Q had far more to reveal.

'The theme park was a big tourist attraction in its day, but it's been closed for the last 10 years. There used to be loads of rides such as The Knightmare, The Tower of Terror, and Excalibur. The site has fallen into disrepair, and many of its rides have been demolished or simply left to decay. It's basically derelict, but they need to keep an eye on it, and that's where I work now, as a security guard. It's a boring job, but it's also my main supply line. You see, it's where the ZMC store their stash.'

'Where? There?' I asked confusedly.

'In Merlin's Magic Hell Ride,' explained Dr Q. 'It's a ghost train that still functions if you crank up the power supply.

Ingenious, really.'

'What is?' asked Samira, with the same level of confusion.

'As a place to hide their stash. You see, they keep it in a coffin that is installed in a section of the ghost train ride.'

And so, the coffin in Dr Q's hallowed library of ancient comics came flooding back into my vision.

'Which means,' intervened Danny, 'that we're going to join this zombie fest carrying a coffin. We then swap it over and march out of there with the stash.'

'No!' said Samira, as abruptly as I tried to respond, but felt it wise to keep quiet.

'Shut up. You do as I say.' Danny asserted his less-than-benign leadership role.

Samira folded her arms and crumpled onto the sofa.

'It's a win-win,' said Danny, seeking to restore calm. 'We put the junkie in the coffin and leave him there, and take out the other coffin with all the drugs in it. Dr Q here has an exact replica, so we walk in as pallbearers, and we walk out the same way.'

'You will need to dress up,' Dr Q added.

'We can all be zombies!' Janet exclaimed, seemingly focused on the event rather than the potential consequences of stealing the stash belonging to a nasty flesh-rotting, killer-zombie biker gang.

'Danny,' I said, mildly adopting a collective voice for all those concerned, 'if we do manage to get away with this, won't we have the ZMC on our tail all the way up to Scotland?'

'They won't know,' said Dr Q. 'Well, not for a while. We should have long enough to get out of here. They do a drop once a week, and they did that last night, so that will give us plenty of time.'

I scratched my forehead with a flood of questions swirling around inside my brain, trying to calculate which questions would be permissible and which ones would not, when Samira posed the one question I had at the forefront of my mind.

'If you let us live,' she said to Danny, 'this now means we will also have a crazy biker gang who will want to kill us all.'

'Listen,' he said, leaning forward, 'if you do this for me, and the money's good when we get to see your gran, I'll leave it up to you to sort yourselves out – there'll be no opposition from me.'

Then Janet had to ask Danny a more obvious question. 'Why do you want to kill them?'

'He doesn't,' I said, trying to play down the murderous tone of things.

'It's complicated,' Samira added.

Danny sat back in his chair, knowing full well that we did not have a choice, and gave us time to mentally prepare ourselves for what lay ahead. On one level, it would only require a little cosplay, a little bit of muscle, and a discreet exchange of coffins – one in, one out – in order to comply with what was either a hastily arranged opportunity or a long-anticipated plan that now had the means to be implemented.

To let Danny know we would comply, I decided to ask one less pressing question. 'Were you going to do this anyway?'

'We accelerated,' said Dr Q. 'Once Danny told me what he was up to. You could call it a confluence of circumstances, an accumulation of requirements, which were perfectly suited for this little operation.'

I nodded, thoughtfully. 'Are you going to sell the drugs in Manchester?'

'No, this is for export into the EU. The goods will be transported by boat. We have papers to say the coffin contains Danny's made-up uncle, whose last dying wish was to be buried back on the Emerald Isle.'

'Not that it's any business of yours,' said Danny, giving me a dirty look.

'I'll miss Trevor,' said Janet.

'How do you know his name is Trevor?' asked Samira.

'I heard you talking,' she replied unconvincingly.

'He's just a junkie!' Danny blurted out in desperation.

'*Was*,' I added, raising my eyes to the ceiling. Not in prayer, but in a generalised state of despair.

# CHAPTER TEN

## NIGHTMARE APOCALYPSE!

We laid Trevor to rest in the duplicate ZMC stash coffin with his arms across his chest. Oddly, although I can only account for my own observation, I thought he looked calm; at peace with himself and the rest of the world, as if he had finally achieved something in a thoroughly unrewarding life. As we nailed down the coffin lid, I made the sign of the cross, only for Samira to slap me, admonishing me for my lack of coherence as an avowed atheist.

After that, Dr Q offered us more fish paste and chicken liver pâté sandwiches, but we all respectfully declined. He seemed to take it well, as he lay out in front of us, in the small living room, a basket full of black suits, top hats, and a children's face-painting kit, the latter of which Janet pounced on and proceeded to lather her face with thick white paint. She promptly added in streaks of blood from gnawing through flesh and bone.

By 6:30 p.m., we had transformed ourselves into zombie-eating pallbearers as we lined up in front of Dr Q's living room mirror to gauge the height of each of us and agree on who would be front and back for carrying Trevor to his ghost train resting place.

There was a degree of equivalence in height between Danny and me, and an equitable height between Samira and Matt, the latter being wobbly and vague, but seemed to understand he had to do something at some point later. We all agreed that it would be best for Janet to walk in front of us, with Dr Q performing his security duties, having gotten us into the theme park.

*Who would have thought*, I said to myself, *that only a few days ago I was worrying about financial reconciliations not adding up, when all along it was just a dress rehearsal for zombie re-enactment in the heist of the century!*

As we all stared at ourselves in the mirror, taking in our gentlemen-of-the-nineteenth-century-grave-robbers look, the words bizarre and surreal didn't quite adequately encapsulate how dazed and confused we all felt. (Although I would accept that Janet seemed to display an enthusiasm that was distinctly missing from the rest of us.)

There was no backing out, no turning back, as we piled into Danny Boy's UK Tours Ltd. coach. Dr Q drove solo in his white security minivan, with its silent orange siren flashing and guiding us for a 30-minute journey through Manchester and into the countryside.

As I'd mentioned, death, or dressing up dead, had brought Janet to life, as she asked a number of questions about who we should scare, who we should kill, and who we should let live. Danny was keen on keeping as low a profile as possible and told Janet to just focus on getting the job done and not to get involved in the entertainment. All of which seemed perfectly functional but also highly unlikely, if not wholly contradictory, given our state of dress for the Nightmare Apocalypse.

'Listen,' said Danny, who seemed to be stressing about

the whole thing, 'we're not playing zombies, ghouls, ghosts, monsters, or jibber jabber jabberwockies. We're in, and we're out.'

Samira, who was sitting in front of me, was shaking her head, presumably raising her eyebrows and looking thoroughly annoyed at getting involved in something that had as much credibility as a Victoria sponge without buttercream and jam.

I was sitting next to Matt and asked if he was feeling any better, and he mumbled something about fish paste and feeling sick. I requested a sick bag and was told we were not on an aeroplane, and so I told Matt to stick his head between his legs. This accelerated the problem, as the unmistakable sound of chunder and involuntary muscle movement indicated that Matt was vomiting.

In fact, he was vomiting a lot.

Oddly, everyone seemed surprised and disgusted that the stench-clenching sick was clogging the air and rolling all the way back down to where Trevor lay in his coffin on the back seats. Matt groaned and pulled his head up, swaying gently as Danny swung around the corners of the country lanes, trying to keep up with Dr Q.

'He looks pale,' said Samira, who tried to cover her nose and take a closer look at the somnolent Matt.

'Don't you mean paler than us?' I asked, seeing as we were all covered in white face paint.

'I don't care how pale he looks!' shouted Danny from his driver's seat. 'He's still carrying that bloody coffin with us.'

'We need air,' said Samira, who went along each window, pushing them open to let the cool, cold winter breeze begin to fumigate.

Whilst it brought minor relief to everyone's nostrils, it also seemed to revive Matt, who was able to utter the immortal words: 'Blimey, now I know what it feels like to be pregnant.'

'Are we there yet?' asked Janet, as she continued to look forward to parading in front of the coffin.

Danny didn't answer, but we did turn off the road and start following Dr Q along a frozen, rutted track. It meant we were getting near to implementing Danny and Dr Q's hairbrained plan, which I was convinced would lead to the rotting flesh of a deadly motorcycle gang tracking us down, removing our limbs, and stuffing us into a sewage pipe. Really, it was just an extrapolation of the many ways I thought we were all going to die one way or another if we ever met Mavis Grind.

We bumped along until we both pulled up next to what Dr Q had described as an abandoned farmhouse, which he had reliably assured us was uninhabited. The reason for being here, and not at the entrance to the Nightmare Apocalypse, was due to the farmhouse being located next to the old theme park, and just a short walk through some woods to an opening in the fence. In other words, we needed as short a walk as possible to the ghost train because we would be carrying the heavy load of Trevor and the stash. Dr Q had made a hole in the fence for us to crawl through so we could then, as discreetly as possible, remove and replace the coffin.

Given Matt's contribution to the evening so far, we all hurriedly rushed out of the vehicle to breathe in the fresh air, free of semi-digested fish paste and white bread.

There was no time to wait, apparently, as Dr Q wielded his special-issue security guard torch that belted out ten million lumens into our faces.

'What's wrong with you lot?' he asked, flicking his interrogation tool from face to face. 'Not got the stomach for a bit of robbery?'

'Well, we've just seen Matt's stomach,' I replied, fiddling with my top hat because the rim was half the size of my considerably large head. 'And it smells of fish paste.'

'That will be the Xylazine,' said Dr Q, as he shone his torch back towards the farmhouse.

'Now he tells us,' Samira groaned, still visibly traumatised by the vomit.

We all glanced over at the creeper-infested farmhouse next to a battered barn with chunks of metal farming tools scattered all around us.

'Is everything here rotten and abandoned?' I asked, beginning to feel the chill of winter through my waistcoat.

'Up north it is,' said Dr Q, smiling.

'I've noticed,' I said, although I was sure Basildon could be a potential contender for soulless dereliction.

'Right,' said Danny. 'Let's get your junkie friend on the move.'

We hauled the coffin out of Danny's tour bus and used straps to carry it across a wet and muddy field. There was some cursing, complaining, allegations of insufficient contributions, and further recriminations for failing to effectively carry the load, but as we approached a treeline, Dr Q told us to stop.

'Once you get through the trees,' Dr Q informed us, 'you'll find the old theme park.'

I looked up and could just make out vague structures that criss-crossed the cloudy night sky as we all sat on top of

Trevor, catching our breath.

'I've got to leave you now,' said Dr Q, sounding a bit like an army officer who had led us as far as he could on a suicide mission. 'Just remember, go under the fence, and then take a left, and in about 500 yards you'll come to Merlin's Magic Hell Ride. The coffin is on the mid-level, sitting in an alcove with a skeleton behind it. Just swap the coffins over, and I'll meet you back at my place when my shift is finished. Oh, and don't forget, act casual, like you're part of the show. Don't mess with the guys in fatigues either. They mean business and will shoot to kill.'

'What do you mean, shoot to kill?' Samira asked, taking in deep breaths.

'He's joking,' said Danny, as we watched Dr Q disappear into the night, so he got to work on time.

'Why don't we just go through the front entrance?' asked Janet. 'We're only going to be doing what everyone else is doing.'

'Because it's quicker and easier this way,' Danny explained. 'Plus, this is all last-minute, and we're not down on the staff list for tonight. We only need to look the part for five minutes and then get out quickly. That also means we don't get involved in anything. We're not here to play or scare anybody. We're here to get the stash.'

*Point taken*, I thought to myself, and the way Danny had put it made it sound far simpler than when the mission was articulated in Dr Q's living room.

So, after five minutes of rest, we picked up Trevor and stumbled through the woods.

Things seemed to be a bit more tangible as we got to see

floodlights illuminate the fencing, beaming down from the wreckage of the old theme park rides. It was Janet who picked out the hole in the fence as we fumbled around hauling the increasingly heavier coffin across the rutted lumps of grass and mud.

'I wonder if Burke and Hare had this kind of problem?' I groaned, as again we all rested on top of Trevor to catch our breath.

'Didn't they dig up the dead?' asked Matt, who had valiantly managed to sustain the physical effort.

'Yeah, but this is more of a commodity exchange than simple graverobbing,' I replied, fiddling with my top hat to make sure it was still firmly stuck to my head.

'OK, ladies,' said Danny. 'Let's get this over with.'

With a great deal of huffing and puffing, straining and objecting, we pushed Trevor's coffin through the hole in the wire fence.

We waited behind a large wooden building while Janet did some recon in the floodlit part of the theme park. Once she had confirmed there was no one around, we dragged Trevor into the light and emerged into the dilapidated landscape: a tumble-down world of bright lights and surreal imagery, broken shapes, gaudy pictures, ironic laughter, and entropy – also known as UK PLC.

As we picked up Trevor, pushed the coffin onto our shoulders, and walked like the zombie pallbearer actors we were meant to be, the gaudy failure of the theme park shone brightly into our eyes. Janet led, smartly marching until we reminded her to behave like a zombie, as we passed the oversized teacups, toddler spinning cars and trucks, and the small stalls to shoot cans nailed down to the shelving. Behind all of this loomed the oversized theme park rides, the grunting metal, the rusty crisscrossing frames that held up short-term thrills for extortionate prices.

*If ever there was symbolism*, I thought to myself, *this had to be it: the run-down carcass of a once happy time, beaten into the ground by the reality of economics and social decay.*

Did I care?

Not much.

Although I wasn't sure if I should have a conscience. But why should I cry over an abandoned theme park when I was disposing of my old junkie friend to steal a crazy biker gang's drug stash? If I was supposed to make sense of anything, I knew that times had changed, they were always changing, and if you tried to stand still because you were sick of the rat race, you'd end up like this place, rotting away and rusting into a mockery of redundancy.

But fear not, because if you can't get off the merry hamster's merry-go-round, there's always a swarm of zombies to drag you laughing and screaming into the pit of nothingness, failure, and alienation. We should be happy, pretending that the world of rotting corpses, rotting hope, and rotting futures is all just an illusion, not meant to be seen, not meant to be heard, not meant to be thought about; pretend it isn't there, and the world doesn't seem such a bad place.

Looking around the Nightmare Apocalypse, it did remind me of places like Basildon and Coventry, and every other soulless hellhole we call home.

Or something like that.

Well, perhaps I did care after all, but then again, maybe

I didn't, as we marched onward, looking for Merlin's Magic Hell Ride.

Suddenly, we were shouted at, rudely and abruptly. A military man in fatigues was going to shoot us.

'All zombies are going down!' he shouted.

Janet was the first to react, in fact, the only one to react, but this is where she may have overreacted.

With her coattails flailing behind her, and a manic shout that seemed to echo off the rusty metal edifies surrounding us, Janet drop-kicked the playacting military guy. It was poetry in motion, or maybe madness in motion, as the guy's toy gun went flying up in the air and his body bolted about 6ft backwards. Janet landed on her arse and sprang up like a flexible gymnast. The same could not be said of the military fatigued zombie killer, who lay prone and unconscious – if not dead.

'Janet!' Samira scolded as we all stood motionless with the weight of Trevor's coffin on our shoulders.

'What?' she asked, which almost seemed like a reasonable question.

'Why did you do that?'

'He was going to shoot us.'

'With a toy gun!'

Janet looked back at us, bemused and mildly resentful.

'Someone check to see if he's breathing,' said Danny, as we all lowered Trevor to the floor. Not that any of us were particularly responsive.

Samira looked at me.

'No way,' I said. 'You're the qualified First Responder.'

Samira didn't thank me as she bent down to check the

guy's pulse and listen for signs of life, also known as breathing.

'He's not dead.' She shrugged.

'He's not conscious, though,' I replied.

Samira looked at me dispassionately. 'Are you sure you're qualified to give a second opinion?'

'In my opinion, yes.'

'All right, you two!' intervened Danny. 'Let's move.'

Janet had something more positive to contribute as she pointed. About 100 yards ahead of us was our objective.

There seemed to be very little about Merlin's Magic Hell Ride that was cogent with the legend and mythology. There was a papier-mâché figure of Merlin, who had been demonically personified into a waving wizard of monstrous proportions, looking down ominously onto all those who dared enter the ghost train of purgatory on the way to Hell. Which was beside the point and probably irrelevant because we needed to get Trevor and his coffin up to the mid-level of the hell ride, and we didn't know how we were going to do it.

I didn't wait for Danny to tell me to have a look, as I knew that I was always meant to be "on point" for all operational matters. Behind some tatty hoarding, I found a line of what looked like two-seater goblets on narrow rails, ready to be launched into the mysterious world of Merlin's hellish castle and round table. There was also a control panel, which seemed to offer a potential solution to heaving a coffin through the narrow passages of a ghost train. All I had to do was flick the power switch.

I suppose at this point I could have consulted, but I was feeling thoroughly uncooperative and keen to get the whole thing over and done with. I grabbed a large red lever and pulled on it, first with one hand and then with both. At the third or fourth attempt, I was able to force it into the "on" position. I had no idea what was going to happen next and was grateful for the profound silence that followed my weak muscular exertions.

'What are you doing?' asked Samira, as if I were touching things that only grownups should.

'I've turned the power on,' I replied, slightly satisfied I had managed to work something out for myself.

However, I immediately began to wonder if it was really necessary, but felt thoroughly vindicated when Danny also appeared, looking relieved.

'Good, let's get the coffin loaded.'

'It's not a freight train,' Samira groaned, her eyes as wide as tennis balls, expressing her concern at reactivating a rundown rail track through an unknown Arthurian Hell ride.

'I'll go,' said Janet, who appeared with Matt.

'What do you mean, you'll go?' said Samira disdainfully, who obviously thought flying kung fu kicks had little to offer right now.

'Come on, let's get it working,' said Danny, who wandered over to have a look at the control panel.

As we both examined the switches and thought about what would ignite the ghostly monolith, Janet squeezed in between us and pushed the one button we had both been staring at because it was green. I think we were both impressed with her decisiveness as we waited for something to happen.

The silence was deafening, ghostly even, punctuated only by Samira scoffing loudly, and then almost choking as the strangest sound emanated from within the bowels of the hibernating beast. Like a re-awaken Iron Man, the clanking, clunking metal struts, gears, cogs, and levers began to switch and *click*, *clack*, and bolt. Then, multicoloured lightbulbs began to flicker; greens and reds, blues and yellows, oranges and purples sporadically lit up the whole façade.

'Christ,' said Matt. 'It's alive!'

'Unlike you, then,' said Samira, who had regained her scepticism.

'Well done!' said Danny, who ruffled Janet's hair as a reward for her fearless competency.

Slightly frustrated that I hadn't been given any credit for breathing life into the inanimate object, I offered to give it a go, meaning to see what happened when I flicked the start switch.

Almost immediately, a train of six two-seater goblets sprang into life and shunted their way along, pushing open the swing doors into the belly of the beast. Behind them soon came another set of goblets, ready to take on board their next set of paying customers.

'All aboard!' said Matt, grinning like *The Fat Controller*.

Danny mumbled something under his breath and told us to grab the useless junkie and strap the coffin onto the goblets.

'Right, you two eejits,' Danny said, referring to myself and the prolapsed anus. 'One in the front and one in the back of them goblet things. Use your phone, and when you see the skeleton and the coffin, tell us to stop and we'll cut the power. Swap them coffins over and get back down here so we are job done.'

I decided I would be better off in the front and leant

against the coffin. Matt was helped in by Janet as he tried to complain that he suffered from travel sickness.

Samira's phone rang.

'It's me,' I said as she answered, smiling malevolently.

'Why do you still have my number?' she asked down the phone.

'Give it to me,' said Danny, who grabbed her phone, stood by the control panel, and flicked the switch.

The goblets shunted and then proceeded as I watched Janet waving us both goodbye before we pushed through the plastic doors.

'I feel sick,' said Matt, as we were plunged into darkness.

'Keep it to yourself,' I hissed, as we were confronted by a swooping witch who passed over our heads, and then I heard an almighty chunder as Matt began spewing his guts out again.

Danny screamed down my phone at me. 'Have you found it?'

'No,' I replied, as we passed a boiling cauldron with errant bats hanging by a thread.

After a moment, in front of us, a light shone down on what I thought might be the Virgin Mary, until I clocked that she was more than likely the Lady of the Lake, with her hand and finger pointing upwards. The goblets twisted violently to the right and struggled to turn a tight corner and gradient, as we were pulled up to the next level and a bright, shiny knight, sitting on a rock, flicked open his visor and grinned its skull head at me.

*This could be the mid-level,* I thought to myself, as the goblet train shunted and shifted.

‘I think we might be here,’ I said, over the phone.

‘Are you there yet?’ asked Danny, which meant he wasn’t listening, as I waited for a coffin and a skeleton to come into view out of the darkness.

A few more pushes and shoving, and then I shouted down the line, ‘Stop!’

There it was, the coffin Dr Q had said would be here, placed next to a gravestone with the unimaginative blood lettering of RIP.

However, we came to stop a few yards too far forward and were left in the darkness. I turned my phone torch on and looked back to see Matt transfixed, as if he had seen a ghost.

‘You look like shit, mate,’ I said, as I sidled up to him.

‘What do you expect?’ he managed to say. ‘I’m a zombie.’

That was good, I thought, because it meant he could understand and compute. I helped him out, and we fumbled our way over to the ZMC stash. I could hear Danny screaming down the phone, obviously anxious to know what we were doing, and so I reassured him that we had found it.

‘Let’s have a look,’ I said, handing Matt the phone, intrigued to know what a stash of pills inside a coffin looked like.

Well, as you would expect, as I levered open the lid, a stash of pills hidden in a coffin looked exactly like a stash of pills hidden in a coffin. In fact, there was a very large quantity of pills, all in sealed plastic bags, bound in clingfilm bundles. Which kind of depressed me, because the value of the merchandise would be considerable, which meant that once the ZMC realised their stash had been stolen and made the links to Dr Q, the risk of our mortal coil being severely severed had exponentially increased. Especially considering that Danny and the Dublin gang would also have gutted us first and fed us to the seagulls.

I looked up at Matt, wondering if he fully comprehended the magnitude of what we had now gotten ourselves into.

'What?' he said, which was his standard gormless response.

'Nothing,' I replied, resting the coffin lid back down.

'Must be worth something,' Matt said, blinding me with the torch as he looked at the lid.

'Our lives,' I muttered. 'Probably.'

'Yeah, but we need a new career,' said Matt, as he shone the torch back down on the coffin.

'Have you got a death wish?' I said, manoeuvring back along the track towards the goblets.

'I think it's how we survive,' whispered Matt, more to himself as I jumped into the goblet and looked to untie the straps that bound Trevor's coffin.

I yelled at Matt to get down here to help, but as I looked back, he was talking to Danny.

'Come on,' I shouted. 'Let's get started!'

'What?'

'Let's get started on this,' I said, untying the straps, before I felt the trucks shunt, pause, and then pull abruptly away.

'What the—'

And that was it. I was off.

I lurched forward to grab hold of Trevor because the coffin was sliding, and before I knew it, the goblet train was turning left and up another gradient.

Danny must have restarted the bloody train, as vampiric Merlin waved his wand close to my face, and eerie demonic sounds rattled through a cave-like tunnel. As I clung on, desperate to keep Trevor from flying off, a happy-as-Larry skeleton wobbled in front of me.

*Not scary*, I thought to myself, before I had to swallow my own words as the goblet train pushed and shoved and took another sharp left before descending at a rapid rate on a rollercoaster hell ride…

'Ahhh!'

I flew out into the bright, brilliant bulb-lit light, passing Samira, Janet, and finally Danny, as they all looked on, confused as to why I looked so petrified.

'Cut the power!' I screamed as I felt the goblets had taken on a ghostly life of their own.

Danny managed to put two and two together, as I looked back at him pushing buttons and turning all the switches on the control panel, but nothing was stopping this runaway ghost train as I was pulled back through into Merlin's Magic Hell Ride.

*Here we go again*, I thought, as the witch swooped down to nearly take my head off. It felt like the goblets had been given a shot of electrical adrenaline as we flew along the track and spun around the corner and gradient again.

Matt was there, with phone in hand, being screamed at by Danny.

Instinctively, I felt I had no other option.

As the goblets pushed and shunted, I let go of Trevor and stood up.

I screamed at Matt to get out of the way and dived headfirst into the alcove, aiming for the graveside next to the ZMC coffin. I was expecting to land with a hard crunch, as I shut my eyes and went flying through the air.

But oddly, I kept falling, falling ever deeper into the grave pit.

# CHAPTER ELEVEN
## INVISIBLE MAN

'Take your clothes off!'

At least, that's what I think I heard as I started coming round with a blinding headache penetrating my eyeballs, like a brilliant bright white light shooting through my brain and smashing into the back of my skull.

'Get naked, man, so I can see you all over.'

Perhaps that was Samira, whispering gently to me, as I awoke from a disturbing dream where I had lost my job in the City, car-crashed a load of coke, had a knife to my throat, and travelled across the country ripping off a crazy zombie biker gang.

Yes, that's it, it's all just a dream.

Maybe not…

I desperately tried to open my eyes, but was actually being blinded by an intense white light rather than imagining a bright, intense light. I put my hand up to shield them.

Then the voice came booming out again.

'Are you bitten?' he demanded to know, in a heavy Caribbean accent.

I kept my hand over my eyes. 'What do you mean?'

'Don't mess with me, man,' he said aggressively. 'I don't mean no bee sting. I need to see if them zombies have bitten you. I need to know if you're going to turn.'

No, this wasn't a dream, I realised, it was a nightmare, and I was in the Nightmare Apocalypse.

So where were Matt, Samira, Danny, and Janet?

'Listen,' I said, desperate for my thumping headache to stop, and hoping that my recalcitrant colleagues would suddenly reappear and rescue me from something that I didn't quite understand. 'Can you turn down the light? Do you have any paracetamol?'

My request was met with a loud hysterical laugh, as if I had said something so profoundly absurd only an eejit would say it.

'Paracetamol won't stop you turning,' the voice said, beginning to come into focus between my fingers.

'Look,' I replied, trying as best I could to gather my thoughts. 'You really don't have to do this zombie thing with me. You know, I'm an injured participant and need some kind of medical attention, you know, first aid, first responder, resuscitation… That kind of thing.'

'You think that's all you need?' he said, as I spied a black guy at the other side of this intolerably bright white room.

'Yes,' I said indignantly. 'And for you to turn the lights down. Don't you have a dimmer switch?'

'Don't you fool with me!' he said, as he stepped forward with a blade sparkling.

That made me pull my hand down, and instinctively I pushed myself up on my elbows.

The blade was real; a long kitchen knife that he wielded all the way up to my face.

'When a white man drops out of the sky and says he ain't no zombie,' he said, his crusty creased face bristling with grey stubble, 'then I have the right to command you!'

I wasn't going to disagree as I began to wonder if this guy was possibly on another planet and was on holiday from reality, but if I had fallen out of the sky, how far did I fall through Merlin's magic grave pit? Was I now dead and living in Hell?

'Look,' I said, desperate to bring some rationality into the conversation. 'This is just a game.'

'This ain't no game!' he shouted into my face, thoroughly agitated. 'No white zombie man starts telling me that I can't see with my own eyes, that I can't see that what is out there is not the truth.'

'OK, enough,' I said, trying my best to be assertive, and annoyed that yet again I had knives being wielded around me like mistletoe. 'This is face-paint, which is why I look like a zombie, which is why some of us look like zombies, and there are also some of us dressed up like the military, and we're all here to scare people who have paid good money to be scared.'

His face came closer, his bulging bloodshot eyes looking deeper into my soul, which I'll admit has been on vacation for quite some time.

'Take those clothes off!' he said again, with the knife now sticking into my chest.

'OK, OK,' I said, turning my face away from the deadly menace.

He continued to stare, up close and personal, no doubt wanting to make sure that he meant business.

As I began to unbutton my pallbearer's waistcoat, he stepped back and positioned himself on the other side of what I could now determine was a compact room, decked out with dozens of bright white lightbulbs covering every inch of the walls. There was also little else in the room, and when I looked up, I could see the ceiling above where I had fallen through when jumping off the runaway ghost train.

As I took off my trousers, he was leaning against a door. Whatever madness was going on in here, that was my way out.

'Is this some kind of maintenance room?' I asked, hoping he'd let me keep my underpants on.

He didn't reply as he stared at my feeble, white body, no doubt unhappy that I was not fully complying with his instructions.

Oh well, if he wants to have a good butcher's at my half-hearted manliness, who am I to complain? I whipped them off and stood proud.

The man motioned with his knife for me to step forward, and then circled around, poking his knife into my skin, where I assumed he found some anomaly. He didn't look satisfied, but neither did he look ready to stab me in the head to disable my zombie brain.

I had to ask. 'Can I put my clothes back on, then?'

'I need to wait,' he replied.

'Wait for what?' I cried, exasperated at the denial of my inalienable rights.

'To see if you turn.'

'But you've checked me over. I have no bites. I am not a zombie! I am pretending to be a zombie because this is the Nightmare Apocalypse!'

'You've seen the zombies, have you?' he said, which included me in his delusional conspiracy, which is what I assumed I was dealing with: a thoroughly irrational man who had shacked up underneath a derelict ghost train.

'To be honest with you,' I said, feeling distinctly chilly from my ongoing nakedness, 'I haven't seen any zombies, real or playacting.'

'Oh, white man, they are real! I've seen them. Inside here. Biker guys, zombie guys, with all their flesh peeling off. Pus and sores, ugly as hell.'

That's when it all made sense.

If he was living here – although I had no idea why he would want so much light – he must have seen the ZMC sorting out their stash, and by the sounds of it, looking none too healthy.

'You know, if you mean the guys that come in here, they're not zombies, the ones with biker jackets,' I said, using a patronising tone that made me think that was how I used to talk to my deaf uncle. 'They're just ill, taking drugs that are not good for them.'

'You've seen them,' he said suspiciously. 'The zombies.'

'No,' I insisted, regretting I had some prior knowledge. 'It's just that, you know, I think it's known that there are some very unattractive-looking bikers that like to come here and wander around the ghost train.'

Why did I say that? Now he took to laughing quietly to himself, assimilating, and no doubt formulating an ever more convoluted delusional system.

'I know you,' he said, dangling his knife in front of my face again.

'Trust me,' I said, ready to fight for my life if I had to, 'this is the first time we've met.'

'Hybrids!' he said defiantly. 'Evolution!'

This wasn't going anywhere, and so I decided to try to introduce myself.

'Look, my name's Jamie, and I know it's weird that I just dropped through the ceiling, but you know, this is because there's this thing with people playacting: it's just all made up. There really are no zombies, and there's no apocalypse, and everything's pretty normal, really, apart from me standing in front of you naked, but I'd like to be your friend… And put my clothes back on… And we could have a cup of tea… Or something like that.'

I was running out of things to say, but I hoped he'd listen to some kind of reason, even if there was a distinct lack of it.

But the man wasn't having any of it as he got up close to my face again, all mean and nasty.

'You sound like a hybrid zombie, telling me there's no apocalypse when you ain't been seeing with your own eyes what I can see. What I can tell you is they don't want you thinking that people can see what I see. This is the apocalypse! You can't walk down them streets without seeing that things ain't right. Them zombies are eating the flesh, and we are letting them get away with it.'

I closed my eyes, hoping that he might just disappear in a puff of smoke. I was torn between confronting him or just going along with his craziness, just so he might put the knife down, or even have that cup of tea with me, but when I opened my eyes again, he was still there, knife in hand, a danger to himself and others.

'Can I ask you a question?' I asked because there was one thing that was seriously bugging me. He didn't say yes, but

I asked anyway. 'How can you live with all these lights on?'

'That's easy, white man,' he said, sounding as if he didn't mind explaining his insanity. 'So I can examine the body, like your body, to keep me safe from the zombies.'

'How do you sleep at night? I mean, do you ever turn the lights off?'

'Them lights go on when the zombie falls into the spider trap. In the dark, I am the Invisible Man!'

'True,' I said. 'But I can see you now.'

I shouldn't have been so cheeky, because he suddenly let out a roar, exactly the roar you'd expect from a caged crazy guy, and slashed his knife across my body.

I saw the blade coming and dodged it, as I tried to keep my footing.

He then lifted his head up, speaking through the hole in the ceiling. 'No white man can see the black man, however white the light. You see, I am invisible!'

He wasn't, but I wasn't going to wait for him to clarify.

With his head still up in the clouds, I made a leap towards the door and grabbed the handle.

Whether what happened next was divine intervention or just a bit of good fortune, the bright light that had illuminated this madness went out.

'Heh, man, who turned the lights out?'

I didn't stop to ask as I twisted the doorknob and fell onto the ground outside. I also didn't look back and started running like a naked white man being chased by a bunch of zombies.

# CHAPTER TWELVE

## QUACK, QUACK

I have a claim to viral fame that I can exclusively reveal! It was me who was captured, photographically speaking, by a phone camera, and posted as the meme of the naked zombie running as fast as a jet plane through the Nightmare Apocalypse!

That said, I did find a tarpaulin and a piece of string to cover up the obvious, and some clown shoes to protect my feet. I then slipped back through the fence, breathing a very heavy sigh of relief.

As I crouched down in the woods, fuming that I had clearly been deserted, betrayed, and neglected to fend for myself by friends and non-friends alike – it had to be Matt who was to blame overall, I decided – I heard a strange duck-like noise quacking in the distance.

I began to wonder if ducks were migratory, so therefore, the sound of a duck quacking was incongruous with the time of year, when the quacking acquired a far more distinct human quality.

It was also very near, very close, so I decided to reply.

'Quack.'

'Quack, quack,' came the response.

'Quack, quack.'

And then they replied, 'Quack, quack, quack.'

I popped my head up.

'Dr Q, I presume,' I said, holding out my hand to Dr Q, who was approximately six inches from me.

'Oh, it's you,' he said, surprised.

'Yes, it's me, and you're standing on my feet.'

Dr Q looked down and noticed my shoes were two feet long.

'You've got clown feet,' he noted, even more surprised. 'And why are you wearing a toga?'

'It's a tarpaulin. I am also wearing clown feet because I fell through a hole to save my life on a runaway ghost train and ended up having to deal with a madman who thought I was part of a zombie apocalypse, who stripped me naked before I could run away.'

'But weren't you supposed to—' Dr Q started to say, before I put my finger to his lips, begging for silence, peace, and tranquillity.

I laid my hands on his shoulders so he could sit down with me. He respectfully resisted asking more questions for a few minutes while I gathered my thoughts.

Eventually, I was ready to speak.

'OK, so, I hope you're going to tell me that this nightmare is just a hideous dream, and I am going to wake from my sedation having successfully had my appendix removed.'

As I looked at Dr Q, I could tell he only had more bad news for me.

'I've got a text,' he said, pulling out his phone. 'From Danny.'

He showed me his screen, and the text message said the following:

abjtuieb bcbejuebcvjwoe jnvjudfkbvhnn inmhsnhdcna.

'Yeah, I think that describes how everything went,' I said, scratching my arse because it was being tickled by wet blades of grass. (Nothing sexual here, they were just really annoying.)

I then told Dr Q about the whole sordid debacle, with no knowledge of where anybody was, the coffin, Trevor, or the stash.

'Something's gone wrong,' said Dr Q, stating the obvious. 'And who was this crazy man hiding in the ghost train?'

'Who knows,' I replied, throwing up my arms. 'But if I was to speculate, he must have been living underneath the tracks, you know, a homeless guy just keeping out of the way and thinking it was the zombie apocalypse for real because he'd seen ZMC going in and out.'

'That's unfortunate,' said Dr Q, as he reflected on his failure to adequately provide effective recon and intel.

'For me it was,' I grumbled, shuffling around on my bum because the grass was being seriously inappropriate.

'I wonder what Danny meant.'

'In his text message?'

'Yes.'

'Let me have a read of it again.'

I sarcastically informed Dr Q of its meaning promptly. 'It means both of you, that's you and Danny, are bigger eejits than Matt and me.'

Dr Q seemed unmoved by the less-than-glowing assessment of their so-called mission and focused again on the meaning of Danny's message.

'Do you think he's in trouble?'

'Why, because the crazy guy found them all and stabbed them in the head with a kitchen knife?'

'Did he have a knife?'

'Yes, he had a knife!' I said, exasperated. 'And he kept swinging it around in front of my face and stabbing me with it to see if I was still human.'

'But did you find the coffin?'

'Yes, we found it, and that's when things got a bit out of control… And I mean *before* I was being held captive by the Zombie Inquisition.'

'These rides haven't been working for years,' said Dr Q. 'You probably had a power surge.'

I raised my eyebrows, barely able to respond.

'Let's head back to the farmhouse,' he said, standing up and brushing down his security guard uniform. 'Hopefully everything will be all right.'

Now that seemed exceedingly unlikely.

Dr Q began walking back through the woods as I waddled behind him in my clown shoes, still feeling aggrieved that I had been abandoned to fend for myself. Which then got me wondering if Danny had done a runner with the ZMC stash, had stabbed Samira, Matt, and Janet in the head, and was munching his way through zombie pills before he exported them into the EU via Belfast and Dublin.

However, there was a crumb of comfort in finding Danny Boy's UK Tours Ltd. parked up, and although there was no sign of any of the deserters, we could just see the coffin lying in between the seats.

'You've got your stash,' I said to Dr Q, as I adjusted my tarpaulin toga.

I was expecting some kind of thank you when Dr Q suddenly pulled me down to the ground.

‘What?’

‘Keep your head down,’ he said, staring over at the farmhouse.

As I stared, I noticed there was a light on.

‘I thought it was abandoned,’ I said, trying my best to keep my voice down.

‘Yeah, so did I.’

‘So?’

Dr Q then offered me a look that, decoded, told me there’s probably more to this than meets the eye. That or, “I should have told you this earlier, just in case things go slightly awry, seriously awry, or seriously south”.

We watched a pale shadow in the window pull a barely functioning curtain across, dampening down the light. Dr Q grimaced and shuffled around to the other side of Danny’s tour bus, inviting me to join him so we kept out of sight.

‘What is it?’ I asked in exasperation.

‘I think there might be a problem,’ he said, in a calm and reflective tone.

‘You mean the farmhouse? How is the farmhouse a problem?’

‘Danny should be here,’ he said, as he continued to reflect and calculate.

‘You mean because the coffin’s here?’

‘Well, that and his text message. Danny was always good at spelling, so that text message doesn’t make sense.’

‘You don’t say,’ I said sarcastically. ‘So you think they’re in the farmhouse?’

‘Could be—’ Dr Q trailed off, with an ever more rueful expression.

‘Well, why don’t we just knock on the door, or ring the doorbell, and ask if they’ve seen a gay Irish man with an Indian woman, a man with a hand wrapped in clingfilm, and a teenage misfit?’

‘Probably not a good idea,’ Dr Q whispered as he began to look vaguely back into the fields and the woods behind us.

‘Why would that not be a good idea?’ I asked, dreading what Dr Q was about to reveal next.

‘Well, if it is who I think it is, and Danny and the others are in the farmhouse, then you could say we have a problem.’

‘OK, what kind of a problem?’

‘I would call it,’ he said, bringing himself back from wherever his mind had wandered to, ‘a solution that requires extraction.’

‘You mean, like teeth?’

Dr Q’s face reacted spontaneously, as if he were revisiting a deadly horror he’d rather not recall.

‘Don’t ever mention teeth,’ he hissed, like it was going to raise the *Candyman* if I said the word five times.

I promised not to ever mention the word that shall not ever, ever be spoken again, and waited for Dr Q to regain his composure, before then demanding, angrily and explicitly, that he tell me what he should have told me before we parked up next to the farmhouse.

‘They’re strange,’ he said, glancing towards the farmhouse.

‘Who? The people that live there? The people who aren’t meant to live there but still do?’

He nodded sagely.

‘How strange?’ I wondered.

‘Oh, I’m afraid they’re a lot worse than me.’

‘You mean, like *Texas Chain Saw* strange or *The Larkins*?’

‘Who are *The Larkins*?’

‘It doesn’t matter,’ I said, as the thought of ever having to watch *The Larkins* on TV filled me with the same level of horror that teeth extraction initiated in Dr Q. ‘What matters is you telling me the truth, the whole truth, and nothing but the truth.’

‘The truth,’ Dr Q began, sighing gently, ‘is that I knew the family, or I should say the brothers and the sister, when I was practicing as a vet.’

‘Weren’t you training to be a vet?’

‘Same thing,’ he said dismissively.

‘And?’

‘That’s where things started with’ – Dr Q paused, remorsefully raising an eyebrow – ‘you know, Dolly.’

‘You mean, Dolly the sheep?’

Unfortunately, he did.

‘But,’ I mumbled as I struggled to join the dots.

‘I discovered,’ he said, in as objective a veterinarian tone as he could, ‘that the relationships between the brothers and sister and the animals was not based just on breeding, but had evolved into something more *intimate*. Initially, I did consider doing the right thing, but I was so messed up, so intoxicated with grief, anger, and substances, that I was drawn inexplicably to their favourite sheep. So, when they found out that I was cheating on them, they reported me – although I might add they were far worse than I.’

I was tempted to repeat the phrase Matt had so obligingly used – “You’re all a bunch of sheep shaggers” – but clearly Dr Q was contrite, if also in need of therapy.

However, I still had no understanding as to why we should be crouched down and out of sight.

'It might be,' Dr Q continued, drawing in a deep breath, 'that the brothers have abducted Danny and the others.'

'Samira, Janet, and Matt,' I added for completeness.

'Yes. So it might be that they are' – he paused again – 'guests.'

'OK,' I said warily. 'How do they treat their guests?'

There was yet another pause. 'We've probably still got enough time.'

'Enough time for what?'

'Before the Tooth Fairy comes.'

'The Tooth Fairy?'

'Well, she likes to dress as *The Sugar Plum Fairy*, but her interest is in teeth.'

'Teeth?'

Dr Q made a popping sound with his finger in his mouth and nodded.

'Are you trying to tell me that these brothers kidnap people and then get their sister to remove people's teeth? Why would they do that?'

Dr Q shrugged unapologetically. 'She'll go for the gold ones first,' he said. 'I know Danny has a few.'

I held my head in my hands and wanted to weep uncontrollably, beat my fists on the ground, and howl like a demented wolf. This should not be happening! In fact, none of this should have been happening ever since Matt was dumb enough to think he could think for himself.

'"I think we can take them. Do you think we can take them?" That's the title from *Superman, Batman* issue three,

December 2003, by Jeph Loeb and Ed McGuinness,' Dr Q said reassuringly.

'OK,' I said with a heavy, heavy sigh. 'What do we need to do?'

# CHAPTER THIRTEEN

## THE TOOTH FAIRY

'Oh, hi, I was wondering if you could help me? I was just passing, and I noticed you had your lights on, and, as you can see, I am not wearing proper clothes. I was wondering if you'd be so kind as to let me borrow some, if you have any trousers, shirts, pants, socks, and shoes. I'd pay you back, of course.'

'Heh, Bob!' the man shouted. 'There's a guy in a tarpaulin wearing clown shoes.'

People, just in case you haven't put two and two together, that's me introducing myself to one of the brothers, having knocked on the door of the farmhouse. The brother who had answered the door was the size of a mountain. He had hair so thick and wiry he might have just been electrocuted, with a red rustic bulbous face which indicated that he was either consuming copious amounts of cider or failing to regularly apply moisturiser, which I highly recommend for any age category.

Also, the man-mountain was called Clinton, because I heard another voice, a female voice, at a high-pitched, wailing scream out, 'Clinton! It's another one of them. Get him in quick!' Which meant, as a large man's hand grabbed my ill-fitting toga and pulled me over the threshold, that Stage One Part A of Dr Q's plan was working. (If you are wondering where Dr Q is, you need to know that Stage One Part B means he is, or he should be, sneaking around the back in order to infiltrate from the rear, something I said he should be familiar with, while I act as a decoy/distraction.)

However, none of this was going to help me, as I was dragged unceremoniously into a foul-smelling house, which I might add did nauseate me when Clinton opened the door, and was thrown into another room full of noxious body odour and farm animal-type smells.

As I tried to orientate and understand my new surroundings, I quickly surmised that the brothers and sister were hoarders, because wherever I looked, there were piles and piles of magazines and newspapers. It actually kind of reduced my fear and anxiety for a few seconds, as I thought that at least these people were able to read, also known to indicate some degree of intelligent lifeform, which might mean they could be reasoned with.

But as you would expect, such faith in humanity is often misplaced, as I was hauled onto a chair and told to shut up. A bit rude, seeing as I hadn't said anything since I'd entered the house.

'Are you one of them?' asked Clinton aggressively.

'In what way do you mean one of them?'

'The zombies.'

'No,' I said, unconvincingly, realising I had failed to remove the face-paint.

'That means you are,' he said, although I wasn't entirely sure if he thought we were zombies.

As he stood over me, I was desperate to hold my nose so I could avoid the foul stench of manure and alcohol, but he was keen to survey me like a fly caught in a spider's web.

'What's with all the stupid clothes?' he asked, which I also assumed referred to Danny, Samira, Matt, and Janet dressed as zombie pallbearers.

'It's fancy dress,' I said. 'We're just playacting for the Nightmare Apocalypse, over in the old theme park.'

'Yeah, so why have you got clown shoes on?'

'I lost my costume. A long story. Well, a short story, but too long to explain.'

However, that seemed to be irrelevant, as Clinton's massive hand grabbed my face and prised open my mouth.

'You've got good teeth,' he said, smiling at me with blackened pegs.

'They're implants,' I replied. 'Well, most of them.'

This brought an even bigger smile to his face.

'Heh, Sis!' he shouted out. 'We should start on this one. He's got real implants!'

Clinton turned my head left and right so he could get a different angle on my tooth-pegged treasure.

'How much did you pay for those?' he asked.

'On average, two grand per tooth.'

'Yeah? I bet they're titanium pegs as well.'

Well, he knew his dentistry.

Our brief consultation was soon cut short by the appearance of what I can only describe as a child's worst nightmare, an adult's fevered hallucination, and a weapon of mass destruction secretly developed by an obscure arms manufacturer.

It was The Tooth Fairy. The Tooth Fairy, who had the shiniest teeth I had ever seen; so white, so sparkly, they could probably be observed from the International Space Station, or from the point of the singularity. However, they were the only thing bright and shiny about Sis, dressed up in a hip-hugging tutu and constricting corset, and, just like Clinton, had familial facial traits that would put the shits up John Wayne Gacy.

Nice…

Anyway, I wasn't going to verbalise my first impressions, just in case she asked me out on a date.

Fortunately, that wasn't going to happen, as she made a beeline for my mouth, pushing Clinton out of the way, pinching my cheeks so I was yet again being treated like a slave commodity, which is what I was used to, having worked in the city.

'Implants,' she said, breathing her sinister alcoholic breath all over me.

'That's what he said,' said Clinton.

And I was ready to confirm if it helped expediate The Tooth Fairy releasing her iron-like grip on my jaws.

'We'll do him first,' she said ominously. 'Let me get my kit.'

Now, at this point, you may be wondering where Dr Q was in all this self-sacrifice for the greater good of others, and you know what, so was I. Although he had assured me that Stage One Part B would be underway, while I occupied the numpties drooling over my teeth, which, by the way, Dr Q said, they extracted from unsuspecting strangers and then sold on the highly lucrative community-based informal dentistry market.

Now, my fellow travellers, let me indulge you in my thoughts on dentists and dentistry whilst the excitable Tooth

Fairy retrieves her toolkit. I know it hurts, decay and abscess, wisdom and otherwise, and so I believe that it should be written into the Geneva Convention of Human Basic Needs and Other Stuff, that anyone and everyone, including even the most despicable human beings ever invented, should have the right to have their teeth sorted. I mean, come on, what has happened here, folks? For people to go running around the country in excruciating agony and pain, resorting to DIY teeth extraction because dentists need to make as much as they can to pay for one skiing trip a year, and two summer holidays, and a spring and autumn city break?

Anyway, that's what I was thinking: developing a much-needed campaign and disruptive social movement calling for dentists and dentistry to be held to account.

Then the hideous Tooth Fairy told Clinton to check on his dumb brother because he was making a lot of noise down in the basement. Which I hoped meant Dr Q was vigorously implementing Stage Two, with no Part A or B.

I needed to play for time.

'Has anyone ever told you that you have very good bone structure?' I asked, using one of my best chat-up lines that, I might hasten to add, I've never used and never intended to.

The Tooth Fairy snarled as she threw a sack down on the floorboards that made an unsettling clunking sound. This meant hammer, saw, and chisel, and I take back all the above regarding dentists and dentistry.

'Titanium,' she said, licking her lips, as if it was something she devoured for breakfast, lunch, and dinner. 'And don't think any smarmy in-me-panties talk is going to save your pretty little pegs from getting extracted.'

It sounded painful, and if I was going to remain supine while I waited for the cavalry to arrive, she would probably have removed all lower and upper pegs with a hacksaw and pliers.

So I stood up.

It was a defiance that lasted one second, as she promptly pushed me back down with a level of ease and force that told me I needed the cavalry. Then, out of her sack, she unravelled a thick yardage of rope and wrapped it around me and the back of the chair.

'OK, pretty boy, open wide,' she said, with all the menace that your bog-standard dentist applies whilst sounding mildly interested.

I replied by keeping my mouth firmly shut, but like a skilled practitioner, her hand prised open my mouth, as she pinched and stuck her stinking breath into my vulnerable orifice.

What happened next is difficult to describe, not only because I am revisiting horrors best left buried, but also because it is prefaced with the dulcet tones of a slightly deranged song sung by the twirling tutu-wearing Tooth Fairy.

She pulled her face away from mine, spun precariously around on her tiptoes a few times, and then sang:

'Om diddly om, pom, pom, pom,
The teeth are mine
If they shine.
Om diddly om, pom, pom, pom,
Now open wide
And don't be shy.
Om diddly om, pom, pom, pom.'

However, just as she was about to sing even more of her puerile, demented, and ritualistic horror anthem, an almighty crash was followed by the unmistakable cries of, 'Charge!' bellowed from the bowels of the farmhouse.

It stopped little ole fairy tots on her tippy toes and produced one less drop of nervous sweat running down my face, as I prayed this was the cavalry organised by the release of the enslaved.

A few seconds later, this was confirmed by Clinton, who rushed into the room and screamed at his sister, 'We're under attack!'

I knew what he meant, but Sis was confused, so Clinton clarified. 'By a zombie penguin!'

That had to be Dr Q.

I think The Tooth Fairy still needed a bit more convincing, as she narrowed her eyes at Clinton and demanded to know where their brother Bob was, and as if on cue, he duly appeared, screaming like a baby, followed by a raging torrent of Dr Q, Danny, Samira, Matt, and then Janet.

*Time to make my exit*, I thought, as the zombie pallbearers threw themselves at the farmhouse bullies. With fists and kicks flying, I stood up with the chair still tied to me and started doing the Charlie Chaplin walk towards the door.

Just as I thought I had made it out, pulling on the handle of the front door, I felt myself being inexplicably restrained from escaping into the freedom of the night.

I was hoping I had got myself snagged on something, but instead had the revolting face of The Tooth Fairy, all bloodied and raging on her hands and knees, trying to pull me back into the maelstrom.

It needed affirmative action.

Having thought my highly valued implants were going to be extracted and distributed through some community food programme, I didn't need any further encouragement to swing around to confront her. This, fortunately, led to the chair I was tied to hitting her squarely in the mush, her head rocking backwards by the force of my anger, and I believe her front teeth making a traumatic exit.

As she moaned and groaned, putting her hand to her mouth to confirm the damage, I got up close and personal.

'Schadenfreude, you messed up piece of—'

I would have finished my sentence with a flurry of expletives, but I was suddenly lifted in the air, still attached to the chair, and carried out into the night.

I was being held up by Danny and Dr Q as we made our escape, with Samira, Matt, and Janet running ahead of us.

'Thanks,' I said, enjoying the ride.

'I am vengeance and the night, and I am *Batman*!' shouted Dr Q, quoting indirectly, and followed by triumphant whoops and hollers.

*Fair enough*, I thought, even if he was more closely related to The Penguin.

# CHAPTER FOURTEEN

## LYING ON THE ROAD

As the sun rose in the east and shone through the windows of our happy and relieved crew, so Dr Q handed out pills that he said would keep us going until we got to Aberdeen. It was a six-hour drive up the M6. We had enough time to get the seven o'clock night ferry to Lerwick, which meant we would be on the Shetland Islands by Friday morning. That, according to Danny, would be good enough to keep his boss happy, and that we were on schedule to get the money from Samira's gran.

However, whether it was due to last night's trauma or the amphetamine kicking in, I was feeling seriously nonplussed, beginning to stew and close to boiling point. The heroic status I had achieved with Dr Q had lasted approximately two seconds, as everyone else thought they were just as justified in claiming a far greater role in defeating the Munsters from Texas-tooth-saw farm.

What nobody seemed to appreciate was the hell ride I had been through, or acknowledge that they did not follow through with the commonly held operational principle of no man left behind. Matt offered some garbled nonsense, which, it must be said, is par for the course, about having to deal with getting the coffin out because Danny was "going into one", and then when I explained to anyone who was prepared to listen that I had been kidnapped by a paranoid deluded homeless guy, stripped naked, and held hostage to see if I turned into a flesh-eating zombie, I was met with a shrug and a highly inconsiderate lack of concern.

That's when I really began to stew, because the way I saw it, I had been taking the brunt of all the things that had turned this little road trip into the realms of off-the-scale insanity. After all, I fumed inside my head, it had been me guiding us along the coastline so we didn't drop 1000 feet to our deaths only to be chased by a hungry panther into the arms of the police; it had been me who had sorted out the old dears from the care home and fed them a meal they probably forgot within 10 seconds; it was me who had made a fool of myself trying to buy Matt some antibiotics, and me who had yet another knife swung in front of my face whilst everyone else thought about themselves and ran off with the ZMC stash. And yes, me again, who had put my titanium implants on the line so they could all be freed from captivity to take on and defeat The Tooth Fairy and her crazy brothers.

Yes, it was all me, me, me.

What kind of thanks do I get?

Nada, nothing.

Just everyone else thinking they were the ones who had done this and done that.

Well, they hadn't.

At least, not the way they told it, and would no doubt be telling anyone and everyone who cared to listen, about the mad adventure they got up to in the cold, cold month of January, travelling right across Britain and all the way to Shetland to get a load of cash from a little old lady. All of which, it is worth saying, was going into the coffers of a less-than-reputable Dublin drugs gang.

Not happy, I said to myself, as I folded my arms, and offered Dr Q a thoroughly disgruntled grunt. I think he understood the personal sacrifice I had been through and had been kind enough to lend me some of his clothes, ill-fitting because I was half his size, before we headed up the motorway.

'"All men have limits, and I ignore mine",' he said, smiling jovially. 'That's from *Detective Comics* issue 663, July 1993, by Chuck Dixon and Graham Nolan.'

'Christ, you're a walking encyclopaedia of *Batman* comics,' I said, which was meant as a compliment, as much as I found the constant references rather annoying.

'Well, you look as if you have reached your limit,' he said, placing a hand on my shoulder like a fatherly priest. 'Would you like me to give you something to bring you down?'

I did, but Danny had seemed insistent on all of us staying awake. Although Janet was excused because she was too young to take drugs, although she had then reeled off the drugs she did take which put my junkie days to shame.

Dr Q read my mind and slipped into my hand a couple of pills, which I took on top of the amphetamine Danny had insisted we all consumed. I thanked Dr Q for the offering and slipped them down my throat. I looked around the tour bus to see Janet lying across the coffin on the back seat sound asleep, while Matt and Samira were hissing and bickering in the only way that couples tend to do, without wanting to appear that was all they do when they are together.

I leaned my head against the window and waited for something to reduce my grinding teeth to a more tolerable grind. I won't bore you with the highly colourful dreamscape I wandered off into, but just to say there were images of pigs in tutus, sheep found in uncompromising positions, and random clown feet chasing me along the railway tracks of an abandoned coalmine. Who says dreams bear no relationship to reality? Suffice to say, as I emerged from my troubled slumber, Dr Q said I must have slept like a baby because I didn't wake, even after Danny had apparently told him to punch me in the face.

So that's why my face felt sore, and not because I was leaning into the window like a squashed tomato.

I then resorted to offering a childlike question. 'Are we there yet?'

'Yes and no,' said Samira, who was sitting behind me.

That's when I realised that we were not moving.

'The ferry terminal's five minutes away,' said Dr Q. 'But everything's come to a standstill.'

I tried looking down the side of the window to see what was holding us up but was none the wiser.

Then Danny shouted out my name.

Well, at least he didn't call me an eejit.

'I'll go look,' I groaned, without waiting to be told what to do.

As I jumped down into the traffic jam, with all the car engines turned off, I assumed there had been an accident. I sidled between a few cars and felt my oversized shirt being tugged.

It was Janet, who was just curious and bored, or bored and curious, and had decided to follow me.

Just ahead of us was a small crowd, and as we approached,

it became obvious what the problem was. Sitting in the road were half a dozen climate change activists, or eco warriors, or existential existentialists, being severely abused by a group of drivers.

Now, before everything I had been through over the last few days, I would probably have ignored them and hoped they would annoy somebody else. But I was still steaming inside over my mistreatment and the general lack of respect I believed I should have been afforded by my so-called friends and acquaintances, and yet again I was being asked to "go sort it out".

Well, sod them.

I'd had enough.

I pushed through the small crowd and sat down next to the reverend, or the priest (the guy who had the dog collar on).

A small cheer went up from the hi-vis vest protesters, followed by a volley of abuse from the drivers and further demands for the police to come and do something about it.

Janet pushed her way through. 'I'll be back,' she said.

'Take your time!' I shouted after her.

I felt a few congratulatory slaps from my fellow protestors, and then the reverend welcomed me to my new gang.

'That's all right,' I said. 'I need a good protest.'

'Well, my son, there is no better place than to sit here to stop what is going on,' he said, his eagle eyes and prominent forehead amplifying his intellectual demeanour.

'What *is* going on?' I asked.

'We are opposed to new oil drilling licenses. There should be no more new extraction of these deadly fossil fuels. We cannot go on like this, destroying the planet. It is that simple.'

Actually, I kind of agreed with him, even if I was just taking advantage of the situation to piss off Danny, Samira, and Dr Q – mainly Danny and Samira. However, it was seriously cold, and my bum was already beginning to feel like it had been left in the fridge freezer overnight.

Just as I was getting truly uncomfortable, Janet reappeared, with the full entourage of Danny Boy's UK Tours Ltd. She promptly sat down next to me, followed by another cheer from the protestors, and general abuse and spittle from the inconvenienced drivers. Then Samira came over, with Matt and Dr Q.

'What are you doing?' she said, in the same way my mum would say it when I was doing something very, very, annoying.

'What does it look like?' I replied in the same way that I would have replied to my mum.

'Danny's fuming,' she said.

'Of course he is, but you can tell him from me that I am not running around putting my neck on the line for anybody anymore. This is my protest!'

'You're an idiot,' said Samira dismissively. 'And you're leading minors astray.'

'I want to be here,' insisted Janet.

'Up to you,' she said. 'But if you're interested, the ferry leaves at 7:00 p.m. tonight. Check-in closes 30 minutes prior to departure, and we're going to go shopping in Union Square.'

Samira strutted off, with Matt and Dr Q following sheepishly behind.

'Your girlfriend?' asked the reverend.

'Used to be,' I said.

'A strong will is hard to keep or possess,' he said, like a good old wise owl.

'I didn't try to possess her,' I said, correcting him. 'In fact, I think it was my lack of possession that led to things going wrong. You see, it was me who dumped her.'

'Ah, dumping,' said the reverend, as he avoided a beer can coming straight for our heads. 'Far too much of that. Not good for our relationships or the planet.'

I checked on Janet, who was being given the full sermon on climate change by a friendly-looking granny, and then the reverend homed in on me.

'Why did you decide to sit with us?' he asked, having probably worked out that I wasn't wholly committed to the cause.

'I'm pissed off,' I said. 'About everything. So that can include destroying the environment, exploitation, capitalism, and every other form of oppression and expropriation, which is mainly all about me feeling shat upon from a great height.'

'You feel you are being individually targeted?'

'Kind of. But that makes me sound selfish, self-centred, and greedy.'

'Are you?'

'Probably,' I said reflectively. 'Or probably was, until I lost my job in the city. Which was my own fault. Probably.'

'And you think you have begun to see some light?'

'I don't know. Kind of depends if I get to live.'

'Why do you think you might not get to live?'

I knew why, explicitly, but I wasn't going to tell the reverend, so I kept it vague. 'Well, all I mean is, we're all going to die, sooner or later.'

'It may be sooner, if we continue to be in denial about the future of our planet. Armageddon is only around the corner, and yet you would think by the way some of our leaders speak, there is nothing wrong with the world we live in today. They refuse to accept the facts and the truth, and then they turn lies into a new kind of truth.'

'Yeah, I've had some experience of that,' I said obliquely.

'It is out of control,' said the reverend, who was very much moving into pulpit mode. 'We destroy anything and everything, to the point where there will be just this polluted rump of a rock spinning around and around, like a dead planet, occupied by only a distorted detritus of fumbling lifeforms known as homo sapiens; us, the higher beings, the ones at the top of the pile, who can't see beyond the end of our noses, desperate, so it seems to me, to leave what is left of our overheating, extinction-driven system, to the little furry animals, scurrying along the abandoned tunnels of artificial structure and civilisation.'

*Christ, don't hold back, Rev,* I thought to myself. *Let it rip!*

'And it occurred to me,' he continued, 'over these last few days, travelling through this poisoned city, although in truth this thought has been occupying me for quite some time, that we care less for each other as each day, week, month, and year passes. We are meant to revel in the characteristics of selfishness, greed, arrogance, and corruption. I struggle, my little group of like-minded agents, in understanding anything. So distant, it seems to me, to be linked any more to any kind of meaningful higher purpose. I feel like we are all adrift on a little life raft, thankful we did not sink when the ship went down, whilst in the full knowledge that all that lies ahead of us is starvation, degradation, cannibalism, and death. And then, the raft tips over the edge, into the black hole of extinction.'

The reverend's little speech was cut short (thankfully, because I was ready to slit my throat without Danny's help) by the first sight of the police. The frustrated drivers began to clap, as well as remonstrate with the police for not being there earlier.

'Oh well, looks like we've had it now,' I said to the reverend.

'Far from it, my son. We have glued ourselves to the tarmac. We will not be moving.'

'Are we going to fight?' asked Janet excitedly, as the police ventured into our compact group.

'Passive resistance,' informed the reverend, as the police tried to pull up one or two, before realising they were going to rip off their skin.

However, had they picked on me, they would have discovered that I was easily removable, having failed to apply any adhesive to my hands.

After a futile 10 or so minutes, the police retreated and started to tell all the drivers to get back in their vehicles. There were alternative routes people could use if they all just followed the police's instructions.

As I watched the drivers trudge back to their vehicles and dispute who was going to back up first, I had an overwhelming sense that I was possibly free at last: free from the burden of following orders of a Dublin gangster, free from having to do anything. I had asserted myself, and there were no recriminations, not that it would have been easy for Danny to march down to the protesters and extract me like a recalcitrant toddler, but if he really thought I had to be part of this absurd journey to the Shetlands, he would have done something by now. He would have made sure I was compliant.

As if to confirm my thinking, Samira passed by with Matt and Dr Q in tow. She didn't stop this time, abuse me, scold me, disdainfully look down on me as if I were worth little more than a good kicking for being a useless human being. She just gave me one look that said, "It's up to you if you want to come, but no one's asking you to come, and you can stay here if you want, if that's what you want to do."

I felt Janet tug on my sleeve.

I smiled at her. Here was the hope, the next generation, the sliver of light that would provide hope for us all.

'I need to go now,' she said, switching off the light of hope.

'You don't have to,' I replied, looking like someone who had lost all his friends.

'Sorry, but I need to look after somebody.'

'Who?' I tried to say, but she had jumped up and was heading back to Danny Boy's UK Tours Ltd.

'Is that your daughter?' asked the reverend.

'No,' I replied, annoyed that he should think I was old enough to have a teenage daughter. 'Just part of the crew.'

For the next hour or so, I continued to sit there with the reverend and his protestors. The police came and went, came back again, and tried to negotiate as all the vehicles in front of us were backed up and sent on their alternative routes. By the time I could see clearly up the empty road surrounded by granite buildings, I was alone, and my shackles had been released.

*Perhaps I have always been free*, I thought to myself, *that I could at any time have just walked away from the Pink House without consequences*. Perhaps I was suffering from a variant of Stockholm Syndrome, called Pink House Syndrome, and the only prison I was in was the one I had constructed for myself through fear and anxiety. Perhaps that was the root cause of all the things that had happened to me: I had become overly compliant in order to compensate for the waywardness of my junkie years and short spell of incarceration. Perhaps I had bent the stick too far the other way in order to keep on the straight and narrow, to make sure, absolutely sure, that I did not go off the rails again.

Had any of it been good for me?

Had I not become a product of the system, leading a life that was a million miles from who I am, who I should be?

As I stared at the empty road in front of me, I felt that drug addict compulsion swarm all over, rush through my body, and pump through my heart and my blood.

I stood up and started to run.

I was running to get the ferry.

I was running to catch up with Samira.

# ALL AT SEA

# CHAPTER ONE
## THE TRUTH

There was one cabin between the six of us, so we agreed to take it in turns to get some sleep. Danny and Dr Q went first, and then Samira and Janet would be next, followed by Matt and me. Danny gave us orders not to sleep in the passenger lounge because he wanted all of us to keep an eye on the stash, which meant sneaking down to the vehicle bay and checking the coffin was still there. I did wonder why anyone would be motivated to steal a coffin on a ferry bound for the Shetland Islands, but I decided to keep my own counsel on that one, mainly because Danny had glared at me ever since I bulldozed my way through check-in. In fact, I concluded it was unlikely I would get any shut-eye before we docked, so I got a load of amphetamine off Dr Q and shoved it down my neck.

We had a 12-hour journey, which meant we'd get to Shetland by Friday morning, on time and on schedule. I was expecting a choppy journey over to Lerwick, with my previous experience of ferries very much along the lines of lying in corridors and avoiding the chunder from seasick tummies, but as we headed out to sea, the waters were surprisingly calm.

I bought a round of coffees, hoping that all this madness would be over by some time tomorrow. Samira would visit her gran and cough up the dosh for Danny, and for a few seconds, I clung naively to the belief I would be free to wander off into the sunset, penniless and unemployed, but at least with my head still firmly fixed to my body. But all things considered, I felt there was no way Danny or his boss would let us go. I had put my life in jeopardy again, all for the sake of wanting to try to fix things with Samira.

Admittedly, this was my own fault, because I could, and maybe I should have, walked the other way from the ferry port, although I did also suspect that Danny and the Dublin gang would still go out of their way to track me down even if I ended up homeless on a remote Scottish island. In other words, if I had hoped I might have garnered some trust and respect from Danny during our little road trip, my belligerence outside the ferry port in Aberdeen had put me back to square one.

But as you now know, I had a far greater motivation.

I needed to talk to Samira so that we could come up with a Plan B to mitigate the consequences of Plan A. Because Plan A, the way I saw it, was me and Matt getting killed because we're eejits, and Samira buys her way out. And Janet? Well, Janet gets to live because she's too young to die. As for Dr Q? Well, he had the stash to profit from, even if the Dublin gang tells him his services are no longer required.

You would think, then, that it would be sensible to reengage with my criminal entrepreneurial colleague and useless only friend Matt. But even if he were mildly cognisant following his toxic blood trip, I was not going to waste my time talking to the eejit (no, two eejits are not better than one).

Samira had proved herself to have a resilience and steeliness that had kept us all alive, and these hidden qualities were what I needed to tap into if I were going to live beyond Friday and potentially win her back from my only friend. I know it would be a betrayal, but Matt wouldn't really know what that meant if it happened.

Which all led to my needing a one-to-one with Samira, beg her forgiveness, and then convince her to hold hands and wander off into the sunset with me. Although I did appreciate there might be a few impediments to the latter: I had no plan other than to grab any moment that might present itself.

After offering Samira and Matt some leftover amphetamine to help maintain consciousness and then arguing with Janet that she wasn't eligible to consume any more narcotic substances, we split up to explore the facilities. We discovered a restaurant, bar, and cinema. We then stood on the deck, tasted the salty sea air on our lips, the freshness of it on our skin, and realised we preferred it inside with all the other passengers.

This left us sitting around a bland Formica table amongst an array of other Formica tables populated by a few other ferry passengers, draining our coffee cups, and Janet resorting to a variety of annoying displays of boredom, frustration, and generalised irritating practices best summed up as bloody teenagers! I was thinking of using her behavioural issues as an excuse to persuade Matt to take Janet down to the vehicle bay to check on the stash, but as if he were reading my mind, he volunteered. It was odd because I had never known Matt to volunteer to do anything unless it was for his own personal gratification, but he said he owed me for all the stuff I'd been through.

I didn't believe that sentiment for one second. However,

with Samira still planted firmly on the chair opposite, it was the perfect opportunity for my planned alone time with her.

I waved them goodbye as if they were going on a gap year around Europe, and once they were out of sight, I started with some small talk to see if she would respond with something close to verbal rather than nonverbal contempt.

'Shouldn't the sea be wavy? Like, you know, up and down?' I said cheerfully.

'Do you want to be sick?' she said contemptuously.

OK, so small talk wasn't going to make the slightest bit of difference to how she spoke to me, but there was a verbal response.

I dived straight in because, first off, I wanted to know how self-interested she was going to be before I got into the more difficult subject area of our failed relationship.

'Will you make a run for it?' I asked, maintaining a steely-eyed focus on Samira's reactions to me across the table.

She didn't flinch. 'Do you mean now, Jamie? How do you think that's going to happen? I don't think I'm capable of stealing a lifeboat unless you've arranged for a helicopter to winch us off.'

I ignored her sarcasm. 'No, I mean, when you get the money off your gran?'

Samira looked thoroughly unimpressed. I was doubting her integrity to make sacrifices for Matt and me.

'You know,' she said, leaning forward so her voice was also lowered, 'all you and Matt had to do was carry out your side of the plan, deliver the coke, and then none of this would have happened. Those Dublin people would have gone away happy.' Samira sat back, cocking her eyebrow at me as if that were all she had to say on the matter.

'I'm not so sure those Dublin guys would have just disappeared,' I said nonchalantly. 'They don't strike me as the kind of people that disappear from your life until they've got a lot more from you than what you first thought you were in for.'

She was listening, so I continued. 'And may I also remind you, that as far as I am concerned, a few days ago, I still had my city job and was siphoning off a few grand here and there to go on annual skiing trips and buy the odd premium squash racket. It wasn't until Matt told me we'd been sacked that I knew what you two were up to.'

Samira shrugged. 'Well, Matt told me you knew what was going on.'

That annoyed me. 'Well, he didn't tell me, because if he had, I would have put the kybosh on the whole thing!'

'No, you wouldn't, Jamie, because you are just as useless and inept as Matt,' she said conclusively. Then she leaned forward again. 'And don't pretend you're the one suffering, Jamie, because at the end of the day, it's me who is doing this to save both your useless necks. I am giving up what I have earned out of this, not you.'

That might be true, but, I wondered to myself, was she really doing all this for Matt and me?

I needed to know more. A lot more.

'OK, I appreciate that you are saving our necks, but you were hiding this money from both of us.'

'I had to, because you two, as you have proved, couldn't run a piss-up in a major financial institution.'

'Harsh,' I said. 'But I do wonder if you would ever have

told us that you had a load of money skimmed off. I mean, would we all have had a share?'

'Don't doubt me, Jamie,' Samira said angrily. 'If anyone lacks integrity, it is you!'

This is the point where things get personal.

'What does that mean?' I asked, curious, and pretending to be mildly offended.

'You know exactly what that means,' said Samira, offering telepathic qualities that had always alluded me.

'No, I don't,' I said, because I was determined to get Samira to spell things out if she wanted some kind of contrition. 'You need to tell me why you seem to think *I'm* the dishonest one, especially when everyone who has a ticket for Danny Boy's UK Tours Ltd. is a pathological liar, probably containing at least one multiple serial killer, and at best, compulsive, impulsive, criminals who morally travel South.'

'I'm talking about emotional honesty.'

Oh, that's what she means.

'Why, because I dumped you?'

'Yes, Jamie,' she said, almost spitting my name in my face. 'Why did you dump me?'

Now that is a very good question, and one that I knew the answer to, but had gone out of my way to avoid having to explain.

But perhaps now was as good a time as any to fess up.

'OK, you want to know why I dumped you?' I said, delaying for just a few more seconds before I had to painfully reveal my emotional dysfunctionality.

'Yes, Jamie, I think you should be able to explain to somebody why they have been rejected. Although you should also know that it happens to be the best thing that has ever happened to me.'

'What, you and me together?'

'No, Jamie, us not having anything to do with each other!'

I delayed for a few more seconds, listening to the ferry boat engines' distinctive rumble punctuated by a passenger bursting out laughing, not at me, I might add, but at her coffee being spilt.

And then I said what I should have said before I told Samira it was over.

'The truth is,' I began, again pausing as I regurgitated in my mind the hideous failings of my emotional immaturity, 'the truth is, I didn't think I was good enough for you.'

Immediately, Samira snorted, thoroughly unimpressed.

'That's pathetic,' she said and folded her arms to form an effective barrier.

True, it was pathetic, but without having to go through 20 years of psychoanalysis, it was as close as I could get to any kind of answer.

'The thing is,' I said, reaching further into my distorted rationalisation, 'I was afraid.'

'Afraid of what?'

'I was afraid… That as time went on, you'd find out all my faults, and then it would be you who dumped me.'

That's when Samira's eyes bulged even more than usual. She unfolded her arms and leaned in menacingly. 'All that means is you didn't want the feelings of rejection, so you got in first, to protect your pathetic little man-boy ego.'

That hurt, but it was true, even though I wanted Samira to understand the mitigating circumstances.

'I know,' I said sheepishly. 'But it needs protecting, my pathetic little ego, because I know that if things hurt too much, I'll go back on the drugs.'

'That's no excuse, Jamie.'

*Well, it is*, I thought to myself, and soundly based on self-preservation.

I had one more thing I wanted to say before I tried to elicit some truth regarding Samira's so-called plan to save our necks. So I said, with my interpretation of a sincere face etched across my forehead and embedded in my pin-pricked eyeballs, 'Sorry.'

Samira accepted this with grace. 'Well, you know where you can shove that pathetic little apology!'

Fair enough, but I felt better in myself. The truth was out there. I had sown the seed in Samira's mind that there might be a grain of humanity in this useless husk of an emotionally damaged ex-junkie.

For the next 10 minutes, we sat silently. I was waiting for Samira to get up and leave me sipping my coffee, yet again, never to speak, but she stayed, fuming, mulling over the truth, as best as I could admit to it, until we reached the point where I felt I could speak, although it had nothing to do with the word sorry.

This was the other thing I had on my mind. 'What happens when you hand the money over to Danny?'

'Sorry?' said Samira, as if she had been rudely woken from a deep sleep.

'The money,' I said tetchily. 'When you get the money off your gran, Mavis, what are you going to do when you give it to Danny?'

'What are you talking about, Jamie?'

'They won't want us to live. They will punish Matt and me.'

Samira shrugged as if I had failed to understand that there was enough oxygen at the top of Everest as long as I held my breath.

'Look, you're no threat to them,' she said casually. 'Danny is not going to risk his time and energy on you two idiots. He just wants you to think he will do something nasty, to keep you scared and obedient, but if you think about it, he's needed you all along, especially you, to do all the stupid things he doesn't want to have to do himself. They'll take the money, and that will be the end of it.'

Perhaps.

She sounded confident, but I didn't know why Samira was so sure about her predicted outcome. Unless I was reading the wrong cup of tea leaves, I was sure there had been explicit death threats whilst there was a knife held across my throat and a toasted human hand.

But Samira added another tasty morsel for me to ponder. 'Look, at the end of the day, Jamie, you could have walked away at any moment. You could have left when we'd got to Aberdeen, but you didn't. There's no threat, there's no risk to your life. Anyway, why did you come back?'

'Janet!' I blurted out.

'What? You came back because you fancy Janet?'

'No. You know, I feel paternal.'

'No, you don't,' said Samira, who eyed me suspiciously.

I feigned some half-truth about there being some kind of connection, how she made me think of myself, what I had been like when I was her age.

'Jamie,' said Samira, who clearly had her fill of my dubious, contradictory worldview, 'Janet is Gen Z, and you are some other generation, just like me. We do not relate. There is no compatibility. It is like two alien species. You are wasting your time if you think your paternalism means anything to Janet.'

Then Samira stood up, took in a deep breath of stale passenger lounge air. 'I'm going to look for those two.' She slid her gorgeous, desirable body between the Formica and the chairs, leaving me with a final thought: you had your chance with her, Jamie, and you blew it!

## CHAPTER TWO
## THE WHOLE TRUTH

Well, that went well, I told myself, nothing like clearing the air and being no further forward. Although on the plus side, Samira was talking to me rather than me having to interpret her dirty looks, and that mean and menacing stare, which had many expletives wound up into a very large hate ball thrown at my weak and heartless face. I felt we had something to work on, even if it was based on a fundamental distrust of each other and our deep-seated self-interest.

As I looked at the bottom of the paper coffee cup and considered the random design of the dregs, I did wonder why I thought I had any hope of ever getting back with Samira. I had been a tosser, and she had every right to be very angry and jump into bed with anyone she wanted, although the tragedy was that she ended up jumping into bed with my only mate, Matt. I suppose I would have done the same if I had been rejected – not that I would have jumped into bed with Matt, but if Samira had a friend just as gorgeous as she was, then I would have jumped into bed with her.

If that makes sense.

Briefly, I tried to think if Samira had ever mentioned she had a best friend, or even just an acquaintance, before putting that one to bed, so to speak, and wishing I hadn't taken so much speed, and slightly anxious that I was tipping over the edge of the ex-junkie threshold for seriously falling off the wagon. It was making me agitated and mildly paranoid as I scrutinised every other passenger who was either awake, talking, or trying to get some shut-eye. Not that I knew what I was supposed to be looking for, or what I was meant to be paranoid about, but my sixth sense, my gut instinct, my carefully calibrated something-doesn't-feel-quite-right radar, was tickling my seventh sense, which is a higher level of paranoia not yet clinically documented.

None of this was good for me, being left here all on my lonesome. So I got up and decided to look for the others, feeling sure I was the only one in the group who everyone had just made excuses to get away from. I then decided that would look just as pathetic as my pathetic ego, wandering around looking for someone to play with, and so instead drifted out onto the deck to breathe in that salty sea air.

However, when I took a few deep breaths, I could taste and smell butter.

Now, this is odd but also pertinent, because it took me back to the one person whom I'd recently forgotten to hate, but who needed a lot more hating now that I had a bit of time to myself. And the smell and taste of butter, which was odd considering we were gently sailing along on the salty brine, reminded me of Bridges.

For those of you who haven't been paying attention ever since you started following me on this insanely mad and highly dubious road trip, I will remind you that Bridges was my boss, and Matt's boss, and he was the one who texted to inform us we had both been sacked.

Butter was his favourite vape flavour.

Strange, but true.

I mean, why anyone would want to smoke butter juice vape on the balcony of our 1000-floored city office is beyond rationality, but then so is Bridges, a man so hard to adequately put into any kind of category, other than the one where he does belong: the unadulterated managerial psychopath. You know the sort, or maybe you don't, but Bridges was the classic sociopathic city boss: trimmed like a razor from head to foot, narrowed down from hair follicle to toenail, a cold callous carbuncle of an excuse for a human being.

Surely not, I said to myself, my face being frozen by the sea breeze. Surely not, no way would Bridges be on this ferry.

But you never know.

I started to think, and I started to wander around every little bit of the ferry, looking for Samira, Matt, and Janet, so I could tell them about the strange butter juice vape I had smelled on the deck, and how it reminded me of my boss. All of which I'll admit wouldn't sound very exciting. Matt might be interested, although I suspect he would probably just thrust his rotting-flesh hand in my face and expect some kind of sympathy, instead of understanding the gravity of the situation if Bridges *were* on board.

Having cleared decks one and two, I was looking down the corridor where Danny and Dr Q were occupying the highly desirable bunk beds. I was checking the ferry map, which helpfully pointed to where I was standing, when I heard a cabin door open and glanced over my shoulder. It was Samira, who annoyed me no end because it wasn't her turn yet to get some shut-eye. I took a few steps forward, about to admonish her for ignoring various principles relating to equality, fraternity, and liberty (replace with equity) when she knocked on another cabin door and walked straight in.

I took one step back. Then I took two steps forward and remembered that our cabin, where Danny and Dr Q were sleeping, was the one Samira had just gone into, and that Samira had emerged from another cabin.

Perhaps she had booked her own cabin?

Perhaps she and Janet had booked their own cabin?

Perhaps Samira and Matt had made up, and they wanted to consecrate their realignment?

Unlikely, all of the above.

I took a few more steps, and then I stood in front of the cabin, the one where Samira had emerged from.

I gently knocked on the door.

And the door opened, and there was Bridges.

He was surprised and I was surprised, but I knew, for once, at last, I did not need to fear the man, because fundamentally, all things considered, and on the basis of all cogent thinking, the boss of a highly reputable financial institution in the city should not be on the same ferry from Aberdeen to Lerwick in the middle of winter, staying in a cabin opposite some of the most dubious characters to have ever traversed the country. The ball, using that overused sporting analogy, was firmly in my court.

'Hi,' I said, smiling inanely. 'I was wondering if you had a copy of my P45 with you?'

Bridges just stared at me, his brown, suntanned, angular face fierce and rigid.

'I tell you what,' I said, continuing to be the more friendly of the two, 'why don't I come in and you can tell me all about your relationship with my ex-girlfriend, Samira.'

Bridges continued to stare, weighing up how he was going to deal with me, when I offered him another solution. 'Or I can go and get her.'

That gave Bridges the only option, as he stepped back inside, let me walk in, and shut the door.

However, before I had a chance to find a seat or request refreshments, Bridges launched into an officious-sounding, legalise-type, citizen's arrest thing.

'I am going to caution you now,' he said, putting his hand on his narrow hips and jutting out his forehead, 'so that you fully understand the serious nature of my presence. You are under suspicion of defrauding the company, illegally obtaining cash assets, utilising known faults in software monitored by our Risk and Compliance Department, demonstrating an active and conspiratorial operation against our business and partners. You do not have to say anything, but if you wish to say anything, this could be used against you in future legal proceedings that are currently ongoing and of which you will be shortly informed.'

I burst out laughing.

'Really?' I said, as sarcastically as I could, whilst taking a pew on the lower bunk bed. 'Thanks for coming all this way to tell me I'm under arrest, Special Agent Bridges.'

He didn't like that one bit, but then he shouldn't have let me into his cabin if he didn't want to be spoken to as if he were just a normal human being.

'Right,' he said, and for some reason, adjusted the waistband of his trousers. 'I have now informed you, and I am now instructing you to leave my cabin.'

Well, there was only one answer to that.

'No.'

Bridges then did this thing he used to do before he launched into an aggressive, bullying dressing-down of some poor schmuck in a meeting that nobody wanted to be in: he flexed his neck muscles from left to right, and right to left.

'You're in serious trouble,' he warned, continuing to maintain this pretence that reality was based on what he wanted. 'It is not in your interests to be interfering, blocking, or belligerently obstructing an investigation into your known financial fraud. I hope you realise that you are definitely facing a criminal court case, and considering your background and known previous convictions, I think it is highly likely that you will be facing substantial jail time. So it really is in your interests that you leave my cabin now and co-operate fully with whatever is requested of you.'

Well, there was only one answer to that.

'No.'

For the very first time, ever since I have had the displeasure of Bridges as my boss, he backtracked. 'What do you want?'

Indeed, what did I want?

Oh, that was simple.

'The truth,' I replied, feeling the reversal of power encourage me to stand up so we were both on a level playing field. 'I mean, the whole truth.'

Of course, equivalence, equality, is a highly subjective thing, especially when dealing with psychopaths, and so having thought I might get somewhere with Bridges, he immediately reverted to the lie he was spinning, and that somehow I was on 1000 wanted posters, and there was a posse out there looking for me that would not hesitate to shoot to kill.

I threw my arms up in frustration and marched back to the other side of the cabin.

'OK,' I said, shrugging. 'I will tell you my truth so that you can then tell me the truth.'

Bridges was confused, but I think he knew what I meant, not that he looked like he wanted to hear the whole truth, but he was going to hear it so he could stop pretending that he wasn't somehow in on all this madness.

'You're right,' I said. 'It is true that I took advantage of a software glitch when calculating the commission between buyers and sellers, and at every transaction that rounded off the numbers, it dumped the 0.001% reconciliation into a suspense account, and that money was not visible because there was a release version of the software that didn't account for it. But I hardly touched the full amounts that were sitting there. The truth is, considering the few grand I did dip into now and then, I was pretty well-behaved considering what I could have taken out and run off with. But I didn't!'

Now, that's what I call mitigation, M'lud.

'And where's that money?' asked Bridges.

Which I thought was odd, because the only people I've known who would ask that kind of question were other junkies who wanted a share of the dope I'd managed to scam off my latest prescription.

'The money,' I said, pulling my trousers and pants down and bending over, 'is right up here. So be my guest.'

# CHAPTER THREE

## AND NOTHING BUT THE TRUTH

Fortunately, I did avoid anal penetration because there was a knock on the cabin door, and then Samira marched in.

'Jamie!' said Samira.

'Hi, you recognise me, then?' I replied, maintaining my anal view for all to see.

'Don't you mean, come right in?' offered Dr Q, who enthusiastically shuffled forward behind Samira and Danny.

'By the way,' I said, pulling up my trousers and being pushed back to the end of the cabin by the tidal wave of nefarious team members, 'in case you haven't all met, this is my ex-boss Bridges, and he's got a few things he'd like to say to you, supplementary, I am sure, to anything Samira has just told you.'

The only thing Bridges managed to say was about me as he pointed, 'This doesn't include him.'

'That must be because I am under arrest,' I said caustically, scanning the faces of Samira, Danny, and Dr Q, who were lined up along the side of the cabin, with Bridges up against the cabin door.

'Why are you under arrest?' asked Dr Q, who clearly thought it was odd that a fine upstanding white-collar criminal like me should ever have to be held to account.

'He's not under arrest,' said Danny disdainfully. 'You're a

free man, Jamie, and you have my permission to go.'

I started shaking my head and smirked. 'No way. I am not leaving here until I know exactly what is going on. If you think I've come all this way and gone through everything I have on this ridiculous road trip only to then be shown the door, you are seriously mistaken. There's the truth, the whole truth, and nothing but the truth, and I want to hear it all. Minimum, I need closure, and maximum, I want to be in on whatever you lot are up to.'

I suppose at this point they could have all jumped on me, wrapped me in a bedsheet, and shoved me through a porthole, but Samira, for whatever reason, piped up.

'He can stay,' she said, as if it were a reluctant but well-earned concession.

Bridges scowled at me, Danny just raised his eyebrows, and Dr Q winked.

'OK,' I said, happy to be selected as a full member of the team. 'So, is anyone going to tell me what is going on?'

Silence is golden, but in this instance, it was excruciatingly painful.

'Don't worry,' I said, feeling mildly empowered. 'Whatever you tell me, it will just be among friends… Excluding Bridges, of course.'

Danny looked at Samira, Bridges looked at the floor, and Dr Q folded his arms as if he were more than happy to hear a reprise.

'Well,' said Samira falteringly, 'the truth—'

'Yes, and the whole truth please!' I added helpfully.

'Is—'

Samira faltered again, so I encouraged her. 'And nothing

but the truth…'

'Yes, yes, yes! Will you stop with the whole truth thing? We're not in a bloody courtroom!'

'Oh, I don't know about that,' I said, lapping up every second of Samira's difficulty to articulate the truth. 'Perhaps we can call it the court of the moral compass.'

'Whatever,' she said, exasperated with me yet again. 'The truth is that you and Matt were going to be killed, so, rightly or wrongly, I decided to save your lives.'

I looked at Danny, and he smiled back at me and half-jokingly drew a finger across his throat.

'At the Pink House?' I asked, narrowing my eyes as Danny then shrugged.

'Yes, Jamie, while I was waiting for you two knobheads, I had to do a deal with Danny and his boss.'

'OK, but I know that,' I said, recalling the hideously unpleasant moment. 'I mean, that's why we're here, to collect the money off your gran.'

Then Samira took a very deep breath and sighed heavily.

Clearly, there was a lot more to the story.

'They,' said Samira, who meant Danny and his boss, 'were still going to kill you, after I made the offer to bail you out.'

And then Danny enlightened me.

'But you were lucky,' he said. 'I had this idea of doing the Manchester job, and I needed at least two eejits to help me with it, so that's why I let you live.'

That was interesting, because Danny was referring to himself rather than his boss, who I assumed was ultimately the arbiter of thumbs-up or thumbs-down.

'So does your boss know about the Manchester job?' I asked Danny.

'Yes and no,' he replied ambiguously.

*That means no*, I thought.

'But why did you put a knife to my throat and toast Matt's fingers, if at the end of the day you were going to use us, and probably needed Matt to have both hands available?'

'Because you needed to be scared shitless and at least one of you needed some kind of punishment, and according to your girlfriend here, the prolapsed anus was the one who deserved to be toasted.'

We said in unison:

'She's not my girlfriend.'

'He's not my boyfriend.'

After that, I took a deep breath, paused, and as quickly as possible tried to assimilate what I had learned, which wasn't anything that different from what I already knew: both Matt and me were lucky to be alive, and had effectively served our purpose.

What now needed explaining was why Bridges was here on the ferry, and what he had to do with any of this.

'So why is he here?'

Bridges looked like he was going to keep quiet, as Danny indicated it was back over to Samira to explain further the intricacies of the known knowns, the known unknowns, and the known known unknowns!

'So,' said Samira uncomfortably. 'Before you and Matt used to come to the gym, Frank was also a member, and that's how we met and got talking.'

Frank was Bridges.

As Samira drew in a deep breath, I had to ask. 'You aren't...?'

'No, Jamie, we are not an item, going out together, or

having an affair.'

Phew, that was a relief!

'But we have been collaborating.'

'Collaborating?' I repeated back to her.

'Yes, Jamie, collaborating.'

'And what does that mean exactly?'

'It means exactly what the word means!' she shouted at me. 'Unless you need a dictionary.'

'No, that won't be necessary,' I replied, as the cogs began to get up to speed. 'But it is a very interesting word, and one I must try to use more often when engaging in criminal enterprises.'

'Don't get on your high horse with me, Jamie!' said Samira, as she looked over at Bridges, who looked as if he needed to go on a proper holiday.

'I'm not,' I said unapologetically. 'It's just that I suspect I might come out of this looking more like Mother Theresa.'

Dr Q made the sign of the cross. 'I've always been a fan.'

'Get on with it,' said Danny, ignoring Dr Q and clearly losing patience with Samira's convoluted approach to revealing the truth, the whole truth, and nothing but the truth.

'And,' said Samira, who then paused again, 'Frank had been skimming the pot long before you.'

'Busted!' I shouted at him.

'Calm down!' said Danny. 'There's more to it.'

'I can't wait,' I said, as my mind started racing ahead, thinking how I'd be back at my desk, on the top floor looking down on Bridges, bringing me coffee and croissants every morning, shining my shoes, as I ridiculed and humiliated from 9:00 to 5:00 p.m.

'And,' said Samira, who paused again, 'we struck a deal.'

'A deal?' I asked, as the wheels and gears of my mind began spinning as fast as a Formula One car.

'Yes, Jamie, a deal, to siphon off the money.'

'Laundering?'

'Kind of. More along the lines of investment.'

'Oh, please don't tell me you were buying Argentinian pesos?'

'No,' said Samira, as if I had belittled her. 'The deal was based on what I knew, and who I knew, and part of that deal was to keep it away from any kind of financial investment because all of those things are totally corrupt.'

She had a point.

'The investments I made for Matt were already in place. It was always strictly cash, and the drug deals were done between London and Dublin.'

'You already knew Danny?'

'No, Jamie, there's more than one organised criminal gang in Dublin.'

I took her word for it.

'But I've never known you to go over to Dublin,' I said, wondering whether I should be thinking that perhaps Samira was also a secret agent with a licence to kill.

'No, I never got directly involved. I was just supplying the money Frank gave me, just like I did for Matt. There's someone else who does all the dealing. They used to come to the gym, we got to know each other, and one thing led to another. It worked perfectly. Well, until you two came along.'

'You mean, Matt and me,' I said, scoffing. 'I don't think we came anywhere near the level you've been operating at.'

'Precisely,' retorted Samira, master criminal, kingpin, big boss, bad boss, boss of bosses.

I decided to be generous and help fill in the blanks. 'And so you and Bridges are here to do what?'

'Collect *all* the money,' she said, emphasising the final word.

'From whom, your gran?'

Samira nodded. 'She's the only one I trust.'

'But why now?'

As I asked the question, my ability to put two and two together became apparent, and I felt the grease in my cogs and wheels begin to turn freely.

'Ah ha!' I exclaimed in my eureka moment. 'I know what's going on. Danny and his gang thought they were going to collect their £250k, but it turns out there might just be a little bit more, in fact a lot more, by the sounds of it, but you've now been compromised because Bridges has turned up to make sure you, and Danny, and the Dublin mafia don't run off with all your ill-gotten gains that you, Bridges, and whoever, have accumulated.'

'OK,' said Danny, 'so now you know. But what we all need to know is how much money is involved.'

That's when I, Danny, and Dr Q all looked keenly at our co-conspirators and waited to be told.

Unfortunately, Bridges was tight-lipped, so it was up to Samira.

'Five million,' she whispered under her breath.

'*Five million*!'

'Five—'

'Million.'

'Five million?'

'All right,' said Danny, his eyes bulging. 'Now keep your bloody voices down!'

'Then why are you shouting?' said Samira, who was desperate to bring our excitement down a notch or two.

'She's right,' said Dr Q, who was shoving various calm-me-down pills down his gullet.

'OK, now everyone, shut your mush!' said Danny, as if this was what he'd been trying to say all along. 'There's some serious money thing going on, and we need to sort this out.'

'Only if it is to the benefit of us all,' said Dr Q wisely.

'Precisely,' I said, feeling like there was a god after all.

'Not him,' reiterated Bridges, who clearly had a serious grudge against me. I can't think why.

Fortunately, and surprisingly, Danny jumped to my defence. 'That's not for you to decide,' he said, taking charge, because he was the genuine gangster and could kill us all for five million quid if he wanted to.

But I felt confident to add for Bridges's consumption only, 'I can't wait for that end-of-year appraisal.'

'Jamie!' snapped Samira, who must have thought it wasn't the right time for vengeance.

'OK, so, let's sort one thing out,' said Danny, focusing on Samira. 'Is it cash?'

'Yes, it's all in cash. We had a travel plan in place to move the cash to Dubai.'

I had to ask. 'Why Dubai?'

'Because there are no restrictions on the amount of cash that can be brought into the UAE. All you have to do is fill out a form and deposit it in a UAE bank. There are hardly any questions at the UAE border about where the money comes from, then you're free to invest it in gold and property. The only risk is being caught by UK Customs on the way out. It's just a well-trodden path, and we have a cash mule lined up to do it.'

'Let me guess,' I said, acting as interpreter for Danny, 'I don't suppose that happens to be your gran, Mavis Grind?'

'She's not my gran,' Samira replied, as if I was stupid enough to think that when she had told me she had a gran called Mavis Grind, she did actually have a gran called Mavis Grind.

'So what's her real name then, this person?'

'Mavis Grind.'

'But I thought you said you didn't have a gran called Mavis Grind.'

'I don't, but she calls herself Mavis Grind.'

'So you don't have a gran called Mavis Grind?'

'Of course I don't! Why would I have a gran called Mavis Grind?'

'Well, I thought you might have some Scottish thing going on, you know, in the background.'

'OK, you two need to stop,' said Danny, wanting to get a grip on things. 'Where is this Mavis Grind?'

Samira paused as she looked at me with the same angry face she had used ever since I had dumped her.

'She's off the radar, and I need to find her,' Samira said anxiously. 'I need all of you to help me find her, because I know she will still be on the island.'

'How do you know she will still be there and hasn't run off with the money?' asked Dr Q, who was probably benefitting from the calming effect of his pills.

'Because she loves it there. She was supposed to check in with me, but everything went dead last week, and there's been radio silence. Then when this Dublin thing went wrong... Well, I thought I could use Danny's help, his support, in case we have to get heavy. I think something has gone wrong. I think she is in trouble.'

'But can you guarantee the cash will still be there?' asked Danny sceptically.

'No, I can't, but I trust her, and if we find her, then we will find the money.'

It was a long shot, that's what we were all thinking. I mean, entrusting someone with five million pounds is a whole lot of trust waiting to be untrustworthy.

After the initial excitement, what Samira had just told us put a bit of a dampener on things. So I began thinking about the positives and wondering what kind of concessions I could extract from Bridges, when Danny piped up.

'OK,' he said, definitively. 'We carry on. We look for your woman, your Mavis Grind, and we divvy up the cash fair and square when we find her and the money.'

'That's *if* we find her,' said Dr Q, who was being far more realistic.

I did have one more thing I was keen to clarify.

'And assuming we do find her, what does dividing the money up fair and square actually mean?'

Bridges made a huffing and puffing sound, as Danny then explained the quotient.

'A million for Samira and her boyfriend—'

'That means Matt?'

'Yes, that means Matt,' Samira reiterated.

'A million for him,' said Danny, glancing over at Bridges. 'A million for me and Dr Q, and a million for Janet, and a million for you, Jamie.'

'That's not equal!' blurted out Bridges, who pulled out of his pocket a very old-looking Casio calculator and started pushing buttons. 'These things need to be weighted, based on risk and the added value of each person involved.'

'Eh,' I said, not wanting to miss an opportunity to be as offensive as possible to my nemesis. 'No surprise that you need an abacus to calculate equity.'

'Give it here,' said Danny, snatching the digital artifact out of Bridges's hands. 'Five million, divided by seven, equals £714,285.71. Recurring.'

'Christ, this could go on forever,' offered Dr Q.

'No, it's not,' said Samira, grabbing the calculator out of Danny's hands. 'You need to divide five million by eight, which equals £625,000 each.'

'That's not enough,' said Bridges, who clearly needed more to retire to the Costa Del crime beaches.

'Why eight?' I asked.

'Because we need to pay Mavis,' said Samira. 'She's taking on a lot of the risk.'

'Hang on, we've all taken risks to get the bloody money out of the system. What's the going rate for a cash mule?' I had to ask.

'She could be dead,' said Dr Q.

'Aye,' said Danny, sounding like a Scottish fisherman pirate. 'Who would be after her, and why do you need so many of us to sort this out?'

'Because if there's five million in cash floating around, there is bound to be the wrong type of people who could find out about it.'

'You mean, people like Danny,' I said, without fear of the consequences.

'Are you being rude, Jamie Boy?' asked Danny, who was ready to square up to me.

'No, I think that was what Samira implied.'

'But it was you who said it!'

'I'm just being objective.'

'You're just being offensive!'

'Stop it!' shouted Samira.

'He started it,' I grumbled, only for us all to be stopped by someone knocking on the cabin door.

'Shush!'

'No, you shush!' I said, wondering why I should be held to account for something I was not responsible for. Maybe.

Then there was another knock.

'It's me, Janet.'

'That definitely makes it at least five million divided by six,' I said, as Samira opened the door.

Janet burst into the cabin, seemingly out of breath, followed by Matt.

'OK, make that five million divided by seven,' I said, correcting them.

The two of them then filled up the rest of the cabin; they were both breathing heavily, as if they might have run a marathon, whilst dazed and confused by the compressed nature of the room.

'How'd you know we were in here?' asked Danny.

'We could hear your voices outside,' said Janet, trying to get her breath back.

'That was you,' said Samira, to me.

I was about to blame Danny when Janet burst out, 'The ZMC are here!'

'Where?' asked Dr Q, a distinct bead of sweat suddenly appearing down the side of his brow.

'We've seen them in the cinema.'

'The cinema?'

'Yeah, and guess what they're watching?'

'*Easy Rider*?'

'No, *Finding Nemo*.'

# CHAPTER FOUR

## SO HELP ME GOD!
## (IF HE EXISTS)

'We should mess up their bikes,' said Janet, who was struggling to find where to stand, her face buried in Dr Q's stomach.

'Eh, but isn't that the worst thing you can do to a biker?' I wondered aloud, as separate conversations broke out between Samira, Bridges, and Matt, Janet, and Dr Q's stomach, and me and the porthole.

Danny, on the other hand, remained composed and reflective when Dr Q said above the cacophony, 'They're probably in the cinema so nobody can see how ugly they are.'

'I suppose that's why they only come out at night,' I suggested, having twisted around to face the increasingly animated discussions revolving around the truth about Mavis Grind, Bridges, five million quid, cash mules and their daily rates, the estimated rate of flesh deterioration for zombies, whether there was a sequel to *Finding Nemo,* and a moot point as to whether character spin-offs can be classified as sequels.

The shock, horror, revelations, animosity, revenge, fear, and loathing carried on for a good 10 minutes, as Matt was sad then happy, Bridges was really unhappy, Samira was angry and frustrated, Dr Q was alerted to the need to lose weight, Janet was unimpressed with the thought of money – it was the root of all evil – and Danny stayed quiet. I decided to join him in being quiet.

Eventually, Danny called the emergency Danny Boy's UK Tours Ltd. team meeting to order, and for some reason, we all behaved and fell silent.

'OK, so, the first thing I need to say,' he said authoritatively, 'is that nobody speaks while I'm speaking.'

He then waited to see if anyone dared speak.

Inexplicably, we all remained silent.

'OK, that's good,' he said, reminding me of an Irish teacher I used to have for English Literature who used to get us all to behave during readings of Shakespeare by threatening castration.

'Now,' he continued. 'We've all made enough noise to let everyone know in these cabins that there's a bunch of no-good eejits bragging about stealing and being rich, so I suggest we stop shouting about money, millions, and grannies, because they'll be a tribe of Shetlanders on our case as well as a bunch of very angry bikers.'

That prompted Matt, Samira, and Bridges, desperate to say something about the money, only for Danny to say it for them.

'We find this Mavis Grind, we divvy up the money, and then we all go our separate ways.'

'What if we can't find her?' I had to ask.

'Then we all go our separate ways.'

'Without paying the £250k we owe?'

'I'll square it with Dublin,' said Danny, whose benevolence was at last finally revealed, so thank you God, if you exist.

However, I could tell Bridges was fuming underneath his

suntanned, toughened hide and doubted that he would be willing to wander off into the sunset with just an eighth of what he had sliced off the suspense account, combined with whatever Samira had made through the drug deals.

But with Danny as the only recognised professional gangster, no one was going to openly argue with the fairest of fair outcomes, given the sticky situation we were now in with the ZMC on board, literally!

Everyone knew that.

'OK, that means you all agree.'

'Where do we look?' I asked, trying and struggling to visualise a granny from the Shetlands smuggling suitcases of cash and drugs across various borders and custom controls.

'Frankie's Fish and Chip Shop,' said Samira coherently, because as soon as she said that, we all started to disbelieve her, until she went on to explain. 'That's where she said she was when I last spoke to her on the phone, and it only takes about half an hour to get there from Lerwick.'

'Is that where Mavis lives?' asked Matt.

'No,' said Samira, because the idea that anyone would live in a fish and chip shop on the Shetland Islands was really daft. 'She lives outside of Brae, in a croft, but I know she always goes in there for fish and chips, so that's where I think we should start.'

'I bet they do good cod and batter,' said Matt, who yet again demonstrated his grasp of the priorities.

'I think we should go to where she lives,' I said, which seemed like stating the obvious and most common sense-fuelled approach, as opposed to starting at her favourite eatery.

'OK, Sherlock,' said Danny, chiding me. 'We don't need

everyone trying to be a detective here. We've got a few things to solve, and this means searching the island while we make sure them zombie bikers don't go chasing us for their stash.'

'Sugar!' said Janet emphatically.

'What, you mean like, one lump or two?' I said incredulously. 'I don't think that's the kind of limited resource the ZMC would see as fair exchange.'

'No, you eejit!' said Danny, who I think would have preferred I keep quiet. 'Janet, who I might add is the only sensible one among the rest of you eejits, means we put sugar in their petrol tanks. That will mess up their bikes. Put them out of action.'

'But that would mean,' I said, happy to carry on being labelled as an eejit, as I had been living with such a title for the whole week, 'if they do catch up with us, they will be so angry, they will cut off our privates and crucify us, hung, drawn and quartered, and drag us along the seabed by our scrotums.'

'Would they really do all of that?' asked Dr Q, as if some of it was possibly appealing.

'Well, that would be the hors d'oeuvre,' I said, not wanting to contemplate what the main course would feel like. 'Perhaps we should hand over their stash if we find the money. Quids in, so to speak.'

'If you think them zombies are going to say thank you for taking their commodity away from them, you're seriously mistaken,' said Danny, who was probably right. 'What we're going to have to do is get all of them sugar sachets from the bar, sneak down to the vehicle bay, and pour in everything we got into the ZMC bikes. Then we stay low in these cabins until we dock in the morning. After that, we head out across the island, but we go off in two separate groups. One group goes to the chippy and the other goes off to the croft. That way, if the ZMC tries to follow us, they won't be able to track us all down in one go. Plus, we'd be doing a thorough search.'

There was a moment of reflection, a considered silence, as we all absorbed Danny's thinking.

For once, it kind of made sense.

'OK, so where's the croft?' I asked.

'It's near Brae,' said Samira, like it was London, because everyone knows where London is.

'And where is Brae?'

'I told you, it's about 30 minutes from Lerwick.'

'So that's where we are all heading,' I said, thinking about the logistics. 'Why not just all of us pile into the van? Sorry, I mean, Danny's luxury tour bus with premium seating for additional coffins. Then, when we've arrived, we can separate.'

'No,' intervened Danny, still running the operation. 'We need to make sure we have two groups when we leave the ferry. They know Dr Q, and they also happen to know me.'

'How do they know you?' I asked.

'That's none of your business,' Danny snapped. 'Seeing as I drive the tour bus, I'll take Samira, Janet, and that Bridges fellow with me, and you and your eejit boyfriend go with Dr Q.'

'Eh, we're not an item,' corrected Matt.

'OK,' I said, continuing to think through the logistical ramifications. 'I have two, maybe three questions. One, how does the ZMC know we are on this ferry? And two, how do we know they are looking for us?'

'I might have accidentally told them,' Dr Q mumbled.

'You mean, you told them where we were going?'

'Not exactly,' he said sheepishly. 'But they probably went to my house, and I might have left a note of the ferry times from Aberdeen on top of the fish paste sandwiches.'

'Great!' I said, exasperated. 'So that does mean they are after us and we are going to be chopped up into fish bait.'

'We all make mistakes,' said Danny, whose benevolence towards Dr Q seemed in stark contrast to the abuse he gave Matt and me.

'All right,' I said, moving on. 'My final question is for Samira.'

'No,' she said emphatically.

'No what?'

'Well, whatever it is you're going to ask.'

'You don't know what I'm going to ask.'

'Just spit it out, Jamie,' said Danny, who expressed a similar level of exasperation, 'before I put you two in the other cabin together.'

'All I want to know,' I said, avoiding eye contact with Matt because he was staring at me, 'is how are we going to get to Brae without wheels, and do you have an address for Mavis Grind?'

'You get a bus,' said Samira. 'And you can find the croft if you walk northeast from Frankie's for about half a mile. It's remote, so don't start Googling the postcode because I don't have it!'

'The point is,' said Danny, again taking charge, 'is that we can lead the ZMC away if they're on to us and you guys can walk off as foot passengers. We'll get Dr Q a hoodie so he can keep his head down nice and low.'

I opened my mouth, ready to say something, to have yet more questions and clarifications, and then, like a fish struggling to breathe, nothing came out.

'That's settled, then,' said Danny, as he offered me a disdainful look. 'And, seeing as it is me and Dr Q who the ZMC will be looking for, we're going back to our cabin to stay low until the ferry docks.'

'When do we get to sleep?' Matt asked, who until now had been conspicuous by his generalised silence.

'You can sort that out with your boss there,' said Danny, nodding in the direction of Bridges, who had a face boiling with constipated rage and frustration. He wasn't happy, I suspected, about anything.

'Ladies first for shut-eye,' said Samira, desperate to be at the front of the queue.

'But I want to do the bikes,' whined Janet, annoyed she might be being told it was too late and she had to go to bed.

'You all get them bikes done,' said Danny. 'And then you all get some sleep before we dock.'

*That would be nice*, I thought to myself, whilst realising there was no way Samira would let me or Matt have the cabin.

I looked at Dr Q, appealing for more pills to get me through the night. I was wired, so I might as well get fully charged, I thought. He obliged by handing over a blister pack of pills and put a friendly arm on my shoulder, understanding my pain and anguish, wishing me well before I ran towards the bullets.

*"All's well that ends well"*, I thought to myself, although I had a few reservations along the lines of trust nobody because they're all a bunch of thieves and liars.

# SHETLAND

# CHAPTER ONE
## SEPARATION

Having stolen all the sugar sachets from the passenger lounge, whilst reminding Matt that he had previous form when it came to sugar sachets, we did half a dozen of the ZMC bikes. They were easily identified because of the various ZMC branding on their petrol tanks. In the end, Samira offered Matt and me the cabin floor with her, Janet, and Bridges. Matt took up the offer, but I was so wired, having poured another load of amphetamine down my throat, that I took to the decks outside and let the skin on my face freeze as I pondered all of the revelations.

I had to hand it to Samira: she had been the surprise package in all this madness, an astute player, and way out of my petty white-collar criminal league. Then there was Bridges, who had been putting his hands in the cash register way before I'd had the bright idea. In fact, the more I thought about it, I came to the realisation that Bridges only sacked Matt and me because he could then blame us for any of the shortfall from skimming the suspense account.

I had to hand it to Danny, too. He had shown a level of fairness that I wouldn't have thought compatible with his gangsterism. I suppose you shouldn't judge a person by all their previous actions and statements, which kind of made it all rather contradictory, and then, the more I thought about it, the more I realised that I was being seriously naïve to believe that anything Danny had said would ever come to pass.

Why accept a small portion of five million when it really was Danny's job, on behalf of his boss, to secure the maximum return on any criminal activity? Things didn't quite add up, so to speak, unless Danny had received a spiritual and moral revelation from the Virgin Mary or a Post-It note from Mother Teresa. This whole separation thing made me even more suspicious. It was only because Dr Q would be with us that going our separate ways was agreeable. Even if we were forced into running away from the rotting flesh of the ZMC, and lots of angry, hairy bikers did catch up with us, I was more than happy to point towards the coffin in Danny's tour bus as a way of avoiding death by a thousand neck bites.

But if there was one thing that was bugging me more than anything else gnawing away at me, burrowing like an annoying little puzzling worm inside my head, it was the mysterious and elusive Mavis Grind. Why would a drug-dealing cash mule live on an island that was close to the end of the world?

By the way, I should also add that geographically speaking, my compass is kind of set to London-centric, so the Shetland Islands are the frozen north and a stone's throw away from ravenous polar bears and igloos, confirmed by having the most northerly fish and chip shop in the world.

There was something annoying and intangible (known as lacking credibility) about the whole notion, the whole tortuous vagueness about the person we were supposed to be tracking down, that I had serious doubts we would find anyone called Mavis Grind. I had visions I would end up sitting on a snowy beach surrounded by penguins, going round and round in circles trying to keep warm, having been left to fend for myself, whilst Samira and Danny fly off to Dubai to buy a skyscraper in the desert.

It all stank of rotting fish. Yet, I had to go along with it, not least because I wanted to know, once and for all, if there really was anything left between us. Between Samira and me.

I went back inside the passenger lounge and got my head down for a few hours, hoping that if anyone did tap me on the shoulder, it would be Matt or Samira or Dr Q, and not some leather-clad ZMC biker suffering from an acute dermatological disease. Not that I slept. I just carried on thinking about things, about how I hadn't given any thought to my mum dying, about how bad it was to dump Trevor's body in an abandoned amusement park, and about taking too many drugs when I should be on the wagon.

Eventually, I did get a tap on the shoulder.

It was Samira.

'We'll be docking soon,' she said, looking up at the clock that told us it was six in the morning.

I rubbed my face, as you do when you've had a rough night.

Then she said something I never thought I'd ever hear her say: 'I just wanted to tell you, I'm sorry.'

'Yeah?' I said, not sure what it was, in the long list of things I had in my head, she should be sorry for.

'What I mean is,' she elaborated, with a mildly guilty conscience, 'I wish I had told you earlier about the things I was up to.'

'Well, it was a surprise,' I said, stretching and trying to

make myself look casual about the whole thing. 'I mean, things could have been a lot different if you had told me.'

'What does that mean?'

'Well, just that, we could have avoided all this mess, and we could have worked together, and maybe...'

I struggled to finish the sentence, because it was leading to somewhere that I knew would be thrown back in my face.

'No, Jamie,' she said emphatically. 'You need to know it's over, between you and me.'

'Yes, of course, I know that.'

'Do you, Jamie?'

'Yes,' I said, being forced into a denial that was as convincing as pleading innocent to having my hand in a honey pot.

Samira shook her head indifferently.

'Anyway,' she said, continuing, 'the other reason I wanted to see you before we disembark is I have decided to credit you with being the only half-sensible idiot who might be able to understand some useful advice and instructions.'

'Thanks,' I replied sarcastically.

'So, when you, Matt, and that penguin go into Lerwick, I suggest you get something sensible to wear, like waterproofs. Some people seem to think the Shetlands are like the frozen North, but in fact it's just wet, very wet, and very, very windy. Then, you need to get the bus to Brae, but tell the driver to let you off at the last cake fridge. Don't worry, they'll know what you mean.'

'Eh?' I said, putting my hand up as if I was back in the school classroom. 'What's a cake fridge?'

'It's a Shetland thing,' she said. 'But it's basically a fridge by the side of the road with cakes in it.'

'Why?'

'Because people on the Isles are not cold-hearted psychopaths always on the make.'

'Like us, you mean.'

Samira nodded and carried on. 'You can always help yourself to a cake, but make sure you donate. Anyway, the point is, you walk northeast from there. Follow the track for about half a mile, and you'll reach the coastline, and that's where you'll see two crofts sitting right next to each other, in the dip below the cliff edge.'

'You've been there before?'

'Yes, once. Now, the croft you need to investigate is the one on the left as you look out to sea. If that's too difficult to remember, there will be a sign above the door that reads: Mavis Grind.'

'OK,' I said, feeling my sceptical juices fuse through my aching body. 'And what are we looking for?'

'Mavis, of course!'

'What if she isn't there?'

'Then we need to look somewhere else,' she replied, clearly frustrated with what I believed to be a relatively cogent clarification.

'Where will you be?'

'You know where we will be,' Samira said, annoyed that I might be questioning her sincerity.

'Eating cod and chips?' I wondered.

'No, Jamie, we will either be running, driving for our lives to avoid being hunted down by those crazy bikers, or we may have a lead from people who know her.'

'You'll let us know, will you, if you find her?'

'Jamie,' Samira said, indicating that she didn't like me questioning her integrity, which, given all that I knew now, seemed perfectly legitimate.

Still, I wasn't going to argue. After all, I had been credited with being one notch above stupidity, and I had a full set of instructions that would lead me to the edge of the world.

'Is that it, then?' I asked, happy to conclude our one-to-one.

'Almost,' she said, probably just as keen as I not to have to talk to each other. 'Have you seen these ZMC on the ferry?'

'No.'

'Have you looked in the cinema?'

'No.'

Samira was cross.

'Heh, nobody told me I had to keep an eye on them,' I said. 'Plus, if you think I'm going into a darkened room to see if it's full of rotting zombie flesh, then you've got another thing coming.'

'I'll have a look,' she groaned, ready to storm off.

'I wouldn't,' I said, as if it were the best piece of advice I could ever offer anyone.

'I'm not afraid, Jamie,' she said, which kind of implied that I was, and to be fair, that had a ring of truth to it.

'All I'm saying is there's no point poking your nose around in the cinema. They'll be wondering why people keep going in there, looking around, and then leaving after two seconds; it draws attention to yourself. Plus, and this is only an afterthought, if they are trying to hunt us down, you'd think they'd be making more of an effort. Searching the ferry and looking at everyone on board.'

'Jamie, I don't know how sociopathic bikers' minds work, but there is absolutely no other reason why they would be on the same ferry as us .' However, Samira did pause for thought before she tried to rationalise all this cloak-and-dagger stuff. 'Maybe they're just lazy, or they don't want to miss their favourite film,' she said, beginning to look less convinced than she was a second ago. 'But what is true is we helped Danny and Dr Q steal their stash, which I'm also sure is something you can relate to. You can't tell me you wouldn't be seriously angry if somebody stole your stash.'

'Fuming,' I said, although that was usually over a miserable day's worth of smack.

'Exactly,' said Samira, punctuated by a very long, awkward silence.

It was in that moment of silence and self-reflection, as she probably considered herself now far less likely to go looking for the ZMC, that I was captivated once again by all the glory of her beauty. At the same time, as I stared like an inane stalker devoid of the ability to communicate my true feelings, I saw in Samira's eyes that same look she gave me when we first started going out together, that look of acceptance, kindness, and completeness.

Was Samira telling me the truth when she said it was over between us? I wondered. Was she being honest with herself and with me, as we both realised, we were awkwardly suspended in each other's gaze, even as we tried to look anywhere else but at each other?

The moment was brief, but I registered it as a positive sign, even if it turned out I was deluded and hopelessly infatuated and in need of long-term counselling.

'OK,' she said, as if snapping out of a mild epileptic seizure. 'I think I'll just wake up everyone else instead. I'll send Matt up to you.'

'And Dr Q,' I added.

'Yes, right,' she said absentmindedly. 'Good luck.'

I would have returned the compliment if I were able to think of one, but Samira was off before I could say anything.

So that was that, then, the separation, the parting of ways.

I did wonder if I would ever see her again, possibly because she could be caught by the ZMC and chopped up into fish bait, or because I'd just been rolled over again, and there was some other plan that had been cooked up, and this was just a way of getting Matt and me out of the picture.

Which meant I was either always gullible, or I just had to retain a little faith in the goodness of people, and that one way or another, we find this Mavis Grind and come away with enough money to go on a very long trip around the world, in search of eternal sunshine and everlasting peace.

Amen.

# CHAPTER TWO

## ROAD TO MAVIS GRIND

As the sun was beginning to rise and the wind was fresh and breezy, we docked in Lerwick. Matt, Dr Q, and me disembarked as passengers, keeping an eye out for leather-clad bikers with steam coming out of their ears. But there was nothing that looked remotely threatening as we watched Danny Boy's UK Tours Ltd. coach shoot off the ferry ramp at an unsafe speed and disappear into the distance.

That was that, then.

'Hasta la vista, hombres,' I said, as I smiled fatalistically at the hooded Dr Q and the miserable-looking prolapsed anus.

We looked like dispirited lost souls as we wandered into the ancient-looking port of Lerwick. In an effort to rebuild team morale, I tried my best to pay some attention to my ex-work colleague and asked Matt how his hand was doing. Still wrapped in clingfilm, he offered up his limp-wristed, soggy lettuce appendage for examination. It didn't look good, and Dr Q had a brief evaluation that concluded he would probably need some kind of skin graft. Matt wailed in despair at his injury, the injustice of it all, and then demanded that we attend to our stomachs because he was a starving Marvin, whatever that means.

As we strolled along the waterfront looking for eateries, Dr Q revealed that not only was he a walking *Batman* encyclopaedia, but he had an encyclopaedia-like knowledge of Lerwick, obtained, he said, from a holiday with his parents. The old houses, he explained, were built by merchants in the late 17th and early 18th century and were known as Lodberries. Now was also a good time to be on the island, because he was pretty sure there was the Up Helly Aa fire festival next Tuesday, which takes place on the last Tuesday in January, a long night that starts with the burning of a Viking galley.

'Well, if I'm still here by Tuesday,' I said, 'I'll know things haven't gone according to plan.'

'Yeah,' added Matt. 'Let's just get the money and go.'

All of which sounded far easier said than done.

However, we did manage to feed our stomachs, and with the best coffee I'd had since we'd left London for North Devon. It was also warm in the café, which reminded me of Samira's advice and the need to get some clothing to match the environment. Dr Q was quick to say he knew exactly where to go, if the shop still existed, and so we followed him, turning right and left, then left and right, until we entered a shop that had a great deal of artefacts that I suspected were designed for tourists, and not the kind of place to get kitted out for the wind and the rain.

After providing some feeble indication that we would be hiking across the islands birdwatching, the owner was more than happy to retreat to the back of the shop and return with what he described as genuine Shetland fisherman overalls. Or, as he explained, they were good enough for the islanders, and they'd be perfect for us. I was sceptical, but they did look like the genuine article, and when we had pulled them over our clothes, we were trousered and waterproofed, looking like bright yellow circus clowns in a surreal Stephen King novel. I was prepared to go somewhere else to look for something more modern, until I heard the price, and that they were for rent, and so I used what little credit I had left on my credit card.

'By the way,' I said, as we stepped outside to look for a bus stop, 'that's a deduction from your cut of the money.'

'Is he always this parsimonious?' Dr Q asked Matt, as we all looked left and right, and then right, and then left.

'I always buy the drinks,' said Matt. 'You'll never get a pint out of him.'

'That's partially true,' I said in my defence. 'But only because other people are more willing to buy a drink for themselves, and that means they then have to buy a drink for everyone else, and I'm not a fast drinker.'

'Don't worry,' said Dr Q, consoling the prolapsed anus. 'I know the sort.'

'Great,' I grumbled to myself. 'Before we've even started, I've been labelled a penny-pinching freeloader, as opposed to a friendly lender of credit.'

'I was also thinking,' said Matt, who clearly thought he had now found a real friend in Dr Q, 'if this is where you can get Fisherman's Friends.'

'The cough lozenge?' queried Dr Q.

'Yeah, exactly! You can't get them anywhere now. I used to love them. I was addicted.'

'I don't know, maybe,' replied Dr Q wistfully, perhaps realising that Matt had his strengths and weaknesses.

As we continued to walk, I did let myself wonder how

long it would take Dr Q to realise that Matt was short of a few screws that held the crumbling scaffolding of his mind together. Still, it was Dr Q's choice who he wanted to buddy up with as we passed a playing field called Gilbertson Park, which had a football pitch and a games hall, which Dr Q said was also used as a venue for Up Helly Aa. We then got onto a main road and were looking over at Clickimin Leisure Centre and pool which, if you ever find yourself in Lerwick and are so inclined, has a leisure complex with a fitness suite, sauna and solarium, multi-use studio, shooting gallery, bowls hall, football, hockey and rugby pitches, and an all-weather athletics track!

'Where's the bus?' Matt asked, unimpressed with Lerwick's modern sports facilities.

'You catch a bus at the bus stop,' I said, trying to be helpful and informative.

'Where's that then?'

'It's in front of you,' I replied, taking the few steps required to sit underneath the little bus shelter.

Dr Q sat next to me, but Matt remained rooted to the spot, offended, it would seem, by me making him look more stupid than he realised, or an idiot honoured with the Prolapsed Anus Stupidity Order of Merit.

Dr Q then offered his own view on Matt and me, free of charge. 'You know, I thought you city boys were meant to be mathematical geniuses enabling you to justify extortionate remuneration for your specialised algorithms,' said Dr Q, casting doubt on a principle of free market capitalism in financial services.

'As opposed to what?' I asked suspiciously.

'As opposed to being profoundly normal,' offered Dr Q, which might have been a compliment.

'Well, they still need a few donkeys,' I said, willing to accept that included me. 'In fact, most of the city is made up of two-faced donkeys who rise to the top by making the loudest noises when eating at the trough.'

'Hee-haw!' responded Dr Q, who had probably learned how to talk donkey while cuddling up to his favourite sheep.

'You know, he's engaged to be married,' I said, as we continued to look at the fed up Matt, cocooned in his bright yellow fisherman's overalls.

'Hee-haw!' replied Dr Q, who was clearly enjoying reminiscing about his life with the domesticated.

I was about to hold my head in my hands out of despair at the company I was keeping when the rumble of a diesel engine raised my hopes.

*Thank God for that,* I said to myself, as a bus came trundling along towards us.

'Matt!' I shouted. 'Stick your hand out. Use the one that still has skin on it.'

He didn't listen, as strands of peeling clingfilm flapped in the wind.

I had hoped that we would all be able to board the bus in an orderly manner, but as I stepped on, I felt Matt and Dr Q press in behind me like uncontrollable kids.

'Are you going fishing, lads?' asked the jovial driver.

'No, bird watching,' said Dr Q over my shoulder.

'We're looking for puffins,' said Matt uselessly.

'Three singles to Brae,' I said, wanting to mumble something back about how stupid they both were, whilst paying for the tickets meant an additional deduction off their share of the money. 'And can you stop at the cake fridge?'

Fortunately, the driver was more than obliging as he issued us tickets and told us to keep an eye out for those puffins.

Having suffered the idiocy of Matt and Dr Q, I took a seat well away from those two and smiled benignly at the half dozen passengers spread evenly throughout the bus. I settled down for the half-hour ride, pondering whether to dip into yet more amphetamine, but repressed the urge as the bus pulled out and restarted what felt like a slow crawl along the main road.

It was a good piece of alone time, as I stared out of the window at the changing atmosphere in the sky and looked down on the rugged landscape. I could hear Dr Q get excited as he spotted grazing Shetland ponies. I was tempted to announce a safeguarding warning but thought better of it as we rumbled forward, stopping for drop-offs and pick-ups, until it was our turn to stand next to what looked like an abandoned fridge by the side of the road.

'Oh look,' said Dr Q, examining the cakes on offer, 'they've got chocolate orange tiffin!'

'Gluten-free and vegan options,' added Matt.

'Christ! Is that all you two think about, your effing stomachs? Anyway, Samira told me you have to pay, donate, if you take something.'

'Or what, we'll be arrested by the cake police?'

'Maybe,' I said to Matt, trying to get my bearings as I pulled out my mobile.

'No worries,' said Matt, as he then revealed from inside his fisherman's jacket a large, round wood-and-glass antique.

‘What’s that?’ I asked, dreading what Matt was going to tell me.

‘I got it from that shop,’ he said gleefully. ‘We need to know how to go northeast, and so I thought I’d better get us a compass.’

‘It’s a bit big,’ I noted, as he held up the glass face for me to praise his ingenuity. ‘Also, it’s a barometer, so it tells you what the weather’s going to be like, not which way to go.’

‘It’s going to rain,’ said Dr Q, whilst tucking into his gluten-free chocolate orange tiffin.

‘Five out of ten for effort, Matt,’ I said, as I opened my compass app and pointed in the right direction. ‘Onwards!’

And that’s when it began to rain. A lot. Although for once I thought we had made a sensible decision – mine, I might add – and effectively prepared for the mission ahead.

Matt had sensibly left the barometer inside the cake fridge, which he classified as a donation, taking two chocolate orange tiffin with him, stuffing his face, because he tended to miss his mouth, as we navigated our way across the windswept, rugged grassy plain towards Mavis Grind’s croft.

Partially blinded by the ferocity of rain blown into our faces, and on occasion having to stand like statues due to the force of the wind keeping us rigid to the spot, I calculated we were fairly close after a half hour of freezing, bone-chilling hiking. I checked our direction, and as we all stood once more blown back by the power of the wind, we could just make out ahead of us the two croft houses that Samira had described. We moved forward and realised they were perched on the edge of a cliff, looking out into the briny sea.

They were picture-postcard stone buildings, probably

from the Stone Age, according to Matt, although there was distinct modernisation parked outside, as both Matt and Dr Q marvelled at the BMW 3 Series saloon in front of the croft on the left, where Mavis Grind was supposed to live.

'She's cashed in some of her chips, then,' said Matt, as he put his face up against the passenger car window.

'We don't know if it's hers,' I replied, walking up to the front door with the Mavis Grind sign hanging down from a storm porch which designated that we had found the Holy Grail.

The place seemed lifeless as I used a bell with a rope and thrashed it a few times to make sure we could be heard above the stormy weather. I had assumed all along that she wouldn't be there, and we'd have to think of some form of illegal entry, when I heard the metal door lock being levered. I signalled to the two car enthusiasts to come over quickly so we could all be present and correct and potentially offer a welcoming introduction.

Although what were we going to say?

Unfortunately, there was no need to say anything.

'Welcome, gentleman, so good of you to come,' said the Henchman, as we all looked despairingly inside at the sight of the Boss Man grinning from ear to ear.

I think Matt would have made a run for it, were it not for the very large hand of the Henchman stretching out to grab him and throw him to the floor. I wasn't going to try to make a run for it, it was too cold and wet outside, and Dr Q certainly wasn't capable of doing anything other than the egg and spoon race.

'If it isn't three yellow leprechauns, come to tell us where they've buried their pot of gold,' announced the smirking Boss Man as we reluctantly stepped inside and stepped over Matt, who was mumbling some strange infantile distress call.

The Henchman pulled Matt to his feet, and we all stood in line, facing the Boss Man, who was sitting comfortably in one of Mavis Grind's armchairs. (There were two in her cosy little living room that could have been designed by Laura Ashley.)

'Now, I know you, and I know you,' he said, pointing to Matt and me. He then pointed at Dr Q. 'But I don't know you.'

'Dr Q,' said Dr Q confidently, who was perhaps oblivious to the fact that he was being polite to his executioner.

'How do you know these two eejits?'

'I have had the pleasure of their company for the last few days,' continued Dr Q, having just qualified from etiquette school. 'We are on a tour of the British Isles, and very keen to have sight of the Shetland puffins.'

'Puffins, you say?' mused the Boss Man, as if it could be something worth considering in some future enterprise. 'Well, Dr Q, you didn't happen to be in the company of an Irishman called Danny Boy?'

There was a fateful pause, then a very long silence, as Dr Q realised that he was speaking to the man who would enact painful revenge on those who may be out to betray or deceive.

There was no point pretending or making up stories, I decided. Something was up for the Boss Man to be here, and therefore telling the truth, the whole truth, and nothing but the truth seemed our best chance of surviving. At least for as long as it took me to say what I wanted.

'The truth is,' I said, catching the Boss Man's attention, 'we're here looking for the money. We've been on one hell of a journey. I mean, I was chased by a panther, and then we ended up helping some old ladies who needed breakfast, and then we ran over an old friend of mine who just so happens to be a junkie, and then we had to get some antibiotics for Matt because he had blood poisoning and was hallucinating.' Matt held up his limp, cling-filmed hand as further evidence. 'That's when we bumped into this girl, called Janet, and she has tuberculosis, but she gave Matt some of her antibiotics, and then, when we got up to Manchester, we met an old friend of Danny's, Dr Q, here, and then we went to this fairground and it was full of zombies, and I got held prisoner by a crazy guy who thought I was a zombie, but I managed to escape, only to find out that Danny, and Matt, and Samira, and Janet, were being held by another load of crazies whose sister was a tooth fairy and she wanted all our teeth, so me and Dr Q saved them, and then we got to Aberdeen, and I was annoyed about a few things and hung out with these oil protestors, but I did get on the ferry, and I just wanted to say, so you understand, that we've been through a lot to get here, and we're on time, and it's important that you realise this, just in case you make any snap decisions, and that I can guarantee we will still get you your money, because—'

At that moment, I stumbled because I didn't quite understand how or why the Boss Man was here.

Matt and Dr Q nodded their approval at my descriptions of the events, as the Henchman looked at the Boss Man, perhaps ready to take instructions on who he should kill first.

Fortunately, my rambling diatribe had dulled the Boss

Man into contemplative thought.

'OK,' he began, emerging from his two minutes of reflection. 'Where are they, Danny Boy, and the others?'

'They're here, on the island,' offered up Matt enthusiastically.

'Where?'

'We don't know,' I said, 'but they did say they'd pop into Frankie's Fish and Chip Shop.'

There was a moment of recognition between the Henchman and the Boss Man.

'Right, you and you,' said the Boss Man to Matt and Dr Q. 'Stay here.' He then pointed at me. 'You can go next door and talk to the neighbour about where this Mavis Grind is.'

Result!

What I mean is, I wasn't going to die. Just yet.

'He'll go with you,' added the Boss Man, indicating I would have the Henchman with me.

'No problem,' I said, in the same way I used to respond to Bridges (who I thought should best be kept out of the picture for now).

But I had to ask, because there was a question I was dying to ask. 'So, have you spoken to Danny since we left?'

The Boss Man scowled.

He wasn't saying, but the only reason why your boss has to get his hands dirty is because you've done something they didn't know about. I just didn't know how much Danny's boss knew.

# CHAPTER THREE

## BESSIE AND THE LOVERS' TALE

'You do the talking,' said the Henchman, as we stood side by side, having knocked loudly on the neighbour's front door.

I was OK with that, because I suspected that talking wasn't one of the Henchman's strong points. As I rehearsed in my head what I was going to say, which was already sounding like a load of baloney, the door creaked open to reveal a pint-sized little old lady, wrapped in a flowery apron, her hair tied up, and her face looking like a cracked ceramic bowl.

'Hi!' I said, sounding like I was going to try to sell her a variety of domestic cleaning equipment. 'Sorry to disturb you, but we were just wondering if you knew anything of the whereabouts of your neighbour, Mavis.'

She pursed her lips, narrowed her eyes, and looked stubborn as hell.

'It's just that we – my friends, relatives and I – have travelled all the way from London,' I continued, praying I was doing my best to look and sound like a good citizen of the human race. 'Her granddaughter's with us, but she's just getting some cod and chips for everybody. Anyway, we've been sitting waiting, and were surprised Mavis wasn't there when we knocked, and so we thought we'd just pop over and see if she was maybe with you? Or if you knew where she was, or if you knew anything?'

Yuck!

None of what I said sounded particularly convincing, and the woman looked even more stubborn and suspicious. In fact, so suspicious, she moved her head to one side to see if there was anything out there apart from two suspicious-looking men adrift on a remote island in the freezing rain and wind.

Relief came when she uttered a soothing sound, having seen something she really liked the look of. 'Oh, is that a BMW 3 Series saloon?'

'Eh, yes, I think it is,' I said, trying to recall what Dr Q had called the driving vehicle machine.

'That's a lovely car,' she said, licking her lips. 'Did you know, the 3 Series has been on *Car and Driver Magazine*'s annual 10 best list 22 times, from 1992 through to 2014, making it the longest-running entry in the list.'

'Well, yes,' I said, thinking I'd best sound knowledgeable about something I know nothing about. 'Do you like cars, then?'

'German cars,' she said emphatically. 'Wouldn't have anything to do with these Japanese ones, though. You need solid build and engineering.'

I nodded approvingly, hoping the Henchman would join in now that he was being complimented on his vehicle, but he remained silent, trying not to betray any semblance of consciousness.

'I tell you what,' she said, now warming to our intrusion. 'Why don't you come inside for a cup of tea, and I might be able to help you with a few things about Mavis.'

'Oh, thanks, that would be great,' I said, as she widened

her door to let us both in.

The inside of the croft was much the same as the one we'd left: quaint and tiny, with a large wooden table where we both sat down as the neighbour shuffled over to an old-fashioned Aga to put the kettle on.

'Now let me see,' she said, more to herself than us as she looked inside some cupboards. 'Would you boys like some chocolate orange tiffin?'

The Henchman nodded, subdued by the maternalistic tone and presence.

'Not for me,' I said, having been put off by seeing Matt use his mangled hand to devour the cake fridge offering.

However, it didn't stop her from digging out a plate and laying a load of slices on the table for us. The Henchman picked up his delicately and grunted his approval, which satisfied the old lady's desire to be the perfect hostess for wayward travellers.

'I just need to wait for the kettle to boil,' she said, going back into her cupboard to start fishing out cups and saucers. 'You know, you don't see too many people on a day like today, or indeed all winter, if I am honest. It's so nice to see that lovely German car of yours.'

'Do you like cars?' I repeated inanely.

'Oh yes, I like a nice fast car,' she said, as she began to set the table. 'Did you know they've been making them since 1975, although there's been a lot of changes since the 02 Series. You see, it was the E21 that replaced the 02 Series, and was available as a two-door sedan with carburetted four-cylinder engines. However, they did introduce fuel-injected models later on that year, and then they added six-cylinder engines in 1977.'

'Wow! You know your cars,' I said, smiling, genuinely impressed with her depth of knowledge, on a par with Dr Q quoting from *Batman* comics.

'Oh no, dearie, I just have too much time on my hands and like to read technical things. It's all because of my husband, you see. He was an engineer, and like me, loved to see manufacturing done properly. Of course, we don't do too much of that over here.' As she continued to lay out the saucers, she said, 'Oh, by the way, my name's Bessie.

'We moved back here about 25 years ago. I was born and bred on the Shetlands along with my husband, but he parted a few years back, so it's just little old me keeping the fires warm.'

As soon as she said that, it struck a chord with me. I was feeling guilty again, running around like a junkie on speed chasing a pot of gold at the end of an invisible rainbow, while my mother was dying.

'Here,' she said, with a sudden wink. 'I always like to wet my whistle with a wee dram.'

She pulled out from the highest shelf a bottle of whisky.

'I'll vote for that,' I said, as she poured a sizable amount into both our teacups.

'Aye, I thought you would,' she said, as she unashamedly poured half a pint down her throat directly from the bottle.

Now that is more impressive than knowing the complete history of the BMW 3 Series!

Bessie wobbled for a few seconds as the 40% alcohol hit the back of her head, shaking her body like a wet dog jumping out of the river. Rather than look like a couple of lightweights, we emptied our cups with a whisky so strong, it ripped the skin off the back of our throats.

'Tiffin?' she said, clearly inebriated by the sudden whisky rush.

'No, tea's just fine for me,' I said, as the kettle announced its boiling temperature with a steadily rising steam whistle.

Bessie wobbled again, and in order to avoid another painful domestic injury, clingfilm and skin graft, I jumped to her aid and told her to sit down while I filled up the teapot.

As I poured, she encouraged the Henchman to have another tiffin, and he obliged with a level of obedience that was incongruous with his character.

'So,' she said, patting down her apron. 'You say you boys are from London.'

'Yes, that's right,' I said, putting the kettle back down on the Aga hotplate. 'We thought we'd do a bit of bird spotting when we found out our friend had a relative she was going to visit.'

'Oh, you'll find plenty of seabirds on these islands. No bother with that sort of thing, if that's what you're into.'

I sat back down at the table, realising she might like to get pissed in the morning, but she still had the ability to put one word in front of the other.

'What about Mavis?' I asked, desperate to move the conversation on. 'Have you seen her lately?'

'Well,' she said, again smoothing out her apron. 'If you want to know where Mavis might be, then you'll have to listen to the tale of the two lovers.'

'I like a story,' said the Henchman.

'Do you, dearie?' said Bessie, who clearly had the measure

of the gentle giant. 'Well, I'll tell you what I know, as long as you promise to be nice to poor Mavis when you find her.'

'Of course,' I said hurriedly. 'Has she gone missing?'

'That, I don't know, but if there's a granddaughter, so you say, come all this way, then it should only be right that you know some of what I know. Not that this is gossip, mind you, and I'll be only telling you this so she can communicate back to the relative if they cannot find Mavis.'

So, I decided to try one of her tiffins, poured out tea for everyone, and waited for Bessie to tell the story.

'What you boys may or may not know is that these islands have a proud history, and we wouldn't take too kindly to anyone calling us Scottish just because Scotland says we're part of their world. That's because we have a long history, a Viking history, and the reason why I tell you this is because if you boys want to know something about Mavis, or should I say want to know where she is, then you'll need to listen to the story of the past that I'm about to tell you.'

'I like history,' said the Henchman, as he helped himself to another tiffin.

'OK, in that case, you might remember that people have been invading and settling on your island and mine for thousands of years, but it was the Vikings who were keen on coming over from Norway to fish and to farm on the Shetlands. Now, the reason for this is to do with the laws of the Vikings. Because only the oldest son or daughter would inherit the family's land and property, what was a second, third, and fourth child to do? '

The Henchman put up his hand excitedly. 'They had to move out and get their own place!'

'Well, we're not talking about a flat share, but it was about 1200 years ago that these Vikings needed to navigate the seas to come here and settle on the land. They brought with them all their Viking ways, of course, their laws and customs, their stories and their superstitions. But then, once you've fished and farmed and built new houses and set up communities, you're back to the same old conundrum that forced people to seek pastures new in the first place.'

'You mean, everyone left?' asked the Henchman.

'No, not exactly, although you Englanders in the North would have had Viking raiders. The point I'm trying to make here is that families have children who need to get married as well as inherit, and once all those things start happening, not everything runs smoothly. This was the case for families who ended up in a bitter feud over lands and marriage. Now, of course, this is all folklore that I am about to tell you, but there are plenty of people here who still believe it has the power to last through the ages, especially if it is a witch's curse that has befallen a family and their bloodline.'

'I don't like witches,' said the Henchman, sounding as if there was no need to doubt their existence.

'Well, there's nothing too wrong with witches,' continued Bessie, sipping her cup of tea. 'It is the curse that you would need to worry about. Anyway, the story goes that as a marriage had been set between one family and another, a bride-to-be and a husband-to-be, that on the night before they were to be betrothed, a jealous rage came from across the seas to snuff out all these good intentions. It was not a raider this time, but a man who claimed the woman was to be his, by rights, a promise and oath sworn in the name of Odin. The woman's family was unable to dispute this, and in order to make right the wrongs made on the island, there was a marriage that night to the man from the North. Of course, this did not go down well with the family who had lost out on a betrothal, the loss of face, loss of potential land, and property. With the humiliation, the hurt, and with no recourse to the Norse law, as the only law that had been broken was one of deceit, they sought the advice of a witch. It was she who offered some kind of retribution, at a price I suspect, but a curse that would condemn the marriage to everlasting torment and suffering.'

'That's why I don't like witches,' said the Henchman.

'Aye, it was a terrible curse, one that plagued the marriage forever after, a cruel and hurtful burden to prevent the marriage from ever flourishing. So it is said that she invoked the god Frey to inflict forever more a childless coupling, a childless future, and if there ever was a child born, then that child would not live longer than seven years. This, at least, is the story that has been passed down by generation after generation, to the point where today, the McDowells suffer the McAuliffe witch's curse to this very day.'

The Henchman looked shocked as Bessie brushed the apron over her legs and asked me if I could just top up her tea with another wee dram. I filled up her cup of tea with whisky and watched as she didn't hesitate to down it in one, initiating a mild shudder, before she prepared herself to continue this historic tale that seemed completely irrelevant, still clinging to the faint hope we would eventually get to know the whereabouts of Mavis Grind.

'Now, I know you boys will be wondering why this silly old woman has told you a bit of a long story, especially when all you want to know is where poor wee Mavis is, but that's where you need to know about Archie McDowell. I knew Archie from when he was a wee boy, no more than the size of a baby kangaroo. His family was all fishermen, and Archie followed in their footsteps, and to the best of my knowledge, while I was away, of course, on the mainland with my husband, Archie got on with life, fishing, drinking, and seeing women as he pleased. But there is always one, that's what I say, who will be a bigger catch, and so it was the case with Archie, who found love with a woman called Ingrid. So besotted was he with her that they quickly sought to tie the knot, only for Archie to find out that, on the day of their wedding she had kept a secret: she was of McAuliffe lineage. If you are superstitious, you may have at least reconsidered, but in this day and age, you would not let such ideas get in the way of love.

'And Archie was the same; he still married that day, while a few whispered and said it was a bad omen. But what followed, I'm afraid to say, would perhaps prove the doubters on that day to be right about the mysterious curse against the McDowells. As I understand it, Archie and Ingrid had a child, a daughter, and she was the light of both their lives. And she grew, played, and entertained, drawing admiration from all who came across her, for her zest for life and her angelic Nordic beauty. But come her seventh year, all that was to change, because out of the blue, the poor child was struck down with illness. At first, the doctors were unable to diagnose what was wrong with her, but as she grew more and more poorly, the sad news eventually came out that she had cancer and there was nothing anybody could do to prevent it from ending her life.

'Now, I don't know if either of you boys has children, but there is nothing worse than to lose a child. It cuts to the core, I believe, and renders you a distraught and hopeless husk of a human being, desperately trying to comprehend the enormity of the loss, the powerlessness, the injustice of what seems like a random form of natural selection. As was the case with Archie and Ingrid, desperately trying to fathom why it was their child who had been so cruelly taken from them. Therefore, it was no surprise really that the curse of McAuliffe upon the McDowells seeped into their rationalisation, to the point where Ingrid became convinced that her daughter's death was her fault. I understand Archie was not as persuaded by such superstitious explanations, especially as his time and attention were soon spent trying to assure Ingrid that she bore no blame for the tragedy. Unfortunately, that is easier said than done. All I can tell you is that one night, a cold and wet night, in the depths of winter, Ingrid decided that it was time for her to be with her daughter, and she threw herself off these very cliffs and into the sea.'

'Blimey!' said the Henchman, who looked as if he might be close to tears.

'Aye, it's a terrible tale, where only grief permeates the tragedy.'

'OK, but what's that got to do with where Mavis is?' I asked, wondering why I had let myself be taken in by an old, widow woman living on the edge of the world, spinning tales from the Nordic *Twilight Zone*, fuelled with a gallon of whisky.

'Ah, do you not remember me saying that in order to

understand the present, you need to understand the past?'

I did, but it didn't help.

'Archie, bless him,' she continued, 'would come up here every spare day or night and stand on the very cliffs that these wee crofts sit on, looking out to sea, crestfallen, heartbroken by the misery that McAuliffe's curse had wrought upon him and his family. I thought it was only a matter of time before he, too, would leap off that cliff edge and throw himself into the watery brine, to close the circle and be with his beloved daughter and wife. But as fate would have it, there was one person who reached out to Archie, one who took it upon herself to wrap a comforting arm around his morbid soul, to lift his head, and get him to see that there might just be a future'

'Mavis,' I said, imagining Archie being pulled from the cliff in the wind, and the rain, and the snow, and maybe the odd hurricane.

'Aye, it was Mavis who had the heart to go see him, to talk to him at first. Slowly, bit by bit, instead of Archie standing on the cliff edge, he would knock on Mavis's door to be let in, and to fall into the arms of the one who had saved him.'

'You mean…?'

'Yes, I do mean. Archie and Mavis became lovers!'

'That's nice,' said the Henchman. 'I do like a happy ending.'

'Oh, if only it were so,' said Bessie fatefully, whilst shaking her head. 'Tragedy upon tragedy is all I can say really. Archie, as you know, was a fisherman, and it was only a month ago that the terrible news of a fishing boat in distress led to the loss of Archie as well. Such an awful thing to happen, the sea taking what it had probably seen for many nights: Archie begging for death on top of the cliff, and the sea finally having its say.'

'Archie's dead?'

'Aye, he has been remembered this past week, and for the love Mavis has just lost, the death of her fisherman. Although some people now say it was because of Brexit.'

'What's Brexit got to do with it?'

'Nothing, one would think,' said Bessie, in a rare moment of rationality. 'But Mavis didn't get much sympathy, mainly because she had another agenda.'

'Really, what agenda?'

'Oh, did I say agenda? What I meant to say was gender.'

'*Gender*?'

'Yes, you know, male and female,' she said, as if I were an idiot, which has been said quite a lot recently. 'In the case of Mavis, she had gone from being a man to a woman.'

'Really?' I asked, sounding like an idiot.

'Aye, and she's a lovely woman to boot. Although it hasn't always gone down that well with some of the islanders here because she's a woman, a proper-looking lady, even though when she came over, I understand that she had been known as a man. But others, you know, might spot the difference, and then I suppose these others would still say that she is a man, however good-looking she is, and for her age, I might add. Still, her family must have known all along the way Mavis wanted to be, after all, you say you're here because of her granddaughter?'

She had a point, a delicate point.

'Oh, yes, I think it was well known,' I said, sounding like

I wasn't very good at lying.

'Must be complicated,' said Bessie, leaning forward. 'For the family and all.'

'Well, I think they've come to terms with it,' I said, as an imaginary red light flashed inside my head announcing Samira as a big fat liar. 'But maybe it might come as a shock that Mavis has lost her boyfriend.'

'Aye, a terrible shock for Mavis, too, I know that for sure. She has been left distraught. Now she is on a walkabout, grieving for the loss of her lover, walking across these islands in search of some peace and solace.'

'Oh, right,' I said, my ears pricking up, having reached the long and tortuous road to Mavis's whereabouts. 'She's just wandering around the island?'

'No, she's not just wandering around,' said Bessie dismissively. 'She's using the island as a place to heal the loss that she has suffered. She came over to see me, I think a week or so ago. She said to me, "Bessie, I am off to the temple, to bury a few of Archie's things, and then I'll be walking to gather my thoughts, away from everybody".'

'The temple?' I asked, wondering if there had been an influx of religious schools of thought.

'Aye, Mavis and Archie would often go to Stanydale Temple. It's an ancient spiritual site, Neolithic.'

'You say she buried some of Archie's things?'

'Aye. Although I'm not sure that's something you should do, archaeologically speaking. It was strange, because she said she was going to bury his things in a suitcase, and I never knew he had a suitcase!'

'You mean Archie never had a suitcase?'

'No, Archie never went anywhere, except out to sea, of course, to go fishing. The strangest thing, she said to me, was if anything should happen, I should dig it up and keep it! Now, why would I want to dig up poor Archie's things? Better left in the ground, where Mavis said she had buried them.'

'Oh, right,' I said, feeling my nervous system start to tingle. 'Did Mavis tell you where she buried it? I mean, Archie's suitcase?'

'Aye, although as I said, if Mavis were not to return, or, poor thing, she chooses to join Archie, I'll not be trudging out there to dig anything up that doesn't belong to me. These old bones of mine don't have the muscle needed to do digging.'

'Did she specifically tell you where she buried it?'

'She did.'

'And is it easy to see? I mean, surely there's a risk that somebody might come along, and see something, and wonder what it is, and dig it up, maybe.'

'Oh aye, there is that risk, seeing how there are so many curious people about who visit these kinds of things. They may well see it if they were to walk 100 yards north of the main entrance to the temple. That's where Mavis said she had buried the last of poor Archie's things.'

Bingo!

# CHAPTER FOUR

## DÉJÀ VU

I was feeling good about myself for once, having achieved what we had been tasked to do: we had a lead, a strange and surreal one, but nonetheless, a tangible lead to offer the Boss Man. I was also keenly focused on where my allegiances should lie, given that there was very little I could believe about anything Samira had told me, or anything I could believe about anything anyone had told me. I think I just wanted everyone I liked to live, and everyone I didn't like to go away quietly (once all the outstanding issues had been resolved). However, as soon as we opened the door to the Mavis Grind croft, a keen sense of déjà vu came flooding back.

The Boss Man had been busy and devised a cruel and mildly ingenious method of torture for Matt and Dr Q. In fact, it was more of a revival, or a sequel to the Pink House method employed to punish and intimidate.

The Boss Man had found a four-slice toaster and had both their hands in the slots, ready, I assumed, for a three-minute timer to be switched on.

'Well, if it isn't Eejit Number One,' he said, with a smarmy psychotic grin running from ear to ear. 'I hope you had a good time over there?'

'Yes, it was very informative,' I said, trying my best to give a look to Matt and Dr Q, which would reassure their petrified nervous systems. Well, at least for a minute.

'It was very sad,' added the Henchman, who took a pew in a comfy armchair by the fireplace.

'What's got into you?' asked the Boss Man, bemused by the lack of testosterone that had drained from his enforcer.

He kept quiet, which offered me the opportunity to fill the vacuum with a slightly shortened version of the tale of two lovers.

I was hoping for a warm ripple of applause by the end of my report, but there were only flat and bemused faces all round, although I do think there was a tear in the Henchman's eye. I decided to take a seat opposite him and let the Boss Man filter and reflect, a tactic I have used in the past to help managers absorb my ideas so they can claim them as their own.

'So,' said the Boss Man. 'What you're saying, if I got this right, is you believe that the money this Mavis Grind has is buried in the middle of nowhere?'

I shrugged, keen to make it look as if I was merely the messenger and it was up to the criminal genius of the Boss Man to draw the dots.

However, he initially ended up shouting at Matt and Dr Q, who had sneakily withdrawn their hands from the toaster of doom. 'Keep those filthy mitts of yours in there!'

They reluctantly placed them back in.

'Well, it's not so much in the middle of nowhere,' I elaborated, taking a more proactive approach to the Boss Man's synthesis and conclusion of a tragic tale. 'Because, according to this Bessie, it's got a specific location 100 yards north of this temple. The only thing we need to bear in mind is that if we dig it up, there might be only Archie's fishing tackle and a spyglass to recover.'

I thought my calm, casual manner would start to win the Boss Man over to a more collegiate approach to finding the money, but as is the way with the criminal mind, he suddenly turned nasty.

'Right, you bunch of lying toerags! If you don't tell me what's going on, Dr Q here is going to have his fingers toasted, roasted, and pickled!'

I pretended to retain a confused innocence.

'You! Eejit Number One!' he said, glaring at me, ready to plunge Dr Q into the hell of waffled human fingers. 'Speak the whole truth and nothing but the truth, or by God I'll be eating your fried fingers for supper tonight!'

Now, where had I heard that kind of thing before? Anyway, Dr Q's beads of sweat perfectly matched the beads of sweat rolling down Matt's petrified face. I did consider continuing to be a lying toerag, but perhaps it truly was time to tell the whole truth and nothing but the truth, so I said it as simply as I could.

'The money in the suitcase, it's five million!'

The Boss Man snorted, no doubt confirming that his life of bullying and intimidation had reached its zenith. 'I knew it,' he said, more to himself than to those gathered in the room, 'that Danny Boy is always up to something.'

However, Matt and Dr Q didn't look best pleased with the big reveal on the prize money available, so I wriggled all my fingers and thumbs at them to ensure they understood the fate that could still befall them.

'That's a lot of money to have buried out in the middle of nowhere,' mused the Boss Man.

'But we do know where it is,' I said. 'If, as I say, this Bessie story adds up to Mavis burying the money.'

'Where is this temple, then?' he asked.

'I've Googled it,' I began, showing my phone map to him. 'It's about 20 miles, or 30 minutes in your BMW 3 Series.'

'Why do you care if I have a 3 Series?'

'I don't,' I said hesitantly.

'You're a cheeky eejit, aren't you?' he said, which sounded almost paternal. 'Where's all this money come from?'

'It's a long story,' I said, recalling how long it took to retell the road journey up here and the curse of the McAuliffes. 'All you need to know is that the city is corrupt, and all I was doing was skimming a bit off the top so I could go skiing once a year and buy a squash racket, but, as it turned out, Matt was doing a lot more, and then my boss was doing even more, and then Samira was doing a lot of investment in the drug trade. So, I suppose you could say it's been a bit of an accumulation.'

'And you don't know where they are, Danny Boy and Samira?'

'I could message them, if you want.'

'No!' he said adamantly. 'We'll keep Danny Boy in the dark for now, seeing as he's pulled the wool over my eyes this past week.'

*Well, he could keep Danny in the dark*, I thought to myself, *but Danny, Samira, Janet, and Bridges could come bursting in through that door at any minute, which would then mean a nasty confrontation* (although I didn't think we had enough toasters to go around to facilitate the level of torture the Boss Man would have in mind).

'This temple, it must be a bit of a tourist spot,' said the Boss Man, beginning to think it all through.

'I don't know,' I replied. 'But people do come over here at this time of year for some Viking festival, so there's a good chance they'd be people around.'

'We don't want that, do we? We sit tight, wait until it gets dark, and then we head out to see what's buried.'

'I can't use my hand,' said Matt, holding up his wrinkled appendage. 'I mean, if you want me to dig.'

'What happens if this Mavis turns up, or Danny?' I asked, trying my best to sound constructive and on his side.

'That's not your problem,' he said, as I noticed Matt sneakily extract his hands from the toaster. 'All you eejits have to do is what I tell you. If this Mavis comes through the door, she can then tell us where the money is, and it might save me from having to go outside and get cold and wet for no good reason.'

'Are we all going?' I asked.

'No. Eejit Number Two can stay here with Cinders,' he said, which I assumed meant Matt and the Henchman. 'My boy can deal with Danny Boy if he turns up while we go out digging, and the same goes for if that Mavis pops her head in.'

'OK,' I said. 'Shall I look for some tools to take with us?'

'No, you sit there so I can keep an eye on you. We'll sort that out later.'

'Er,' came the sound from Dr Q, who looked decidedly calmer, 'what about our share?'

Oh dear, that really was the wrong thing to say.

The Boss Man grabbed one of Dr Q's hands, put his finger on the toaster slot, then he put his face up close and personal.

Dr Q understood perfectly what his share was going to be, and the Boss Man stated it just in case Dr Q had failed to interpret the fear and loathing.

'Your share is your life.'

'And if we don't find the money?' asked Dr Q nervously.

The Boss Man let Dr Q keep his hand and smiled gratuitously.

'Best not go there,' he said. 'Now, make me some toast with butter and jam on it.'

# CHAPTER FIVE

## ZOMBIES CAN'T DANCE

In fact, we all ended up having butter and jam on very old, toasted, crusty bread. However, the Boss Man took sadistic pleasure in plunging Matt's hand into the toaster slots in between toasting, and when we suggested it was probably unhygienic considering we were still all trying to get as much toast as possible down our throats, he went and sat on his own, as if he had been admonished by a peer group that never wanted him to be part of the gang in the first place.

As we waited for daylight to end and the dark to permeate, I curled up on one of the chairs by the fireplace, desperate for some shut-eye, having abused my body with uppers and downers. There was an eerie quiet inside the croft, as I listened to the rain pounding outside and the wind producing odd, intermittent catcalls as it swirled in, out, and around every crevice in the stone walls. I could have interpreted the constant whistling of the wind outside as an ominous sign for what lay ahead, but I was so mentally and physically exhausted that I managed to find solace in the safest place possible: a very deeply embedded sleep.

Unfortunately, as you might expect when having to share the same place with a couple of gangsters, I was rudely woken by being kicked a number of times. It was the Boss Man who had triggered my sleep alarm.

'Eejit Number One,' he said scowling. 'It's time to go.'

I needed a minute, five minutes, maybe ten, to reorientate myself into the absurdity of the past week and its impending conclusion.

'What about tools?' I said, rubbing my eyes.

'No need to worry about that,' he said. 'We always have a few shovels in the boot of the car – you never know when you might need them in our line of business.'

Of course, how silly of me not to realise what a psychotic gangster likes to pack for a day trip!

I stood up, stretched like a bored and tired orangutan, and noticed Dr Q was standing right next to the cruel and heartless Boss Man.

'These are for you,' said Dr Q, offering me a potpourri of pills in the palm of his hand.

'What are they?' I asked, demonstrating a level of caution that I probably should have had since I started swallowing anything and everything.

'These ones will bring you down,' he said, using his stubby little fingers to point them out. 'And these ones will bring you up. It will create a perfect balance, so you'll feel normal.'

'Listen, I've had enough downs and ups to last me a lifetime, and if there's one thing I do know, drugs don't make you feel normal.'

'You can trust me, I'm a doctor.'

'No, you're not. You're a disqualified trainee vet.'

'Enough,' intervened the Boss Man, as he made his way to the door.

Dr Q continued to hold out his hand, assuring me that it was for the best if I accepted his advice and took my medicine.

'Quack, quack,' I said, just because I felt like being irrelevant, and then shoved the pills down my throat.

'Good luck,' said Matt, putting his thumbs up.

Not what I needed, nor the Henchman waving goodbye through the window as we walked over to the BMW 3 Series.

'At least the rain has stopped,' said Dr Q cheerily.

It had, but the wind was vicious.

'OK, which of you two eejits is going to drive?' asked the Boss Man.

'I can't,' I said, holding up my arms. 'I don't know anything about cars. All I know is the wheels go round and round like the big red bus.'

'I hope you know how to drive,' said the Boss Man to Dr Q. He nodded confidently. 'Right, you two are both in the front, so I can keep an eye on you,' he said as he threw Dr Q the car keys.

The Boss Man watched us take our seats, and I propped my car phone on the dashboard so Dr Q could follow the route. After a few missteps on the pedals and a choking ignition, Dr Q had us out on the road.

There was a serene silence as we drove back along the way we had come before veering off the A971 towards Stanydale Temple. We carried on in silence, as I spent the next 20 minutes contemplating whether I had it in me to beat the Boss Man over the head with a shovel or a pickaxe. However, I knew it was highly unlikely and had to hope that he would keep his word if we found the money and let us live. Although I couldn't think of any reason why he would let us live, suspecting that he would just drive off into the distance with five million quid after burying me and Dr Q in the hole we had dug.

'We can park there,' I said glumly, pointing to a layby.

'How far is it from here?' asked the Boss Man, looking through the car window into the darkness.

'Not far,' I replied, scrolling on the map to check where things were supposed to be. 'There's a track we can follow, and then I think we need to spread out 100 yards from the site and start combing the ground.'

'Maybe we should wait until the morning,' said Dr Q, who was also staring into the darkness. 'It would be a lot easier to see any disturbance on the ground.'

'No!' said the Boss Man. 'No waiting. I've got torches in the boot and that should be good enough.'

'Well, I'm hoping this Mavis has left some kind of mark,' I said, more to Dr Q than the Boss Man. 'You know, like three stones on top of each other.'

'Oh yes!' said Dr Q, who was beginning to rise to the challenge, 'I know what you mean. Why do people do that?'

'Because they're eejits,' offered the Boss Man. 'Now come on, both of you, let's get going.'

*Oh well, at least there are more eejits than just us*, I thought to myself as I got out of the car. We were then handed a shovel each and a torch between us.

'What if we bump into somebody?' I asked before we set off.

'You tell them to mind their own effing business,' said the Boss Man, straight from the manual *How to Make Friends and Influence People*.

'Well, just to say,' I said, feeling all informative and collegiate, 'that it's not much of a temple, more like a bunch of boulders in a circle. Prehistoric though.'

'OK, enough with the archaeological twaddle,' said the Boss Man, who then waited for me to show him the way.

I pointed to a track and took the lead, using Google Maps to guide us. Fortunately, with the rain having stopped, the clouds above us were clearing, even if the wind was still chilling us to the bone. The ground was flat, wet, and soggy as we squelched our way along, with enough moonlight to navigate without turning our torches on. Seeing as we knew we should be looking 100 yards from the temple, we took a wide berth around the insignificant-looking boulders that were no more than knee-high.

'That was the entrance,' I said, pointing back towards the rubble. 'I think.'

'Not much of an entrance, not much of a temple,' muttered the Boss Man.

However, ignoring the disgruntled tourist, I marked out approximately 100 yards. We then stood staring at each other, perhaps wondering why we were standing in the middle of nowhere freezing our bollocks off.

I had an idea.

'OK,' I said, my face being sandblasted by the wind from the sea. 'Why don't we walk in a circle around the site, keeping 100 yards from the temple? We should look for any ground disturbance or marker.'

'Could you not have got something a bit more accurate from the old bag?' said the Boss Man, whose faith in the mission was being sorely tested.

'Well, if we find something odd, I'm sure we'll find the money,' I said positively. 'This Mavis has obviously gone off the deep end, and we need to collect.'

'There's no "we" in this,' snarled the Boss Man. 'Eejit Number Three can come with me, and you go the other way.'

*Harsh on Dr Q,* I thought, *because I would always have put Matt at the bottom of the eejit pile.*

'The clouds have cleared,' I said, as the stars, unimpeded by the urban pollution that usually blights my occasional stargazing, sparkled and brightened the dark vista.

'We'll keep our torches off,' said the Boss Man, who clearly didn't want to attract attention – not that we'd seen a car, islander, or tourist since we'd turned off the main road.

We all did a quick recon around the area, on the basis that this was meant to be the most likely location, and then set off in opposite directions, promising to meet back at the same spot unless any of us found something. With my head down searching the soggy ground, it reminded me of the days when I used to go hunting for magic mushrooms, and I applied the same logic to getting my eye in and scanning the boggy peat. But after trudging around half the circle and meeting up with Dr Q and the Boss Man, we agreed to keep going and check each other's path in case we'd missed something.

To be honest, it was a bit of a hopeless task, not least because this Bessie, fuelled by gallons of whisky, could have just fancied taking the piss out of us, and we were looking for something in the dark that was hardly going to be identifiable, or worse, just didn't exist. And as I trudged over the green sodden bog, kicking at tufts and ruts of grass, I started wondering why Mavis would have buried the money, if that is what she had done. I mean, you would only want to hide something if you were spooked out, if you knew someone was coming to claim it or take it for themselves. The only person, or persons, who really knew about the money, before it all came out on the ferry, was Samira and Bridges.

It kind of got me thinking that at least one of them had prompted Mavis to hide the money. Now, that could be because Samira had told her to do it, because we were coming to collect on the £250k, but then, Mavis could just as easily put £250k on the table and said nothing about the rest of it – we would have been none the wiser, although we were now wiser because Samira had fessed up on the ferry. On the other hand, there were some other complications, like Danny, who was trying to shaft the Boss Man, or at least that's the impression the Boss Man gave.

Then I kind of virtually kicked myself because I hadn't factored in the worst, the most evil and despicable human being to ever walk on this earth. Bridges. It had to be him, I told myself, who had freaked Mavis out enough for her to take the drastic steps of burying five million quid out in the middle of nowhere.

How or what he'd done, I didn't know. Maybe it wouldn't matter if we found the money and ended up handing it over to the Boss Man. I suppose that meant we still needed to find a way to survive and not be thrown off a cliff by a tearful Henchman. After all of that, I decided however we had got here, the clear priority was still one of survival.

This was uppermost in my thinking, as after a good hour of searching, we despondently looked at each other back at the spot where we had started from, with the Boss Man sustaining the kind of grievous look that I suspected might be a precursor to a shovel wrapped around my head.

'Heh!' exclaimed Dr Q, perhaps wanting to be the first in the line for a beheading. 'Look!'

He had his head raised, looking up at the sky.

'It's the Mirrie Dancers,' he said, his face marvelling at the green, orange, and pink lights sparkling across the heavens. 'It's the Northern Lights.'

I'll give him that – it was spectacular.

'Aurora Borealis,' Dr Q whispered as he started walking backwards, as if trying to take in the view through a camera he didn't have, and then fell on his arse.

'I think you've just landed on your Aurora Borealis,' I said, walking over to give him a hand.

'I tripped on something,' he said, as I took his weight and felt my spinal cord slip numerous discs.

'Yeah,' I said, bent over by my selfless act and staring at three large stones that Dr Q must have tripped and knocked over. 'You just might be the greatest treasure hunter since *Indiana Jones*.'

'Who's he?' butted in the Boss Man.

'*Raiders of the Lost Ark*!' said Dr Q, bemused by the Boss Man's lack of cultural intelligence.

'We're looking for the bloody money, not some missing bible,' he retorted.

'Well, I will happily believe in God,' I said, falling to my knees, 'if this is where Mavis has buried it.'

I grabbed the stones and piled them on top of each other, recreating the marker. I then shone the torch and lit up the small area. It was obvious the peat-like grass had been upended and then bedded down again, and we could all see the disturbance and where the topsoil had been removed.

'I think Mavis must be an eejit,' I said triumphantly, 'because these are three stones stacked on top of each other, and the ground has been dug up.'

'No time to waste, then,' said the Boss Man, who dropped the tools on the ground. 'Best get digging, sharpish!' He took the torch from me, which was probably as much as we could expect in terms of a contribution to digging.

'I'll start, shall I?' I said as the turf lifted off easily with the shovel.

We took to digging around the sides, the soil so sodden that it was fairly easy to remove. All of this was done in silence and the odd glance between me and Dr Q, as we both reflected on the various ramifications of finding a suitcase full of five million quid (or Archie's underpants and fishing hooks).

We estimated we had gotten down about a foot or so and agreed that it would be far more practical to stand in the hole and dig by taking turns. I let Dr Q continue with his efforts, as I stood on the other side of the hole and as far away as possible from the Boss Man. His focus was purely on the dig, constantly peering left and right to spot anything that might reveal the suitcase, or a box, or even a Neolithic stone axe. In other words, we could just be digging up a load of earth because of coincidences and be no closer to the money than when we first arrived on the island. At least, that's what I was beginning to think until Dr Q hit something with his shovel that sounded distinctly inorganic.

Everyone's eyes widened, like we had all swallowed a bag full of amphetamines, as the Boss Man told me to help Dr Q.

'It looks silver,' I said, as we scraped the soil off the top of what looked like a hard-shell suitcase.

‘OK, boys,’ said the Boss Man, as if we had suddenly become members of the gang. ‘Pull it out and put it up here.’

So we did, using our shovels to wedge it loose from the soil and heave it up onto the surface of the ground. We wiped away the remaining soil with our bare hands and checked the locks.

‘It’s a combination,’ I said, frustrated by how close we were to discovering the truth.

I was going to suggest we get out of here as quickly as possible and sort the locks out back at the croft, but the Boss Man was too impatient for that and grabbed a shovel and gave the locks a good *whack*.

It was at this point that both Dr Q and me were prepared to offer some constructive advice, when the strangest sound, an eerie kind of chant, floated across the vista. It then increased in volume, so that we all looked back towards the temple, and saw the most peculiar sight that you would ever expect to see on a freezing cold night 66 degrees north of sanity.

‘What da fock?’ the Boss man shouted.

And he had a point.

Because from out of nowhere, and more specifically within the oval boulders of Stanydale Temple, were five or six very naked men holding hands and moving in a circle, chanting like Benedictine monks.

The Boss Man then requested further clarification. ‘Where the *fock* did they come from!’

Neither Dr Q nor I had an answer, and fortunately, we didn’t have to give one, as the Boss Man grabbed a shovel and started marching aggressively towards the naked men.

‘Duck,’ said Dr Q, as he jumped into the shallow hole and

knelt so he was out of sight.

I thought it seemed the most sensible thing to do, so I joined him, watching the Boss Man shake the shovel above his head like an angry farmer complaining about trespassing, his voice raised. By the time the Boss Man had got up close, the chanting had stopped, and the circle of nakedness stood waiting for their interruption to explain himself.

That's when we noticed, as best we could in the dull winter light, that the men were rotund, large, well built, but seemed to have skin that was marked, scaly, and distinctly unhealthy-looking.

'Perhaps it's a dermatological self-help group,' I suggested to Dr Q. 'Communing with the gods to cure their affliction. You know, like a leper colony.'

'No,' replied Dr Q, who seemed deep in reflective thought. 'I'd say they look more like zombies.'

'The walking dead!' I exclaimed, alarmed at the prospect of having to decapitate half a dozen flesh-eaters.

Then he elaborated. 'Zombies on motorbikes.'

'You mean…?'

'Yes. The ZMC.'

'Oh, Christ!'

Which is as much as I could say before we witnessed the Boss Man take a massive swipe with his shovel at the group of nakedness that had now surrounded him. It was probably not the best move, because he missed, and then disappeared into a mass of peeling flesh, fists, and kicks that brought him down.

'What shall we do?' I asked, fearing it would be us who would be decapitated and then barbecued for a late-night feast.

'You know, it reminds me of *Detective Comics* Number 33: *Criminals are a Cowardly and Superstitious Lot,* November 1939, by Bill Finger, Gardner Fox, and Bob Kane.'

'Meaning?' I said, in exasperation.

'That we come in peace,' he said, standing up.

'You mean, we go and say hello?'

Dr Q didn't reply as he picked up the suitcase by its handle and walked straight towards the enemy.

I cursed – a lot – before deciding to take the plunge with Dr Q.

The naked ZMC didn't notice us until we tried to casually walk around the temple site, as if we were just returning from a Sunday stroll along the beach.

Unfortunately, our casualness was noticed, as a generic 'Oi!' stopped us in our tracks.

I didn't want to turn around and look, but Dr Q was bold.

'All right, Reg.' I heard him say.

'Say, we come in peace,' I muttered under my breath.

'Dr Q,' I heard the reply. 'What are you doing here?'

'Puffins,' he said, which sounded almost plausible. 'We've been looking for puffins.'

Hearing that ridiculous reply meant I had no choice, I had to help, and come face to face with the naked ZMC.

It wasn't easy. They looked a right state as did the Boss Man, who was lying face down, at best unconscious, at worst, probably dead.

'Didn't take you for a twitcher,' said the naked postural called Reg, with his ZMC gang members eyeing us up suspiciously. 'Thought you were more into the farming side of things, cuddling up with them sheep.'

'That is an unsubstantiated accusation, and a defamation I will defend rigorously in court if required,' said Dr Q, as bold as a disgraced trainee vet could be.

'Of course you will,' said Reg, chuckling to himself, which then caused his fellow ZMC to also start chuckling.

Then one of the ZMC piped up. 'Must be hard to see them puffins in the dark.'

'Exactly,' said Dr Q. 'Which is why we are on our way back to our hotel.'

'What's in the suitcase?'

'Puffin toys,' replied Dr Q. 'They're very playful birds.'

It was an odd answer, which had us all stumped for a few seconds, which gave Dr Q the opportunity to focus on why the ZMC were communing with the ancient Nordic gods.

'Is this a regular thing?' he asked.

'Every year,' said Reg. 'Cleanse the mind and body. You should try it. Get naked, lie at one with the spirits, and communicate through dance. Although we nearly didn't make it. Someone spiked our bikes on the ferry over here. We've had to walk all the way from Lerwick.'

'That's terrible!'

'Awful,' I added.

'Shameless.'

'Have you got insurance?' I asked.

'No, we just take it out on people who've got no manners,' said Reg, glancing down at the prone Boss Man.

And so I did wonder if they might barbecue the Boss Man after their exhaustive efforts to restore their skin, whilst also wondering why Dr Q and I were having a civilised conversation in a Neolithic temple with a biker gang who should be beating us senseless.

'Anyway,' said Dr Q. 'Funny who you meet in the strangest of places, but we need to get going.'

'Are you sure?' asked Reg. 'You're welcome to stay and join us.'

'Thanks for the offer,' said Dr Q, who thankfully had managed to stay calm, cool, and collected. 'But a hot whisky and a toasted crumpet will cure my—'

'Cold,' I added, as I realised Dr Q might go all dermatological.

'OK, Dr Q, see you back in Manchester. Don't forget to collect and deposit.'

We nodded and waved, like two kids who had got away without a beating from the bullies walking home from school.

'Jesus!' I said, as we continued down the track and up to the BMW 3 Series.

'Close,' said Dr Q. 'And the good news is, we now know that they don't know we've got their stash.'

'True,' I said. 'Plus, there's something else we know.'

'What's that?'

'Zombies can't dance.'

# CHAPTER SIX

## MAVIS GRIND

We threw the suitcase into the boot of the car and got going ASAP, because we still had visions of naked bikers, peeling flesh, and shrivelled appendages running after us, having realised the absurdity of Dr Q and me emerging out of nowhere like we had just popped round the shops to get a pint of milk.

'Come on,' I said, my anxiety matching Dr Q's as he turned the ignition.

But the car didn't start.

Which was not a problem, because he just needed to try again.

But the car didn't start.

'Try it again,' I said, my left eye forced into an involuntary muscle movement.

Dr Q tried again. A third time, a fourth time, a fifth time, and a sixth.

'All right, enough!' I shouted, wishing I could blame Dr Q for something that was clearly beyond his control. 'We need to walk.'

'We can't walk,' said Dr Q, adamantly. 'It's 20 miles.'

'What's 20 miles?'

'To get back to the croft.'

'Why are we going back there?' It was a good question, I

thought, and by the look on Dr Q's face, not something he had considered.

'You mean, we don't go back to the croft?' he said.

I wasn't sure, but it was worth testing the water with Dr Q.

'Well,' I said, as I looked out of the passenger window for naked men coming over the horizon, 'the way I see it, what is the point of going back there?'

It was clear, from Dr Q's reaction, that he wasn't sure why we should go back there either.

'The thing is,' I said, 'we probably have five million quid, and if we split it, that means we can both walk away with two and a half million quid each.'

It was Dr Q's turn to stare out of the window and begin to ponder one of life's dilemmas: what would you do for two and a half million pounds?

He raised one very pertinent question. 'But we don't know what's in the suitcase.'

'So why don't we find out?' I replied, offering the bleeding obvious solution. 'But we can't do it here.'

'No, you're right.'

'Let's just go,' I said, making up my plan as I went along. 'It's the same distance to Lerwick as it is to that croft. There must be buses running, or we can call a taxi, or get a lift from someone. Let's get back on the main road, and then, when we get into Lerwick, we can find out what's in the suitcase.'

Dr Q went back to thinking things through, and as each second ticked by, I began to persuade myself that whatever Dr Q said, I was going to take the suitcase out of the boot and start walking.

Fortunately, Dr Q agreed with me. 'Let's do it!'

We got out of the car, grabbed the suitcase, looked at one another one more time to make sure we fully understood the ramifications of our betrayal, and then started walking. As we headed off, we could hear in the distance the chanting of the naked ZMC.

'Do you think he's dead?' asked Dr Q, as he tried to see if the wheels on the suitcase would still go round and round.

'You mean, Danny's boss?'

Dr Q nodded.

'It would help,' I said, checking on Google Maps which way to go. 'By the way, I think it's better to go back the way we came. That will get us onto the main road quicker. Do you think they run night buses?'

'We'll see,' said Dr Q, who yanked up the handle of the suitcase and started off with a purposeful stride.

We stayed in single file, Dr Q taking the brunt of the wind as I wrestled for half a second with my conscience. I had a sixth sense that Dr Q wasn't 100% behind my potential betrayal of Danny, Samira, Bridges, and anyone else who fancied a few quid, but I didn't care, because in my head, I was heading for the hills, the sunshine, Costa del Spain, and living out the rest of my life running a pizza restaurant with puffin toppings as a speciality. I couldn't see why we shouldn't just take the money and run. After all, what would the others do if they were in our position? Matt, Samira, and Bridges – we were all cut from the same cloth. We had all dipped our hands into the virtual cash till, developed criminal enterprises to increase value, and disguised and lied about what we were up to. In essence, we were all thoroughly untrustworthy grifters who would exploit the smallest crack in the smallest stone to look for blood and water.

Therefore, I couldn't see why Dr Q shouldn't be wholly committed to running off with the money, unless he had some kind of bond with Danny which wouldn't tolerate betrayal or disloyalty. But I bet, if it were Danny who was walking along the side of the road with five million quid, he would be like me, planning how he was going to smear himself with honey, while winged cherubs licked his nipples and carp nibbled his testicles.

I suppose the only one who would perhaps bring a degree of brevity to the situation would be Janet. Perhaps if it were Janet she'd consider some worthy cause, donate all the proceeds to charity, and carry on her merry way with a sulky goth stare. But I wasn't like Janet, and neither was Dr Q, and these kinds of opportunities only come along once in a lifetime, if ever!

There was in my mind, no more debate, no more conscience, as we came to the fork in the road that put us back on the A197.

'I need to sit down,' said Dr Q, who had tested his body against the elements and was breathing heavily.

'Well, we need to go that way,' I said, pointing the way back along the A197 and hopefully to a cozy hotel where we could break open the suitcase.

'Why don't you phone for a taxi?' Dr Q suggested, his head down, all puffed out.

I looked around and spotted a bus stop across the road. It made sense to wait there as I searched for a cab company. Then, just as I was about to ring, we could see and hear a vehicle, its headlights rapidly approaching. It then slowed as the headlights blinded us before pulling into the bus stop. It was at that moment that all my Machiavellian hopes were crushed as Danny popped his head out of the window.

'Hello, boys,' he said, full of smarmy glee. 'Want a lift?'

How could we say no?

But Dr Q perked up as the passenger door was opened, and we took a seat to be scrutinised by Danny, Samira, Bridges, and Janet.

The first question was an easy one, as Danny asked about the suitcase.

'It's a long story,' I said, hoping not to reveal anything until I had little or no choice.

But Dr Q blurted it out. 'We think we've found it!'

'Found what?' they all asked excitedly.

I confessed. 'Archie's underpants and five million quid.'

'Archie's underpants?'

'Five million quid?'

'Yes,' I replied calmly, although my morally dysfunctional heart was weeping inside.

'That means you've found the money?' Samira asked, now part of the crowd that had formed around me and Dr Q.

'Maybe,' said Dr Q, who was probably right to add a degree of caution around the winning lottery number.

'Is that it?' asked Bridges, pointing at the suitcase that Dr Q had his arms wrapped around, and looking as if it would take a pneumatic drill to remove from his grasp.

However, before we could endure any more mild interrogation, I noticed the headlights of a bus coming up behind us.

'We better move,' I said to Danny.

'Why's that?'

'Because there's a bus behind us, and if we don't get going, me and Dr Q will get on that bus and go wherever it's headed.'

'You two aren't going anywhere,' said Danny, getting into gear and pulling away sharply.

Dr Q glanced at me with slight regret on his face. 'Let's go back to the croft.'

'We've been,' said Danny, as he kept his eye on the road. 'And there's no one there.'

'Matt and one of your colleagues should be there,' I said, puzzled.

'Perhaps they went to see Bessie?' offered Dr Q.

'Who's Bessie?' asked Janet.

'She lives in the other croft, next to Mavis Grind,' I said. 'And she makes chocolate orange tiffins.'

'But why go back to the croft?' asked Bridges.

'Because,' said Dr Q, who then paused as he searched for a reason, 'we owe it to Mavis.'

Bridges didn't like that, although I could see Samira wrestling momentarily with her conscience.

'All for one, and one for all,' I said sagely.

'OK!' shouted Danny, above the noise of the engine. 'We'll go back there. It's 20 minutes away and as safe as anywhere else. By the way, you boys didn't come across the ZMC, did you?'

'We certainly did,' I said, prompting an avalanche of issues and concerns. All of which led into a highly convoluted explanation of the day Dr Q and I had experienced, as we also found out about the long and winding road Danny and his crew of wayward urchins had been on in pursuit of the elusive Mavis Grind.

It turned out that they had been given various sightings and steers – some of them bum steers – ever since they had managed to speak to someone in Frankie's Fish and Chip Shop. They had circumnavigated the whole of the island, walked along beaches, looked out to sea, traversed peat bogs, and had wind and rain destroy their body and soul, whilst all the time worried that the ZMC were going to creep up behind them and gorge on their intestines.

But the one thing Danny wanted clarification on was whether the Boss Man was dead, and if the ZMC were in fact on their annual tour of the island seeking spiritual and dermatological purification, and therefore had no idea that we, or should I say Danny and Dr Q, had stolen their stash.

'Were they angry about the bikes?' asked Janet.

'A little. A bit of advice for you: always invest in good insurance cover,' I said commercially.

'But that means we're in the clear, with these biker people,' Bridges said, as Danny drove down the track to Mavis Grind's croft.

'We'll see,' Danny grumbled sceptically, as we pulled up and could see there was a light on in both the crofts.

Danny wanted to get everything inside, which meant Samira grabbed the suitcase, and we struggled to lift the coffin out of the vehicle. Then Danny, Bridges, Dr Q, and I acted as pallbearers, marching the short distance to the door of Mavis Grind, entering to find Matt and the Henchman sitting in armchairs by the fire, stuffing themselves with chocolate orange tiffin.

'Don't get up,' I said, as we set the coffin up next to the fireplace, and Samira and Janet followed in behind us.

That's when Matt's eyes lit up.

'You've got the suitcase!' he exclaimed, jumping out of his easy slumber and causing the Henchman to be distracted from eating for half a second.

'We need to open it first,' said Samira, as she plonked it down on the floor. 'There's a combination lock.'

'Not a problem,' smiled Matt, who for once looked like he might have an answer. 'Mavis Grind is here.'

'Where? Here?' we all asked in unison.

'In the bedroom,' Matt replied, pointing down a short corridor.

We all looked and stared at a very old wooden door.

'You mean, you found her, or she's just turned up?' asked Samira.

'She's just come in,' said Matt, whose focus was now more on the suitcase than the revelation that Mavis Grind had been discovered.

'Did she say anything?' asked Bridges, who seemed to be anxiously staring at what might emerge from behind the door.

'Not really,' Matt said. 'We explained why we were here, you know, and that we'd been looking for her. She said she would wait in the bedroom until you'd all got back.'

'Well, that's all of us back, don't you think?' said Danny, making a few steps towards the door.

Whether this Mavis was listening or could see Danny coming towards her bedroom, we didn't know, but we all kept our eyes fixed on that wooden door as we heard a latch move and then it creaked open.

What happened next is etched upon my memory forevermore. No words can actually adequately describe what emerged from the bedroom, and to say it was revelatory would be a humongous understatement.

Mavis Grind, the mysterious drug mule, the reason for taking the most bizarre and eventful road trip from Ilfracombe to the Shetland Islands, strolled elegantly towards us, swinging her hips; her lips slick with a glowing red gloss, her high cheekbones powdered, her long dyed blonde hair curled down over her shoulders, all put together in a figure-hugging flowered print dress. She smiled, at first, as she came more into the light, but that smile suddenly disappeared as she looked straight at me.

Then I had the strangest thought, a memory of long days past, when I was once part of a family, with my mum and my sister, when everything was normal. It felt like the seconds that went by were minutes, even hours, as I filtered and ran through every other thought that could possibly explain who and what I was looking at. But there was only one word I could use, one word that would test the truth of what I was thinking.

'Dad?'

And Mavis Grind knew.

She knew. It was me, Jamie.

She put her hands to her face and bolted straight back into the bedroom.

After that, I wasn't listening because of the shock to my system, even if I could hear Matt behind me, saying, 'Eh, mate…'

His words drifted off into the mega disturbance that was

invading my head, thrashing around like a cat in a sack, scratching, screaming, and wailing.

Then I heard Samira. 'Sorry, Jamie, I didn't know.'

Why would anyone know? Why would anyone know that my dad, the one who had disappeared overnight all those years ago, was living on the Shetland Islands, drug dealing and money laundering, mourning the death of a cursed fisherman, whilst either pretending to be a woman, or having transitioned into a woman.

Suddenly, I felt a hand on my shoulder, a comforting hand.

It was Danny.

'If that's your dad, you need to go and talk to her.'

Which was easier said than done, because I was rooted to the spot, my legs all trembly, wondering how to start a conversation with my dad, who should be hung, drawn, and quartered for abandoning his wife and kids to fend for themselves. Who, at a minimum, had better show some contrition before we even get down to the reality that probably – and I was struggling to compute the reality – my dad had become a woman.

I looked around the room, at all the faces who were all saying the same thing: you've got stuff to deal with!

My heart sank, all the way down from my chest to my little pinkie toe, but whether I liked it or not, and I certainly didn't like it, I would have to go through that door and look at the woman who used to be my dad.

I took a deep breath and breathed out slowly. There should have been some kind of melodramatic music to accompany my slow and cautious steps to the bedroom door. I looked back at all the faces and received some benign, reassuring nods and half smiles.

*Should I knock*? I thought. *Yes, I'll try knocking*.

'It's me, Jamie,' I said through the door.

There was silence.

Perhaps she had runaway again, jumped out the window and off on another walkabout, but this time contemplating her despicable betrayal of her wife and kids. Plus, it would also get me out of having to deal with this, enabling me to put it back in the mental safe deposit box, never to be opened again.

I turned around to look at the sympathetic faces encouraging me to do the right thing and shrugged, indicating, as far as I was concerned, that I had tried my best and we should just get on with opening up the suitcase.

Unfortunately, they were having none of it, and made nodding movements and raised their eyebrows, forcing me to knock on the bedroom door again.

Reluctantly, I performed the same task, knocking harder but remaining silent.

I waited.

Mavis wasn't there; I was sure of it. She must have escaped.

Phew!

But just as I was about to avoid having to deal with all things personal and psychological, messy and torturous, the bedroom door opened.

It was Mavis. Mavis Grind. My ex-dad. And not so much the return of the prodigal son (because that would be me) but the return of the prodigal dad – as a woman. That was the moment when I wished one of these egotistical tech entrepreneurs had done something useful for once and invented a time machine, and all I had to do was open an app and be miraculously transported back 10 years so the woman in front of me could be turned back into Dad, the dad I had loved and got on with, just before he had done a runner.

Instead, there was this attractive middle-aged woman in front of me, who had sad, weepy eyes. As I looked into her small bedroom, with a large metal-framed bed that took up most of the room, I had flashes of Archie and her going at it like rabbits.

Not good.

As I stepped inside and closed the bedroom door, I remained standing, while Mavis – Dad – sat on the bed.

I know it's rude to stare, but in this instance, I felt it was perfectly justified. Boy, did I stare, trying to penetrate the foundation and the makeup, trying to see through into my dad's mind and find some answers in the back of her head scribbled down on Post-It notes.

'Yes, it is me, Jamie,' she said, looking down at the floor as I continued to stare.

Well, the voice was different, slightly.

'It is you then?' I managed to say.

'Yes, it is me, Jamie, your dad.'

'Are you?'

'Yes,' she insisted, far more assertively, and then raised her head so I could see those eyes, those tell-tale eyes, which confirmed that I had a dad who had now become a woman.

'Wow! You've changed,' I said, continuing to stand by the bedroom door.

'I know it's a shock, Jamie,' she said, using her hands as if she was opening out a book for me to read. 'But I am prepared to explain things to you, if you promise to listen.'

'I'm all ears,' I replied, wondering if it would all end with me ripping her head off.

'Will you listen?'

'Do I have a choice?'

'Yes, you can go and forget you ever saw me, if you'd like.'

It was tempting, but I did also have a stake in five million quid, so I wasn't going anywhere.

I folded my arms and leant against the back of the bedroom door. 'It's not easy to forget that my dad went AWOL and then reappeared years later as a drug mule and woman. That's not something I will ever erase from my memory.'

'No, well, you're probably right,' she said, still betraying some of the behavioural traits of my old dad by stroking her cheeks. 'I think it's best that I tell you my side of the story, before you blame me for all the terrible things you think I am responsible for.'

I merely raised an eyebrow.

'That night,' she said (meaning, the night I left you, your mum, and Brenda), was the worst night of my life. You must understand, Jamie, that I didn't want to do it, I didn't want to run away and abandon you like that, but I was in a tight spot. Two things had caught up with me. As you know, the firm I worked for had found out it was me who was embezzling their funds. They were going to arrest me; I had little or no warning. I had to do something. As you can now see, there was another thing going on with me. It all kind of coalesced into a difficult, but very rational decision, a decision that I thought would cause the least harm for everyone concerned.'

'How do you think abandoning us overnight with little or no money was in our best interests? And anyway, if you were scamming the company, why didn't we see any of it being lavished on us?' I asked.

'Because of this,' she explained, gracefully rolling her hand over her body. 'Because of who I am. Because of who I needed to be. Because of who I needed to become.'

'You mean, you spent all the money on yourself so you could become a woman?'

'No, Jamie, I had other debts, gambling debts, and both you and Brenda had whatever you wanted. At least up until I left.'

That was true. I had always wondered why Santa Claus was so generous when I was convinced that I had made it onto the naughty list every year.

'I suppose you thought we wouldn't be able to cope if you turned around and said you wanted to be a woman?'

'It would have caused a lot of hurt. Far more pain and anguish than if I were caught by the police and locked up.'

I had to think about how I would have reacted if I ended up with Dad, who, on his release from prison, had commenced his transition. How would I have coped with having two mums?

'Well, I'll admit it wouldn't have been an easy one to process,' I said, trying to imagine such a scenario. 'If you had told us.'

'Exactly, Jamie. Can you imagine how devastating it would have been for Stella?' she added, and my brain flicked back to the image of my mother in hospital. 'Not only would there be a divorce, but terrible humiliation for her. All her friends, the neighbours, not to mention her God-awful family. I didn't want any of that to happen. It was for the best, just in that moment, to run away, escape, and let everyone think I was just a bad person for stealing money.'

'And abandoning us,' I added, which I was thinking was far more to the point, rather than my dad's pursuit of self-actualisation.

'Jamie, I know you won't want to hear this, but life hasn't been that easy for me either. The torture and torment I have been through, struggling to understand who I was, struggling to find ways to transition, and wrestling all the time with my conscience, wondering whether I should get in contact, and wondering whether I should try to help financially. All these things have created a life of torment and guilt.'

'Guilt my arse,' I spat, beginning to feel resentful that I should be sympathising with my dad. 'I don't think you realise that my happy, carefree childhood got flushed down the toilet because of what you did. Mum was distraught, and me and Brenda were left to fend for ourselves for months afterwards, until Mum could get herself back on her feet. Everything after you left was a struggle. Mum never recovered from it. Brenda got her act together, but I ended up filling my body with drugs and alcohol.'

'Are you blaming me for you becoming a drug addict?'

'Who said I was a drug addict?' I replied, mildly offended.

'Sorry, I just assumed that's what you meant.'

'Well, if I were a drug addict, then you were a major contributory factor. Plus Basildon, boredom, perhaps some immaturity, and Mum's cooking. Anyway, if a dad walks out on his family and disappears overnight, that is going to have an impact, and it was devastating for me, Mum, and Brenda.'

'I hear you, Jamie, and all I can say to you is I am really, really sorry for any hurt I've caused.'

Damn!

That's not fair. That's not right, he – she – can't get away with just saying sorry. I mean, there must be more than just saying sorry. There must be things like divine retribution, purgatory, and a life of eternal damnation and everlasting roasting over a very hot fire, and then maybe also chronic crippling illnesses like diabetes, or obesity, or athlete's foot just for good measure.

So I had to tell her – perhaps as some kind of retribution of my own – that the wife my dad abandoned, my mum, was dying of cancer.

'Well,' I said, hesitating before putting things in the most hurtful way I could, 'you've got another person to mourn other than your boyfriend, Archie, because Mum is dying.'

That made her scoff, although I didn't think she was scoffing at Mum dying.

'Two things, Jamie,' she said, narrowing her eyes to tell me she knew I was trying to be mean. 'If you're referring to Archie, I couldn't give two hoots. I've been sad and depressed about Stella, your mother, not him.'

'You mean you know? But how?'

'There is one person whom I kept in contact with after I left – your Uncle Gerry. I used Gerry to help Stella out whenever I could, although she never knew, of course.'

'Gerry!' I exclaimed, who I knew to be as untrustworthy as my dad, Matt, Samira, Danny, the Boss Man, Bridges, and myself. 'You knew? You always knew what was going on?'

'No, not always, Jamie. Just the odd thing now and then, in case there was a crisis.'

'And what would you have done if there was a crisis?'

'That would have depended on what kind of crisis it was.'

I leaned forward, so she could understand the full depth of my resentment and fury. 'My whole life has been a crisis!'

Mavis raised her eyebrows, the way that Dad always used to when he knew something that you didn't.

'You got yourself a job, in the end, didn't you?' she said, reminding me of a previous life I had only a week ago.

'I had a job,' I said, leaning back on the door. 'But it looks like I've followed in your footsteps and now everything has come full circle. Which reminds me, I really would like to know how you got involved in all of this.'

'It's quite simple, Jamie,' she said, casually, which I doubted. 'I had one or two contacts from the city myself, and one thing led to another, helping me keep things ticking over, until eventually I was contacted by a young lady called Samira.'

'Samira?'

'Yes, Samira,' she repeated, with a knowing smile that only dads do when they know something about you that you hoped was a secret.

'That's how this whole thing started, with you and Samira and Bridges?'

'Eh, no, yuck! That odious man. I only liked dealing with Samira.'

At this point, there was a moment of clarity, well, more like slowly clearing fog.

'So, just to be clear,' I said. 'One, you had this

uncontrollable desire to be a woman, whilst at the same time embezzling from your employer, and the two things came to a head, causing you to abandon your family in order to avoid total humiliation for your wife and children, whilst leaving the strain of mystery and ignominy to fester in our lives for the last 10 years. Two, you then lived a life of subterfuge, keeping tabs on your family whilst pursuing a life of crime because you were now a fully dedicated professional criminal. Three, during this period or passage of time, you made enough money to facilitate the transition to becoming a woman, using, I assume, this new identity to offer your services as a money laundering drug mule. Four, unbeknownst to you, this last set of illegal engagements or transactions has accidentally led you to finally run into one of your children, me, who, through no fault of his own, has become entangled in a criminal enterprise that is full of absurdities as well as opportunity. So that finally, in a remote croft on the Shetland Islands, we meet face to face, with the prospect of dividing up a substantial amount of cash, if your neighbour Bessie is to be believed, enabling us all to wander off into the sunset to fulfil our heartfelt dreams.'

'Well put, Jamie,' Mavis said, crossing and uncrossing her legs. 'You should consider a career as a lawyer, but perhaps that's for another time.'

'I think you're a bit late on the career advice. It seems like I've turned out just like you. Not a woman, of course, just a dirty, rotten criminal.'

'You know, it's not genetic, Jamie, being a criminal. It's just choices, opportunism, and speculation most of the time.'

'Easy for you to say,' I grumbled, holding my head in my hand.

'OK, Jamie,' she said softly, and picking up where I had left off. 'Why don't you just tell me what Bessie said to you?'

'Bessie?' I replied vaguely, having consciously lost the thread of where I was supposed to be up to.

'Yes, what's that old coot been saying to you?'

'Eh, something along the lines of curses and Vikings and fisherman's underpants, which I know sounds crazy, but we did find where you buried the money.'

'Oh,' she said, as I wondered if my dad had a scheme to run off with the money and we had put the kybosh on it.

'Is the money in the suitcase?' I asked, hopefully.

'I'm sure it is, Jamie,' Mavis said ruefully. 'Although I'm surprised you managed to get any kind of sense out of Bessie. That woman is seriously prone to talking alcoholic gibberish. Just so you know, Bessie is from an institution and is as mad as a hatter. So don't be taken in thinking she is a little old Scottish lady with quaint folktales for the tourists.'

Well, I did, actually, but I was going to pretend she hadn't fooled me. However, there was one thing about Bessie that was bugging my festering neurones.

'So why did you tell Bessie about the suitcase?'

'Bridges,' she said emphatically. 'He'd been trying to contact me, and when I did speak to him, he was all threats and menace. He was after the money for himself, I was sure of it, but I also wasn't sure what was going on. So I let Samira know I was going to hide things and keep away from the croft until she got here.'

That didn't surprise me about Bridges.

'OK,' I said, but why did you still tell Bessie?'

'I don't know, Jamie. I wasn't thinking straight. I'd popped around, and she had poured whisky down my throat, and I just blurted it out. No harm done, though; she doesn't know her arse from her elbow. In a way, it was an oblique message to Samira to find where the money was, which has turned out to be the case.'

It was then that we both took a natural pause in our confrontational conversation. I suppose I wanted to be more angry, more entitled to demand remorse and retribution from her, but it just wasn't there. Perhaps time had soothed the edges? Perhaps the way things had changed over the years meant that having a dad who needed to become who he truly was wasn't such a big thing.

I then started to wonder whether I owed my dad an explanation about how I had got here, and my relationship with Samira and all the rest of the passengers from Danny Boy's UK Tours Ltd. However, just as I was about to say something, we heard a car pull up outside.

Now who could that be?

# CHAPTER SEVEN
## ON THE THIRD DAY

There was a loud knock on the door.

'Is that the police?' I asked, imagining a horde of heavily armed special forces with sniper scopes and red lasers pointing at all our heads.

'Jamie,' Mavis said, standing up and opening the bedroom door, 'the police don't knock.'

I followed behind, with Samira, Matt, Bridges, Danny, Janet, and Dr Q all looking like startled rabbits.

'I'll go,' Mavis said, as I struggled inside my head to think how I should now refer to my dad.

Then there was another loud, angry thud, just as she reached the door and opened it. Light from inside the croft flooded the outside world to reveal the bedraggled and exhausted Boss Man, who lunged forward as if he were desperate to be inside somewhere safe and warm. As he re-orientated, recognising the rest of us, showing panic and displeasure in one grimace, Mavis shut the door and stood in front of the Boss Man, protecting her wayward flock.

'Who da *fock* are you?' he said, each word pronounced like a seething dose of the predictive menace to come.

'I am Mavis Grind,' she said, unintimidated. 'This is my croft. Who, exactly, are you?'

*Nice one, Dad,* I thought, *stand up to the bully for my sake and everyone else's*!

'I'm the Boss Man, and I've just had naked men, covered in pus sores, sticking their todgers in my mouth and sodomizing my arse!'

'Oh dear,' said Mavis, sounding almost genuinely concerned. 'I don't think that's a traditional islander welcome. They must be from the mainland to do something like that.'

'You don't say,' replied the Boss Man, who used his arm to move around Mavis and into the middle of the room. 'Anyway, enough! I've come for my suitcase.'

Now that was interesting, because it had been left on the floor and was now nowhere to be seen.

'Where is it?' he continued, full of rage and trauma, scanning the room and then focusing on Danny and the Henchman.

However, it was Dr Q who had a question. 'How did you get here?'

The Boss Man snorted, his nostrils flaring, as he put his hands in his pocket and threw something at the Henchman.

'I always carry a spare set of car keys,' he said, handing over driving responsibilities to the Henchman, before turning on Dr Q. 'Have you not heard of the phrase, leave no man behind?'

'We thought you were dead,' I explained hurriedly.

'Is that right?' he replied, turning to focus his rage on me by putting his face into mine.

'OK,' said my dad, as she tried to step in between us. 'This is my house, and everyone will play by my rules, and that means we all need to calm down so we can work things out, without any more harm coming to anyone else.'

It sounded like a pretty inane thing to say given the character and predisposition of all those present, but for a moment, the steam pouring out of every pore of the Boss Man seemed to ease off.

'Why don't I make everyone a cup of tea?' continued my dad, who was speaking into the side of the face of the Boss Man.

'Do you have any tiffin?' asked the Henchman innocently.

'I've got some biscuits,' she said. 'In a jar.'

However, the attempt at forming a panel of adjudication was smashed by the Boss Man.

'Nobody moves,' he said, still maintaining his laser-like menace as he attempted to penetrate my soul, 'until I see that suitcase.'

Fortunately, it was at that moment that I saw Danny pull the object of desire from behind a chair and slide it into the middle of the room. It was the only solution, as the Boss Man turned around, and we all looked at the potential treasure trove of five million pounds.

Or, put it another way: *five million pounds!* That's what we were all thinking, calculating, dividing, and subdividing, or plotting betrayal, or considering recrimination. Because, in rare moments like these, as I am sure you can appreciate, the rational, compassionate, collective instincts that have enabled homo sapiens to evolve into the highest known form of intelligent life in the vastness of the universe, go out of the window.

For a second, which felt a lot longer than a second, we all stared at the muddy suitcase. It needed somebody to say something, to bring the temperature down and introduce coherence rather than rage, rationality rather than anger, calculation rather than greed and selfishness.

It was Janet who stepped forward and sat on the suitcase.

'What's she doing?' the Boss Man asked, slightly disarmed, as we all were, by the youthful intervention.

'Making sure that none of us do anything stupid,' said Danny, who really was the only one who probably had the ability to stand up to the Boss Man.

This only sparked recriminations. 'Oh, Danny Boy, you've got the medal for stupidity, that's for sure, turning on me the way you have.'

It was then that Danny looked at Dr Q, who then looked at me, which meant Danny looked at me the same way the Boss Man had been looking at me, also known as the death stare.

'You know,' I suddenly heard Samira say, 'we should think back to the ferry, when we all managed to talk things through and come to an agreement on what was fair and equal.'

'This isn't the United Nations,' the Boss Man hissed. 'And no agreement stands, now that I know what you lot have been hiding from me.'

'But it's not yours, is it?' said my dad. 'And in terms of rights of possession, that suitcase belongs to me.'

'You can have the suitcase,' said the Boss Man. 'Once I've got what's inside it.'

'What do you think is inside?'

'We all know what's inside!' screamed the Boss Man, whose torturous journey had clearly put him at the end of his tether (if he ever *could* be tethered).

'It's the money, isn't it?' stated Matt nervously.

'It is, isn't it?' asked Samira, looking at my dad just as anxiously.

My dad didn't reply immediately. Instead, she walked over to the table where the toaster was and sat at the table. During that time, I had a thousand thoughts and doubts, far too rapid to record, but thematically aligned along the thought that what if the money isn't in the suitcase.

With nobody speaking, I suspected everyone else was just as anxious, wondering what my dad would say. The tension was far worse than having to sit in a dentists' waiting room with a throbbing abscess.

Mavis casually crossed her legs, sighed a little, and then said, 'Yes, the money is in the suitcase.'

'Good,' said Samira immediately. 'So we can now agree to equally share the money.'

You would think at this point, with Samira offering everyone a slice of the cake, that in truth she had accumulated with Bridges, with a minor contribution from me and Matt, that there would be a breakout of equanimity. But self-interest erupted, based on claim and counterclaim.

It was the Boss Man who initially restated that he was going to take all the money himself, which I suppose assumed that he was the biggest gangster among us, and so could use brute force to walk away with all the money. On the other hand, Danny stepped in to assert his rights, who, although he was formally employed by the Boss Man, was now formally offering his resignation and would take his fair share of an equal distribution. The Boss Man then lurched into a tirade of expletives, curses, and obscure insults at Danny, which verged on the homophobic. (I suppose he might have been bitter about the ZMC.) All of which led Samira to assert, quite correctly, I believe, that *she* had acquired the money, along with Bridges and my dad, with absolutely no mention of Matt and me! She then stated that, therefore, if anyone were going to share all of the money, it would be those three.

'Well, hang on a minute,' I said, scrutinising Bridges, who had been remaining ominously quiet and whose face was exceedingly red. 'I do believe that Matt and I may have made a small but not insignificant contribution to the combined pot of embezzlement.'

'Did you?' said my dad, almost disapprovingly.

'It's in the blood,' I replied spontaneously.

'You two eejits,' said the Boss Man, pointing individually at Matt and me, 'owe me £250k for the coke!'

'And you're a drug dealer?' asked my dad, with a double dose of disapproval.

'Look,' I said, struggling to think which issue I should address first, 'Me and Matt have been through a lot since the Pink House, and we have just as much right to what's in that suitcase as anybody else. Danny said equal share, and I support that.'

'I do believe,' intervened Dr Q in a tone that suggested some objectivity, 'that if we divide the money by the number of people present, that would be a sum of five million divided by nine, which equals £555,555 recurring.'

'What are you, a human calculator?' retorted the Boss Man.

'No, just good at maths.'

'Half a million,' I heard Matt hiss, dissatisfied.

He had a point. Half a million didn't seem a lot. I mean,

not if you are left with the prospect of never being able to work again and need resources to live on a remote island with no extradition agreements in place, in case someone eventually works out what's been going on and calls in the law.

On the one hand, no one could be extracted from the equation of dividing up the money, but it did seem to me that not everyone in the room had contributed to the accumulation of wealth. After all, what exactly had Dr Q done to acquire five million? He and Danny were also sitting on a stash of zombie drugs that would cover any perceived losses. Then there's Janet, who had the rest of her life ahead of her and would probably become an online influencer, raking in millions through subscribers watching inane twaddle about going down to the shops to buy face cream. As for the Boss Man, he could have what he was owed, and that would be that.

I made my pitch, just to test the water.

'Perhaps,' I said, seizing the day and all that, 'we should reflect on how and why we all got here, and perhaps be a little bit more objective about who has done the work to accumulate, and who is just here seeking to take advantage of the hard work of others.'

There, I'd said it.

'What does that mean?' asked the Boss Man, who wanted to get up close and personal with me again.

'I think that means,' said Dr Q, who I was beginning to realise might have the highest IQ among us, 'is that if you didn't embezzle, then you're not part of the division of the spoils.'

And with that astute clarification, everyone stood up and

started shouting at each other.

It was the Boss Man and Danny who moved towards me, finger-pointing and shouting, claiming the embezzled money had increased in value due to investments in the drug trade, and that the value of embezzlement was nowhere near the accumulation acquired through drug trading. It was this topic that they declared themselves experts in, and were part of the Dublin drug trading fraternity, which, by association, they were indirectly representing, blah, blah, blah.

This weak argument seemed to embolden Matt to come to my defence – vested interest, you see – and argue that myself, him, and Samira had been the ones to take the calculated risks, and had very little if zero future, and so should have a larger share than those who already had well-established criminal careers that they could seamlessly return to, whatever the outcome.

It was then that Samira stepped in and said we should all consider what the actual size of the cake was because Danny and Dr Q had stolen the ZMC stash, and we needed to also calculate its market value in order to come to an honest account of what should be divided. The Boss Man then screamed in Danny's face, demanding to know why he had been betrayed all along, and that there would be all kinds of heavy prices to pay for things that Danny was guilty of (which we all wanted to hear about, but the Boss Man was unable to list anything beyond the ZMC scam with Dr Q).

All of which made Danny angry, as he began to unleash a torrent of grievances that went back over many years of gangsterism, including the lack of an annual appraisal and annual pay rises, which seemed fair to me.

Although my dad had kept quiet, she eventually joined in, believing some degree of recalculation should be considered after Dr Q had announced that if they were to include the estimated market value of the ZMC stash, it could be equivalent to approximately one million. Matt argued it would more than adequately compensate the Boss Man for his lost earnings of £250k, including interest, which led to the Boss Man and Danny shouting at everyone else, and each other again, because they believed they were apparently being shafted.

I thought we were all going to resort to some kind of fisticuffs, when the shouting was interrupted by a very loud bang, so loud it sounded a bit like a gun being fired. When we finished looking at each other and started looking at where the sound had come from, all we could see was Bridges, who had a small pistol in his hand. There was debris falling from the ceiling and all over his face.

Now he was wearing the expression I had witnessed every day of my city life, a mean and nasty scowl that usually prefaced a targeted rant at anybody in his sights. Only this time, he had a gun and had clearly tipped over the edge into violent psychopathy.

He moved the gun around to make sure that if any of us were brave or foolish enough to run at him, he would shoot first and then say it was their own fault.

Bridges rubbed his face and spat out the ceiling plaster he had swallowed, and then offered his contribution on the suitcase and how its contents should be distributed.

'Right,' he began, addressing us all as we waited in bemused and stunned silence, 'let's get one thing clear, so that all you useless inbreds, social misfits, and cretinous losers know once and for all: that money is mine, and mine alone, and nobody, from here on in, is going to say another word about dividing it up, cutting it this way or that way, because I am the person who has earned it, and it all belongs to me.'

That was a moot point, but seeing as he had the gun, no one was going to argue with him. Just yet.

'Now you,' he said, waving his gun at my dad. 'Get on the floor and open that bloody suitcase.'

My dad elegantly got off her chair and knelt by the suitcase, while Janet swiftly jumped up and stood next to the coffin.

However, my dad didn't immediately do anything, as she looked around at all of us, wanting to make sure we also approved of conceding to Bridges's demands. I noticed Samira nodding, and I think we all wanted to know what was in there, even if it meant we might have to then jump on Bridges and give him a good spanking.

This was the moment, the big reveal, the Holy Grail. After all the madness and absurdity of trekking across the country in a land of surreal purgatory, we would finally get to see the fruits of our ill-got gains.

At least, that was what we thought. But as my dad was about to fiddle with the combination lock, there was a knocking in the room, a few distinct taps, as if someone were knocking on a door so they could come in. We all looked at each other, and Bridges looked at us all as if we were up to something. At the same moment, we all distinctly heard the sound again, and collectively traced it to where Janet was standing, next to the coffin.

'Is that…?' I asked.

'Shh,' Samira hissed.

Bridges crept up to the coffin whilst randomly waving his gun in everybody's face, and put his ear up against the coffin lid.

*Tap, tap, tap, tap.*

It was definitely coming from inside the coffin, although there shouldn't be anything coming from inside the coffin, because it was supposed to be full of the ZMC stash.

But the noise had freaked Bridges out, who took a step back and was ready to pull the trigger.

'Don't shoot!' screamed Janet.

Suddenly, the lid of the coffin creaked and slowly opened on its hinges.

'The Second Coming!' announced Dr Q, with his hands raised in a hallelujah gesture.

'Trevor?' I said, as I stared at the body of the man we had run over in Basildon, his eyes closed, and his arms folded across his chest like an Egyptian mummy.

Then all of a sudden Trevor's eyes came to life, bright and bloodshot, as if he had risen from the dead, although I suppose it is true to say that he *had* now risen from the dead.

'Jesus Christ!' said the Boss Man.

'No, it's not,' replied Danny, who seemed fairly sanguine about it all. 'He's just a dead junkie.'

'Who's eaten all the stash?' said Dr Q, losing a lot of his religious fervour.

Bridges, who was really freaking out, his head like a boiling pustule, took a step forward and peered into the eyes, searching for life in what I considered to be a well-preserved corpse.

At least, that's what I thought, until we all screamed like babies.

'Ahh!'

Trevor suddenly leapt out of the coffin and grabbed hold of Bridges's neck, pushing him backwards, so that he stumbled over onto the floor.

'OMG!'

'What the?'

'How the?'

All of which went unanswered, as the born-again Trevor continued to strangle Bridges, prompting the Boss Man to seize the moment and grab Bridges's gun.

I must admit, I was conflicted at that moment: whilst not able to give a rational explanation for the Second Coming, I was realising a heartfelt ambition in seeing Bridges being throttled.

'He's choking,' said Matt, stating the obvious.

'No, he's not,' said my dad, 'he's having a heart attack.'

Which prompted Samira, first responder, to push Trevor the zombie off Bridges, thump his chest, and start pumping on his sclerotic heart. Then my dad, who did the one thing that I suppose was an act of humanity and kindness that had been seriously absent in all her previous lives, started kissing Bridges on the mouth, which I think was part of that CPR thing.

Now nobody seriously wants someone to die, apart from maybe the odd dictator, but as we all looked on, and as my dad and Samira vainly tried to revive the prone Bridges, they eventually reached a point where Samira took his pulse and did that shake of the head thing, which said Bridges had finally gone to meet his maker and was no doubt struggling to explain why he was such an evil bastard.

For once, nobody knew what to say or where to start as Trevor was comforted by Janet, although the Boss Man and Danny did start arguing over who should have the gun. Perhaps things would have descended rapidly into more recriminations and acrimony, were it not for another interruption, and this time a genuine knock on the door.

'Who's that?' said the Boss Man.

'Aliens,' I said sarcastically, hoping that I might be proved right.

'Well, the only way to find out,' said my dad, brushing herself down after all her exertions from kissing Bridges, 'is by answering the door.'

Although before she did that, she pulled out a tablecloth and threw it over Bridges, whilst the rest of us did our best to look casual, and Trevor sidled over to the coffin. Clearly, he had grown to like where he had been living.

'Bessie!' we heard my dad say.

'Oh, hello, Mavis. I saw your light on, so I thought I might just pop over and check everything is OK.'

'Oh, yes, no, everything's fine, just friends and family over for the weekend, as you can see.'

Which led to my dad opening the door and allowing Bessie to scan all of us sitting like guilty school children waiting to receive our punishments.

'Oh, hello, everyone,' said Bessie, greeting us with a smile as we all smiled back. 'Now, would any of you boys and girls like a chocolate orange tiffin? Because there's a group of boys that have called in on me, and they're all dressed in leather jackets, underpants, and cowboy boots, and they said they've lost their bikes.'

'OK, Bessie,' said my dad, manoeuvring her arm around Bessie's shoulder to steer her back outside. 'That's a lovely offer, but it sounds to me like you have enough people to entertain. Perhaps tomorrow I'll pop over and have a cup of tea with you.'

As Bessie was being gently pushed out the door, we could hear her insisting. 'Now, are you sure you don't want to partake?'

As soon as my dad shut the door, the Boss Man threw the gun into the Henchman's lap. 'Go round and sort them out and put a bullet in every one of their heads.'

'What about Bessie?' said the Henchman, with sad eyes.

'She's not your mum, you eejit,' said the Boss Man, who heartlessly waved the Henchman away to commit the heinous act.

Things had gone seriously pear-shaped.

"Slaughter at the croft" – the headline started flashing in front of my eyes.

Still, there were also other things to consider.

And it started with Trevor.

# CHAPTER EIGHT

## CULT OF THE TIFFIN

'You're supposed to be dead,' I said, pointing an accusatory finger at the hapless Trevor, who was being comforted by Janet.

I suppose I should also have said that I was glad we hadn't killed him, although there were a number of questions that needed some fairly straight answers.

'Why aren't you dead?' Samira asked, who, if I recall, was the one who had used all her expertise as a first responder to pronounce that Trevor was dead, deceased, no longer breathing, and had cut his mortal coil.

'Yeah, and while we're at it,' I added, 'why aren't you in a coffin scaring the crap out of people in Merlin's Magic Hell Ride?'

'He did save our lives,' added Janet, who I suspected knew exactly why Trevor was back among the living.

'Look, before you get into that,' said my dad, glancing at Bridges's body, 'I can confirm that this one is definitely dead.'

'Well, whoever you are,' said the Boss Man, 'dead or alive, you'll not be having any of the money.'

Which sounded like he was reevaluating his ultimatums on the division of the spoils.

'Why don't we let Trevor speak for himself?' said Danny, who maybe had a vested interest because he was the one who had run him over.

Trevor was looking rather sheepish. Perhaps it takes it out of you when you have to come back from the dead.

He tilted his head onto Janet's shoulder.

'I'll explain,' she said.

'Please do.'

'Well, you know when you were in the pharmacy trying to get antibiotics for a urinary infection?' she said, directly to me. 'And then I followed you back to your hotel—'

'By the way,' I said, hurriedly interrupting. 'I didn't and never have had a urinary infection.'

'And you found me in Danny's van—'

'That, by the way,' said Danny, 'is a perfectly respectable passenger transport vehicle.'

'Well, I had a look inside, and there was the coffin,' said Janet. 'I thought that was odd and wondered if there really was a body inside.'

'She saved me,' Trevor whispered.

'And that's when I found Trevor,' said Janet, like she had just discovered a new species.

'Alive?' queried Samira.

'Doh!' exclaimed Janet.

'But you didn't have a pulse,' insisted Samira.

'Sorry,' said Trevor, his voice still quiet and barely audible. 'It's happened a few times, you know, when they've taken me into A&E, and they thought I was dead. I was just passed out.'

'You must have a very weak pulse,' said my dad, who also knew Trevor from when we were kids.

'But why,' I said, rubbing my forehead, 'didn't you just tell us you were alive?'

'I would have done,' said Trevor. 'But Janet said she thought you guys were up to something, and it might be dangerous if you knew I was alive.'

'Us?'

'Nah.'

'Don't think so.'

'Anyways,' said Danny, who looked over at me. 'According to Jamie here, this is something you have a thing for, a bit of a wee scam, jumping in front of vehicles so you can claim the insurance.'

'I did it once,' said Trevor, as a matter of fact.

'I don't believe you,' I interrupted, fairly sure that Trevor had tried to implement the scam on numerous occasions.

'I only count successes!' said Trevor.

'See!' I retorted, whilst wondering if it really was that important to prove Trevor was a compulsive masochistic insurance scammer.

'You're a lucky man,' said my dad, 'for this young girl to have kept you going all this time.'

That's when a few pennies dropped, as I thought back to Janet always keeping close to the coffin and sneaking down to the vehicle bay on the ferry crossing over to Lerwick. She would have been giving him water and snacks, maybe even a brief toilet break.

'OK,' I said, computing a few things. 'You must have gone cold turkey by now. Why do you look so normal for a dead man?'

Trevor tapped his pocket. 'Always have enough stash on me, you know, for emergencies.'

The ingeniousness of junkies never ceases to amaze me.

'Stash!' said Dr Q, all of a sudden. 'Where's the ZMC stash?'

'Please don't tell me you've eaten it,' Danny warned, far more sanguine about the situation than I would have anticipated.

Trevor shook his head, without responding, and looked rather sheepishly at Matt.

We all turned to face Matt, the great ape, and the last surviving member of the little-known offshoot of homo sapiens, more commonly referred to as The Dumbass.

'Shall I put his hand in the toaster?' I asked one and all.

'Why would you put his hand in the toaster?' asked my dad innocently.

'It's a long story,' I replied, as I grinned darkly at Matt.

'I'll put his head in a toaster,' Danny growled, far more menacingly, 'if he doesn't tell me what he's done with my drugs.'

And that persuaded Matt to start talking.

'It was Janet,' he said, passing blame immediately, in good old Matt tradition.

'I was looking after Trevor!' she blurted out. 'And there wasn't a plan, anyway. It just happened.'

'What happened?' asked Danny.

'All I did,' said Janet, who looked as if she wanted to stab Matt right between the eyes whilst pointing at him, 'was tell him about Trevor when we were on the way to that fun fair. I didn't know what to do, but I didn't want to leave Trevor in the coffin on his own like that, so Matt came up with the plan, after he'd done it.'

'Done what?' I asked, intrigued as well as bemused as to how all this subterfuge could have been implemented behind everyone else's back when humping the coffin all the way over to the Nightmare Apocalypse!

'It was a moment of inflation,' said Matt, repeating the nonsensical phrase he had used with me on the way down to Ilfracombe.

'What does that mean?' asked Dr Q.

'It means,' I said, acting as interpreter for the Matt way of thinking, 'that he thinks he had a bright idea.'

'Now that's something I'm going to find hard to believe,' said the Boss Man, presciently.

Matt cleared his throat, no doubt so we could all hear with clarity how the genius at work operates unimpeded from reality.

'I'll admit,' he said, 'my actions were perhaps a little self-interested, but I was only doing what I thought was right and proper at the time, helping save Jamie's old friend, and ensuring Janet's secret was not revealed.'

'Matt does not know what the word altruistic means,' I said to everyone, and then smiled at Matt. 'Do go on.'

'And then it came to me,' he continued, referring to his inflationary concept of stupidity. 'When Jamie threw himself off that ghost train and fell down the hole, all I had to do was pretend to have swapped Trevor's coffin over for the one with the stash. That way, Trevor would be returned to Janet, and he gets to live another day.'

'Hang on,' I said, desperate to kill off the idea that Matt was some kind of saint. 'What you mean is, you pretended to do the swap so you could then go back and steal the stash for yourself once all this madness was over!'

'That,' said Matt, trying his best to look offended, 'is defamation!'

'But also an accurate description of the self-interest you happened to mention a minute ago,' said Danny.

'I suppose that's why you didn't bother to help me,' I accused Matt as I recalled the paranoid zombie killer who had stripped me naked.

'I was keen to get out of there,' Matt retorted, who I thought now deserved to have pins perforated across his eyeballs.

At which point, Samira had her say.

'Matt, you are a total imbecile!'

'OK, enough!' intervened the Boss Man. 'I am grateful for that little bit of intel, which means those zombie bikers still have the stash. None of you is ever to go back there, because once I hear those gun shots, not only will those sodomising bastards be where they belong, but me and the boys know where to seek compensation. However, there is a more pressing issue in front of us.'

'I agree,' said my dad, as she pushed herself off the floor and stood over the genuine corpse of Bridges.

*Poor old Bridges*, I thought to myself, not that I actually meant it, because if there was anyone who deserved to die, it was the nasty piece of work who had spent all his life destroying everyone else's life through constant corporate management bullying. I knew for sure that there would be one big booze up if it ever came out he had passed onto greater things, and it wouldn't be to celebrate his life, but to cheer the demise of the city manager psychopath.

'Well, if we put him in that coffin,' I said, taking a closer look to make sure he was dead, given our lacklustre performance to date, 'is there a risk he could come back to life?'

'It's not the coffin that has magic powers, Jamie,' said Samira.

'Shame,' I replied. 'Because a box that offers you everlasting life would be a bit of a winner.'

'We could have him cremated,' said Dr Q. 'They'll be burning the Viking boat in a couple of days for Up Helly Aa.'

'I'll give you 10 out of 10 for thinking out of the box,' said my dad. 'But asking the authorities to let us burn a body in a coffin on a Viking ship is not a runner.'

'We can throw him off the cliff?' offered Danny dismissively.

'That would ensure a second death blow,' I said agreeably. 'And diminish the risk of Bridges coming back to haunt us.'

Superstition had started to get the better of me.

'His body will wash up on some beach, though,' said my dad, who I suppose knew something about tidal flows, given her relationship with local fishermen.

'Won't the fish eat him?' asked Matt innocently.

'You don't get Shetland piranhas,' my dad replied.

'OK,' said the Boss Man, in a tone that indicated he was going to make the final decision. 'We dig a hole outside big enough for him, the coffin, and half a dozen bikers.'

'And Bessie,' I said markedly. 'But I'm not digging any more holes. Dr Q put in a shift with me to dig up that suitcase.'

'I'm sure we can all help,' said Samira, who nodded

towards my dad and then in the direction of the suitcase.

Which kind of brought everything back to what we all needed to think about and decide on, not that I thought anything was going to be up for debate with the menacing Boss Man and the power he wielded.

'OK, we bury the dead,' said my dad with some finality.

She knelt down by the suitcase, which was what we were all more keenly focused on, as I reflected that if we resort to a little prayer, we might find some absolution for our thoughts, actions, and sins regarding the death of half a dozen people.

But who cares?

This was it.

The moment we had all been waiting for.

All the trials and tribulations, the madness and absurdity, the horrors of travelling through a broken country, beaten and battered, which all came down to opening the lid of a muddy suitcase. I watched my dad turn the numbers on the combination lock.

'That's not original,' I said, as she set the numbers to one, two, three, and four.

'Sometimes the obvious is less obvious,' she said cannily, as she flicked the locks and opened the suitcase.

We all rushed in and gawped at…

Lots of underpants?

Not money, cash, mula, sterling, dollars, or even the effing peso!

My dad started ferreting around, throwing the underpants in the air, desperately looking for something that wasn't there.

Then, with make-up-covered wild eyes, she screamed one word:

'BESSIE!'

'Bessie?' we all replied.

'Yes, Bessie!' screamed my dad again.

At that moment, I realised, perhaps more than anyone else, exactly what the word Bessie meant in relation to underpants and the missing money, all of which was being perfectly synthesised with the sound outside of a car engine being started. She must have wanted us out on the peat bogs and out of the way, waiting for her opportunity to run off with the five million.

As my dad rushed to the window, she announced my realisation to one and all, just in case their brains were not completely in gear and up to speed.

'It's Bessie from next door! She knew about the suitcase; she must have dug it up. I told her the combination. She must have replaced the money with Archie's underpants,' my dad said bitterly.

'That's a pretty significant contribution to underfunded mental health services,' I said, sarcastically.

'We all make mistakes, Jamie,' said my dad, ruefully.

'But I thought she was having tiffin?' said Matt, who probably hoped he would have been invited.

'No, she's not!' shouted my dad, as she flung open the door and rushed outside 'She's driving off with the bloody money!'

And for a second or two, we were all trying to process what to do, when Samira said the most obvious thing.

'We need to stop her!'

'Jesus!' exclaimed Danny and the Boss Man.

'Come on!' screamed Samira, who was rushing outside.

We all ran out the door, including the weak-legged Trevor.

'She's stealing my car!' the Boss Man screeched.

*And the money*, I thought, as Bessie, the whisky drinking, folktale-telling, chocolate orange tiffin lady, was sitting behind the wheel of the Boss Man's BMW 3 Series, trying to get the car started with my dad banging furiously on the car window.

'How did she get in there?' asked Dr Q.

'I gave my boy the car keys,' said the Boss Man. 'Danny Boy, get the tools out of the boot.'

I understood the logic of what the Boss Man said, but as I turned to check with Dr Q if we had left the shovels out on the wild peat bogs, he was running over to Bessie's croft.

However, there were enough of us to stop Bessie escaping, as we all now descended on the car, with Samira, Janet, and Trevor joining my dad, banging on the windows and pulling on the door handles.

Fortunately, Bessie was still desperately trying to get the car started, so she wasn't going anywhere in the next five seconds as the Boss Man sprung open the car boot and pulled out a crowbar. He then slammed the boot down and started thrashing at the rear window. Which kind of left me wondering what I should do to help retrieve the one thing that mattered most to us all.

I had to do something as the Boss Man was shattering the glass and Danny was on the car boot jumping up and down, when the worst sound of all was punctuated with a scream of elation from Bessie.

The engine of the BMW 3 Series roared into life.

Bessie put the pedal to the floor, but instead of moving

forward, the car spun on its back wheels, throwing Danny off and sending everyone else onto their backsides.

Except me, and I did the only thing my desperate brain thought possible: dived through the rear window where the Boss Man had shattered and removed the glass, falling into the car and landing between the driver and the passenger seat.

I was squashed and wedged, but at least I was a lot closer to our demented nemesis, who looked down at me with utter contempt in her eyes.

'Where's the money!' I shouted, the only thing I could think to say.

'Shove it!' Bessie replied, stamping down on the accelerator pedal and continuing to rev and spin.

*Fair enough*, I thought, as I considered how best to prevent her from driving away with only my right arm. Not that I knew what I was doing, but it seemed to make sense to stop her revving the car, so I put my hand on her leg to stop it moving.

But that was a mistake. Because all of a sudden, the car shot off into the dark. At great speed.

In one way, that could have been the end of the story, Bessie and I driving off into the sunset, agreeing to become partners in crime, dividing the spoils, and settling down on separate islands thousands of miles apart.

That isn't what happened, though. Instead, within a very short space of time (it was difficult to estimate due to shock and trauma) we were launched like a space rocket into the air. Now, some of you, if not all of you, may recall a similar incident at the beginning of this story, involving the prolapsed anus known as Matt, some £250k of coke, and some very disinterested cows in a field just outside Ilfracombe. The journey had all the similarities of my previous experience of weightlessness, as we landed upside down, skidding for an eternity on the soft boggy surface of the Shetland Islands. Really, it could be classed as a soft landing.

Was I alive, a bit like Trevor, with a weak pulse pretending to be dead? Or was I in Heaven?

It seemed, for better or worse, I was alive, having benefitted from being wedged painfully in between the driver and passenger seat, meaning I was thrashed around but remained relatively stable as the BMW 3 Series had hurtled through the air before landing and spinning like a washing machine at 1400 RPM.

After a moment, gravity played its part, as I suddenly dropped onto the inside roof of the car, with Bessie's unconscious face hanging far too close to mine.

All of which would have been perfect, but for the smell of petrol, smoke, and the flames which jogged me out of the now familiar shock of flying through the air in a German-made car. If there was one thing I had learned from watching documentaries about how to survive a crash landing, it was to get out quickly.

Of course, being close to sainthood, I had to take Bessie with me.

Unfortunately, when I unbuckled her seat belt, she fell like a large sack of potatoes, pinning me down. So I rolled her over and then pulled her body out backwards, through the smashed rear window.

That was when the car blew up, and I landed on my arse, and Bessie landed on top of me again. At which point, I was going to give up, resign from life, and seek solace with the crazy man who lived under an abandoned fairground ride, until I felt myself being dragged away from the heat and the flames engulfing the BMW 3 Series.

For once, I was grateful to see Matt, as Samira and Dr Q pulled Bessie away.

Dazed and confused, Dr Q started checking me over as if he were a real doctor, not a disqualified trainee vet, whilst everyone else, who had been involved in the scramble to thwart Bessie, arrived.

'That was brave of you,' Samira said as I was surrounded by one and all.

'But also reckless,' said my dad, which is what you would expect from a parent.

'Did you get the money?' asked the Boss Man, who was obviously far more succinct.

I couldn't really speak, as a profound sense of déjà vu overwhelmed me. All I could do was shake my head and point at Bessie lying a few yards away from me.

'You eejit!' screamed the Boss Man, as everyone turned to look at the car that was burning five million quid.

'Did you see the money in the car?' asked Danny, who raised a salient point.

*No*, I thought to myself, as a sudden rush of hope, of optimism, brightened my eyes.

Which actually could have sustained us for at least another novel, but as is the way with these things, the answer was in the banknote that was whipped up into the air, the note that floated around in the cold, windy night, before settling on the prone body of Bessie.

‘All I can say,’ I said, croakily, ‘is perhaps it’s for the best.’

‘I agree,’ said Janet. ‘We should try to be nicer people.’

‘A moral compass stated by the young has a ring of sincerity and should be reflected on, me thinks,’ said Dr Q. ‘But before we all cry ourselves to sleep, there is another matter we need to deal with. Although, you’ll be glad to know, I do have a plan.’

‘A plan for what?’ asked Danny, who looked like he would need a lot of crying before he could get to sleep.

‘Well, said Dr Q, ‘while you were trying to stop Bessie, I had a look inside her croft. I was curious as to why the ZMC were not following us outside.’

He then paused, as if at least one of us should ask the question so he could provide the answer.

But we didn’t.

So Dr Q continued.

‘Bessie had poisoned them all with her chocolate orange tiffin. Arsenic, I would say, by the look of things.’

‘Oh my god,’ said my dad, shaking her head.

‘But a blessing in disguise,’ said Dr Q reassuringly. ‘We have many bodies to dispose of. In fact, far too many, I think, to realistically achieve our objective. So, I suggest we don’t pretend anymore and contact the police.’

‘Are you crazy!’ said the Boss Man.

‘It has been said, once or twice,’ replied Dr Q. ‘But the only way out of this is to bite the bullet, so to speak. Now, this Bessie is a certified lunatic, and it would not be beyond the realms of possibility that we spin the story to the police of the ZMC and Bessie indulging in strange occult practices. After all, there must be sightings of the ZMC, and we can back that up with sightings of them dancing naked around the Neolithic temple. Mavis can add some colourful renderings of the oddness of Bessie, and if we throw in Bridges's body, we have what I would call the Cult of the Tiffin.'

'That's ridiculous,' said Matt, which was odd coming from him.

'Well, you can do what you want,' said the Boss Man. 'But I'll not be seeing or talking to any of you lot ever again.'

He started walking towards his burning car and then beyond it, moaning about the loss of his henchman. And that was the last I ever saw of him.

'The Cult of the Tiffin?' I mumbled, hoping it would make it sound tangible.

'Now that is what I would call a crazy long shot,' said Samira.

'Crazier than what we've just been through?' asked Dr Q.

And you know what? He had a point.

# CHAPTER NINE

## UP HELLY AA

By design, or by accident, we had managed to find and lose five million pounds in less than a week, which is small change in the financial services industry, but that's another story. Somehow, we weren't under arrest, but helping the police with their enquiries. We were not allowed to stay at my dad's croft because of its proximity to the crime scene, and all the alternative hotel accommodation in Lerwick was full due to the tourists visiting for the Up Helly Aa. They had just enough police cells in Lerwick for all of us, although alternative arrangements had been provided for Janet because of her age, and Bessie, who was hospitalised. We all had a police cell to ourselves as we waited to answer questions about what we knew regarding the Cult of the Tiffin.

Not that any of us had too much to say. We had decided that my dad would be the one to spin the story about Bessie and her alcohol-infused psychosis, and that we all considered ourselves lucky to still be alive, which was true in one sense, but not for the reasons given to the police. We also had the freedom to roam between the police cells, but there was little desire on my part, or from anyone else's, to mix and mingle. It was probably because we had all seen enough of each other, and maybe we all just wanted the madness to stop, and being alone in a cell surrounded by plain tiled walls seemed a suitable way to seek peace and tranquillity. In fact, I was so keen on not talking to anyone that I was happy to be left until last to be interviewed and to provide a witness statement, because I could declutter, de-filter, and get some desperately needed sleep.

It wasn't until the second day that I was in the police interview room, sticking to my story about a fun road trip to Shetland, having been invited to stay at the croft. There was no mention of my dad and her biological origins, there was no mention of Danny and his gangsterism, just a tenuous linkage that loosely bound some of us by attending Samira's gym in the city which could be verified by checking membership records.

Of course, I was shocked, like everyone else, that my boss Bridges had been sucked into some ridiculous occultist menagerie, mixing with druggie bikers who were no doubt satanists and evil-doers. As for Bessie? I did meet her once, I did have one of her chocolate orange tiffins, and it was truly shocking when we discovered the dead bodies in her croft. Of course, we had no idea what had happened and had only been curious when the car she must have stolen was driven away at great speed and crashed into the boggy fields. Who knows what was going through her mind? At least she might now get the mental health interventions that were clearly lacking to prevent such a tragedy.

Anyway, as weak and absurd as it all sounded, we were not guilty of poisoning the ZMC, or the Henchman, and Bridges's heart attack was probably going to happen at some point. Plus, we didn't kill Trevor, and it was hardly his fault that his resurrection triggered a cardiac arrest in Bridges – it was just perfect timing to save us all.

And as for the money?

Well, there never was any money, because there never was any discrepancy, coke deals, Pink Houses, kidnapped old ladies, urinary tract infections, zombie bikers and zombie drugs, paranoid zombie hunters and psychotic tooth fairies. Such events were so crazy that it's the kind of thing that gets made up for a bit of a joke, turned into a novel, turned into a movie. I wouldn't recognise this tale if someone told me, and if anyone says otherwise, they would be conflating fact and fiction, because the only fact that I am aware of is that I left my job in the city because I have a higher moral code than the kind of people who work in financial services.

Er hem…

Eventually, we were all told we could leave once we had signed off on our statements. Some of us could stay back at my dad's croft because they had finished with the crime scene, but the prospect of staying with my dad filled me with dread, so I asked to stay one more night in the police cell. They were obliging, and I slept for the next 24 hours in a deep state of unconsciousness that was only disturbed when I was encouraged to go out and enjoy the festivities.

Up Helly Aa!

I still felt mentally and physically exhausted as I left the police station and immediately found myself surrounded by a Viking invasion. It was a strange reintroduction to reality, plunged into a world that had gone back 1000 years.

The streets were lined with tourists and onlookers, as torchbearers were formed in ranks in the darkened streets of Lerwick. They were dressed in the most bizarre and grand-looking costumes, each holding what looked like a fence post wrapped in sacking, the strong smell of paraffin wafting in the night air.

I mingled aimlessly, with a sense that everyone was waiting for something to happen, and this was suddenly confirmed when a firework shot up out of nowhere and burst high above everyone's heads. This was the signal, because the fence posts were lit, and I could hear a band strike up, and the blazing procession started marching.

With little else to do, I let myself be carried along by the crowd as the fires in the massed ranks lit up the streets. We snaked along, and I could see ahead of me what looked like a squad of Vikings at the head of the procession dragging a large Viking galley, and someone standing proudly at the helm of this replica longship wearing a raven-winged helmet, and holding an axe, and shield, which I thought was probably what any self-respecting Viking king would do for a well organised stag night. I suppose the only difference was that he hadn't hired a long white limousine for his mates, because they were dragging the galley through the streets.

In the midst of the throng of people, and the chatter and the noise, I didn't notice that I had inadvertently stumbled into Danny and Janet's orbit, who, like me, were watching the procession as it sang and moved along behind the Viking and his galley.

'They let you out, then?' asked Danny cheekily, as we stood on a corner of the narrow path.

I shrugged, as if I didn't care, which was fairly accurate in terms of how I felt about everything.

'You should cheer up,' Danny added, as I looked down at

Janet's impish face. 'Things could have been a lot worse than they turned out to be.'

I didn't see it like that.

'What's worse than losing five million quid and finding out your dad is a drug mule whose ambition was always to be a woman?'

'There's nothing wrong with being a woman, Jamie,' said Danny, admonishing me.

'You know what I mean,' I replied, whilst being buffeted by people wanting to get past.

'If I were you, I'd be thinking that I'm lucky to still be alive,' said Danny, who stood his ground, forcing people to walk around him. 'After all, I could have cut your throat and let you bleed to death.'

'Then why didn't you?' I asked defiantly.

'Because I like you, Jamie,' said Danny, who was looking directly into my face. 'You're a good person, and there aren't many good people in this world of ours. I think if you realised that about yourself, you'd do all right.'

That was an odd thing to say, a gangster believing that you need good people in the world. Still, I had always thought that there was also a seed of goodness in Danny, but I wasn't about to tell him that as I looked down at Janet again.

'So, what are you guys going to do?' I asked them, sensing that they had probably teamed up.

'Danny said he'd look after me,' said Janet, who looked pleased by the arrangement.

'She'll be coming back to Dublin,' added Danny. 'She's got potential, if you know what I mean.'

'Is that what you want?' I asked, wondering if, as a "good

person", I should be contacting Social Services.

'I wouldn't be doing it if I didn't want to,' Janet smiled.

*Fair enough*, I thought to myself.

Danny turned away as he saw a gap in the procession and darted across with Janet in tow.

'We'll see you on the ferry tomorrow!' Janet shouted across to me.

I held up my hand, acknowledging the arrangements that had been put in place for all of us to leave the island the next day. Not that, all of a sudden, we would be free of Bessie's genocidal chocolate orange tiffin rampage, as the police calculated how to manage the anticipated news coverage and the spotlight that might focus on us, and for obvious reasons we were keen to be as far away as possible from all the lies we had concocted.

After all, we had no guarantee that Bessie wouldn't regain some level of lucidity if she recovered from her injuries, and would point the finger at some, if not all of us, in a possible court case. It was in all our interests to maintain a conspiracy of silence and the proverbial principle of the three wise monkeys.

Watching Danny and Janet weave their way through the crowds on the other side of the street, separate from where I was standing, symbolised the status our association was going to be from now on: keeping our distance whilst being in sight of each other. I was OK with that, to some extent, although I was wondering how I was going to navigate my relationship with my dad, and let Samira know that the reason why I had gone along for the ride all the way to insanity was because of how I felt about her.

Still, the festivities kept my mind from wandering off into a morose self-indulgence, as I caught the end of the procession and began to push my way through the crowd to get closer to the Viking galley. Having apologised a few times for bumping into people in the heaving streets and got up close to what I assumed was the main event, a circle of flaming fence posts had surrounded the galley. Another rocket exploded overhead, and a wall of cheers filled the heated amphitheatre. A bugle call sounded, and the torches were hurled onto the galley. I was slightly worried that I was witnessing a Nordic seafaring *Wicker Man,* until I noticed the Viking king had abandoned his ship before the flame-throwing.

Within minutes, the galley was a blazing inferno, serenaded by the crowd singing a stirring hymn in a language as obscure as the rest of the proceedings.

And that's when I heard a voice inform me, which I recognised as Dr Q's.

'It's called *The Norseman's Home*, what they are singing, if you are interested,' he said, with Matt and Trevor.

I nodded, turning back to face the raging fire.

'It's like a catharsis,' continued Dr Q from behind me. 'Don't you think?'

'What is?'

'The burning,' he said. 'It feels like a cleansing, a purification of the soul, relieving us of all our burdens so we are renewed again.'

All I could think was that the heat was keeping me warm, because I didn't particularly share Dr Q's emphasis on the psychological benefits of burning a wooden ship.

'You don't look happy,' mused Dr Q, who was now

standing by my side, looking curiously into my firelit face.

'No, I don't think I am,' I answered reflectively. 'I just saw Danny and Janet together. I thought Danny would be hopping mad about the whole thing, but he doesn't seem that bothered about losing five million quid and a stash of drugs.'

'Well, that's because Danny has other outcomes to feel cheerful about,' said Dr Q, as he winked at me. 'He's got his Boss Man off his back, and I think he would like to take young Janet under his wing.'

'What, like adopt her?' I replied, showing my bemusement.

'Danny is a sensitive man underneath all that gangster stuff. I think Janet has a better life chance with Danny than rotting away in some juvenile care home where no one cares.'

'But she has tuberculosis!'

Dr Q burst out laughing, as if I had said something really stupid. 'Janet is a canny young woman,' he said, glancing behind me at Matt and Trevor, who stood together watching the Viking galley burn. 'She'd tell you whatever you wanted to hear in order to get what she wants.'

I had to think for a second or two, remembering how altruistic I thought Janet had been to give up her meds for the hallucinating and sickly Matt. I decided to assume that Janet had probably handed over any old pills in order to get in with us, and that Matt's recovery was down to a placebo and his innate idiocy overcoming psychosis.

'What about you, then?' I said. 'What have you got planned?'

'Oh, that's easy,' Dr Q replied, pushing his hands down into his jacket and looking supremely smug. 'There's a fortune in the ZMC stash that only a few of us here know about. I have drawn up a contract with our two brethren behind us, and we will be returning to Manchester to initiate the business of meeting demand and supply in communities across the land.'

It was my turn to laugh at the absurdity of Dr Q doing anything with Matt and Trevor.

'You do know,' I said, lowering my voice slightly, 'that neither of those two know how to put one foot in front of the other without being run over or driving off the edge of a cliff?'

Dr Q shrugged, fatalistically, but appeared content with his new business partnership.

'Let me offer you one more indirect quote: "I chose this life, and I know what I'm doing", *Identity Crisis*, issue four, November 2004, by Brad Meltzer and Rags Morales.'

That made me chuckle; Dr Q was always good for a quote.

'Is it your dad?' he asked, querying my despondency.

'I won't pretend it's not an issue,' I replied, as I looked around at all the happy faces glowing in the light of the cleanse. 'Maybe the future is gender realignment.'

'I doubt it, I think it's a bit niche, you know, important to those who need it, but I don't see it as a solution to climate change, World War Three, poverty, or an alien invasion.'

That was that then, as we all nodded at each other sheepishly, as if we had done things together that should remain unsaid.

'Where's Samira?' I asked Matt.

He pulled a face, the one he would pull when things weren't going well with Samira, which had been quite a lot ever since they got together.

'We've divorced our engagement,' he said stoically.

I tried my best to hide a brief sense of joy and satisfaction that Samira was now free of the absurdity known as the prolapsed anus, but made sure I offered my sincerest condolences.

'Maybe it's for the best,' I said. 'Given everything that's happened.'

'She's a force of nature,' intervened Dr Q. 'Not one to be tamed by convention or rules.'

'Let's face it,' said Matt, as he looked at me with those dull, unimpressive eyes, 'she's more capable than either of us. She was scamming with Bridges before we had thought of it.'

I was about to correct Matt and inform him that I had initiated the scheme to siphon off the money, and there was no "we" at all, but I thought better of it, because fundamentally, Matt was right for once. Samira was more capable than either of us.

'I've got tickets,' said Dr Q, 'for one of the parties. Difficult to get. We should celebrate our freedom, enjoy our last night here.'

I didn't feel like celebrating, but felt the arms of Dr Q push me forward as we all moved off as a group.

After winding our way around the streets of Lerwick, passing a few halls that had parties in full swing, I recognised the Gilbertson Park playing field. We didn't have much further to go as we crossed over the main road and into the Clickimin Leisure Centre.

Dr Q produced the tickets as we all piled into a hall that had the Up Helly Aa celebrations in full swing. At one end was an ABBA tribute thrashing out their greatest hits and a multitude of islanders displaying bizarre dance configurations, missing the beat, and filling up the space. Like a reluctant attendee at my first school disco, I found a haven in the corner while Dr Q and his new business partners sought out the whisky and a wee dram. I wasn't in the mood for drinking, and the mutton soup was even less appealing.

As I scanned the crowd, I picked out my dad, who was chatting up a local fisherman. Samira was next to them, enjoying the attention of a couple of Vikings. Danny and Janet, Dr Q, Matt, and Trevor were surrounded by locals, all animated by their arrival. Perhaps we were famous, having survived the horrors of the chocolate orange tiffin poisoning, and people were desperate to hear from the horse's mouth.

Not that I wanted any attention. I was ready to leave and call it a night, when I received a text that put the final nail in my coffin of misery and despair.

It was from Brenda.

Mum had died.

# ALL'S WELL THAT ENDS WELL

# CHAPTER ONE
## ON TOP OF THE HILL

It took most of the next morning to recover from drowning myself in booze, so that I was just about able to use my jittery legs to walk over to the meeting point before we all headed down to the ferry terminal in time for the 5:00 p.m. crossing back to Aberdeen. Fortunately, I was not the only one who looked rather sorry for themselves, as our motley crew of reprobates were continuing to rehydrate with cups of tea or coffee in a local café. In fact, things were so bad that there was little or no recognition of my arrival, as I bought myself a cup of tea and sat down next to my dad.

She had lost the glamour of our first encounter, with no make-up, wrapped in a warm winter coat, and looking as bad as I felt about finally losing Mum. I remember my dad being tearful when I gave her the news the night before, and then after about ten wee drams, all of us ended up in a conga around the leisure centre, everyone desperate to feel relief and joy from the accumulation of events.

I knew my dad was hurting, and I was hurting, as the sadness of Mum's death seeped into our consciousness and was made real when we woke up this morning.

We were now going to travel back home together, face the music, and help Brenda with the funeral arrangements (after she had got over the shock of my dad's reappearance).

I had replied to her text with a few cryptic lines so that at least she knew what was coming. I had a crude calculation for it: one in, one out, one gone, and one found and returned slightly different from when she left. We had lost Mum but found Dad, and she could be as good as Mum, if she stood by her sense of regret that she had offered me when we had discovered each other.

I didn't say anything as I sipped my tea and looked over at Danny and Janet sitting at one table, and Dr Q, Matt, and Trevor sat at another.

Oddly, I think I felt a strange sense of pride in my fellow suffering souls, whom I had travelled with, through all the desolation and destruction that we had driven through, a sad country feeling sorry for itself. There was a sense of accomplishment in our little road trip, as if we were Knights of the Round Table having reached the end of our quest. However, if we had found the Holy Grail, we had also managed to burn it, and were only left with a small consolation that more personal matters may be more resolved than material ambition. I suppose that's the point of these sorts of things: it's not the destination that counts, but the journey.

There was, in that, some kind of solace; a cold comfort for all of us that there was a personal resolution or self-realisation.

Danny had found a young disciple in Janet, and she would be a willing apprentice. Trevor had been lost and gone to Heaven – or maybe that was purgatory – and been resurrected. Matt had found a new friend and business partner in crime in Dr Q, and Dr Q had two people he could bore with quotes from his mildly tedious obsession with *Batman* comics.

All's well that ends well, I suppose, although I didn't feel things had ended that well for me. Sitting next to my dad, we now faced the prospect of burying my mum and singing hymns in the crematorium, whilst relatives close and distant looked my dad up and down, trying to figure out what it meant to become a woman. Although I was thinking my dad's presence might have to be a discreet presence, as I was not entirely sure how much police interest would be shown in the female known as Mavis Grind.

Which got me thinking along a tangent.

'So,' I began, dunking a biscuit in my tea, 'how did you come up with the name Mavis Grind?'

'That wasn't me, that was Samira,' my dad answered, pulling the collars of her winter coat up towards her face. 'I used to call myself Alice, but then Samira came to visit. She said she had been for a walk and discovered a strip of land, an isthmus, and she said it was called Mavis Grind. She liked it, I liked it, and so I got a new passport, and everyone got to know me as Mavis. I think it suits me, and it makes me feel like I have a home on the island.'

'You let Samira give you your name?' I said, sceptically.

'Of course,' she replied, surprised that I would question her being anointed by Samira. 'She's more of an islander than me, so why wouldn't I?'

'What do you mean she's more of an islander?'

'Don't you know? Samira's been coming here since she was a kid. She knows this place like the back of her hand. All the nooks and crannies, all the sights and sounds, all those places like the temple. She loves it here, so she told me. If she didn't have to be in London to get the business, she'd have her own croft just like me.'

This was a revelation, not least because Samira had pretended that she had hardly been this far north more than a couple of times.

'Are you all right?' asked my dad, who could tell I was beginning to go paler than the sickly paleness from last night's intoxication.

'So,' I said, thoughtfully and aloud, 'where is Samira now?'

'She'll be out and about, I suspect. She's certainly not coming back with us to London. In fact, it wouldn't surprise me if she calls it a day with that place and settles down here. You know, she just wants to be independent, and that's what money can do for you. She wants to be as far away as possible from her family, because sooner or later they will arrange a wedding for her, and I don't mean to that useless specimen Matt Chubb. That whole engagement thing was something Samira cooked up to frustrate her parents.'

I was frozen, for half a second, or maybe a minute or so, as my brain began racing, going over and over in my head the mantra: judge people not by their words but by their actions. What had Samira consistently proved by her own actions? That she couldn't be trusted to be honest, truthful, or sincere. Perhaps, much like my good self. But that was not the issue here. The issue was one far greater, far more pertinent, far more meaningful, because my dad, whether she knew it or not, had provided a great insight, a minor revelation, and one I needed to act upon immediately.

'I won't be long,' I announced, standing up and heading towards the door in a trance-like state.

'Where are you going?' asked my dad. 'You don't want to miss the ferry.'

'Not a problem,' I said, seeing that there was an hour or two to go. 'I'll be back!'

I was out of the door, walking rapidly, and then running through the winding streets, all the way up to the bus stop near the Clickimin Leisure Centre. As luck would have it, and I needed a bit of luck, there was a bus in, and I hopped on with my mission to get to Brae as fast as the driver could get me there.

It was a frustrating half hour as we jogged along over bumps in the tarmac, with me constantly looking out at the sky to see how quickly the day was turning into dusk. However, this time I didn't stop off at the cake fridge. I let the bus take me closer to Brae. I jumped off and started following the A970, with Google Maps as my guide.

It was a long shot, a gamble, a risk that might end up with me stranded in the middle of nowhere once again, but I had a hunch, a stomach-churning gut instinct, I would find Samira where I would expect her to be right now.

The walk wasn't that long, as I arrived at the isthmus of Mavis Grind, with the road crossing over to another part of the island, and not too far from that was marked a scenic point, a spot where you could look out over the land and the water swimming around the rugged grassland and heath.

At the top of the hill, topped off with a small triangle of rock, I spied Samira, looking out across the vista and the water.

Who would have thought it? My gamble had paid off, as I stumbled up the hill, keeping my eye on Samira, hoping she would stay put and not run off.

I kept my focus, with the sun dipping and the day ending.

At least she had waited, which was a positive, as I struggled to catch my breath, my hands on my knees.

'What are you doing here, Jamie?' she asked, calmness and self-assurance personified, standing next to three stones piled one on top of the other

'I'm going birdwatching, to see if I can find some puffins,' I replied between large intakes of breath.

'You're talking rubbish, Jamie,' Samira said, with her usual deft admonishment.

'No, I'm not,' I said, with a fair degree of fake honesty. 'I've got an idea for a pizza topping.'

'Gross, Jamie, how could you think like that?'

'Well, I blame the people I hang around with.'

Samira kept her poise as she homed in on the obvious. 'Jamie, you need to go back home and say goodbye to your mum.'

'It's too late. She's dead. Anyway, I said goodbye on the way up here, remember? Just before Danny ran over Trevor.'

'That's not the same,' she said, disapprovingly. 'What about the funeral? Shouldn't you be there for that?'

'Don't like funerals. Don't like death. Don't like the thought of dying, either.'

'Nobody does, Jamie, it's just about paying your respects. Will your dad be there?'

'She's not my dad; she's my other mum.'

Samira raised her eyebrows. 'You should go back and help your family heal,' she said, offering a faint smile and a genuine sign of sympathy.

'I don't want to go back,' I said, able to stand up straight so I was level with where Samira was standing. 'I like it here.'

'Rubbish! This is not you. You need towns and cities, trains and cars, tall buildings and people rushing around bumping into each other. You'd be bored here with nothing to do.'

'I could fish,' I said hesitantly. 'You know, cod, herring, crab – that sort of thing.'

'When have you ever done any fishing, let alone proper fishing?'

'I've got the overalls.'

Samira started shaking her head.

I don't think she had anything else she could say to me.

So instead, I said something.

'Well, you know what they say, no man is an island.'

'That's right, Jamie, and fortunately, I'm not a man, I'm a woman. So the best place for me is to be as far away as possible from man-boys like you and Matt.'

'I've changed,' I said, desperately. 'This last week has taught me a lot. You know, about myself, my shortcomings and all that.'

'Why does that matter to me?'

'Well,' I said, clearing my throat. 'I know you've buried more than the five million, but, hey, it's yours. That's not why I'm here.'

'Why are you here, Jamie?'

'To ask you a question.'

'Go on, what's your question?'

'Will you marry me?'

'No.'

'OK. How about getting engaged?'

**END**

# ABOUT THE AUTHOR

Simon Marlowe is a darkly comic crime thriller author and a consummate wordsmith, skilfully blending social and political issues into compellingly relevant narratives on a par with the best in modern crime fiction today. He spent his formative years living in South London, indulging in political activism and music, before graduating from several universities in politics, education and management. He eventually moved back to his home city in Essex, and after briefly studying for a creative writing MA, settled down to producing contemporary fiction, before turning to darkly comic, fast-paced and action-packed crime thrillers, in the *Mason Made* trilogy, now followed by the hilarious criminally comic road trip *Road To Mavis Grind.*

Keep up to date with Simon's books via:


Instagram: @simonmarloweauthor
X: @simon_marlowe
Facebook: Simon Marlowe Author
TikTok: @simonmarlowe5